Praise for Georgia B...

The D...

"You can count on Beers to give yo... ...ach and every time."—*The Romantic Rea...*

"*The Do-Over* is a shining example of the brilliance of Georgia Beers as a contemporary romance author."—*Rainbow Reflections*

"[T]he two leads are genuine and likable, their chemistry is palpable... The romance builds up slowly and naturally, and the angst level is just right. The supporting characters are equally well developed. Don't miss this one!"—*Melina Bickard, Librarian, Waterloo Library (UK)*

Calendar Girl

"*Calendar Girl* is a perfect masterclass on how to write a breathtakingly beautiful romance novel...Georgia Beers had me captivated from the start with this story. Two skilfully crafted characters, an enthralling plot and the best kissing scene ever!"—*Kitty Kat's Book Review Blog*

"*Calendar Girl* by Georgia Beers is a well-written sweet workplace romance. It has all the elements of a good contemporary romance... It even has an ice queen for a major character."—*Rainbow Reflections*

"A sweet, sweet romcom of a story...*Calendar Girl* is a nice read, which you may find yourself returning to when you want a hot-chocolate-and-warm-comfort-hug in your life."—*Best Lesbian Erotica*

The Shape of You

"I know I always say this about Georgia Beers's books, but there is no one that writes first kisses like her. They are hot, steamy and all too much!"—*Les Rêveur*

The Shape of You "catches you right in the feels and does not let go. It is a must for every person out there who has struggled with self-esteem, questioned their judgment, and settled for a less than perfect but safe lover. If you've ever been convinced you have to trade passion for emotional safety, this book is not you."—*Writing While Distracted*

Blend

"Georgia Beers hits all the right notes with this romance set in a wine bar...A low-angst read, it still delivers a story rich in heart-rending moments before the characters get their happy ever after. A well-crafted novel, *Blend* is a marvelous way to spend an evening curled up with a large glass of your favorite vintage."—*Writing While Distracted*

"You know a book is good, first, when you don't want to put it down. Second, you know it's damn good when you're reading it and thinking, I'm totally going to read this one again. Great read and absolutely a 5-star romance."—*The Romantic Reader Blog*

"This is a lovely romantic story with relatable characters that have depth and chemistry. A charming easy story that kept me reading until the end. Very enjoyable."—*Kat Adams, Bookseller, QBD (Australia)*

"*Blend* has that classic Georgia Beers feel to it, while giving us another unique setting to enjoy. The pacing is excellent and the chemistry between Piper and Lindsay is palpable."—*The Lesbian Review*

Right Here, Right Now

"The angst was written well, but not overpoweringly so, just enough for you to have the heart-sinking moment of 'will they make it,' and then you realize they have to because they are made for each other."—*Les Reveur*

Right Here, Right Now "is full of humor (yep, I laughed out loud), romance, and kick-ass characters!"—*Illustrious Illusions*

"[A] successful and entertaining queer romance novel. The main characters are appealing, and the situations they deal with are realistic and well-managed. I would recommend this book to anyone who enjoys a good queer romance novel, and particularly one grounded in real world situations."—*Books at the End of the Alphabet*

"[A]n engaging odd-couple romance. Beers creates a romance of gentle humor that allows no-nonsense Lacey to relax and easygoing Alicia to find a trusting heart."—*RT Book Reviews*

Lambda Literary Award Winner *Fresh Tracks*

"Georgia Beers pens romances with sparks."—*Just About Write*

"[T]he focus switches each chapter to a different character, allowing for a measured pace and deep, sincere exploration of each protagonist's thoughts. Beers gives a welcome expansion to the romance genre with her clear, sympathetic writing."—*Curve magazine*

Lambda Literary Award Finalist *Finding Home*

"Georgia Beers has proven in her popular novels such as *Too Close to Touch* and *Fresh Tracks* that she has a special way of building romance with suspense that puts the reader on the edge of their seat. *Finding Home*, though more character driven than suspense, will equally keep the reader engaged at each page turn with its sweet romance."—*Lambda Literary Review*

Mine

"From the eye-catching cover, appropriately named title, to the last word, Georgia Beers's *Mine* is captivating, thought-provoking, and satisfying. Like a deep red, smooth-tasting, and expensive merlot, *Mine* goes down easy even though Beers explores tough topics."—*Story Circle Book Reviews*

"Beers does a fine job of capturing the essence of grief in an authentic way. *Mine* is touching, life-affirming, and sweet."—*Lesbian News Book Review*

Too Close to Touch

"This is such a well-written book. The pacing is perfect, the romance is great, the character work strong, and damn, but is the sex writing ever fantastic."—*The Lesbian Review*

"In her third novel, Georgia Beers delivers an immensely satisfying story. Beers knows how to generate sexual tension so taut it could be cut with a knife...Beers weaves a tale of yearning, love, lust, and conflict resolution. She has constructed a believable plot, with strong characters in a charming setting."—*Just About Write*

By the Author

ONE WALK IN WINTER

by
Georgia Beers

2019

ONE WALK IN WINTER

ISBN 13: 978-1-63555-541-7

THIS TRADE PAPERBACK ORIGINAL IS PUBLISHED BY
BOLD STROKES BOOKS, INC.
P.O. BOX 249
VALLEY FALLS, NY 12185

FIRST EDITION: OCTOBER 2019

CREDITS
EDITORS: LYNDA SANDOVAL AND STACIA SEAMAN
PRODUCTION DESIGN: STACIA SEAMAN
COVER DESIGN BY ANN MCMAN

Acknowledgments

Spending my entire life in the Northeast, I am no stranger to winter. Snow, ice, wind, blizzards, subzero temperatures? All very familiar to me. And while I don't hate winter (like a lot of people I know), it's always been kind of a mixed bag for me. I hate being cold, but I love the white freshness of new fallen snow, the way it seems to offer a clean slate. I don't enjoy driving in winter weather, but big, fluffy flakes falling quietly from the sky? One of the most beautiful sights I can think of. And walking through the woods in the winter can be mesmerizing. It can be poignant, make you look inward. But could it be life-altering? I decided I wanted to find out. I hope you enjoy the journey as much as I did.

As always, thank you to Radclyffe, Sandy Lowe, and everybody at Bold Strokes Books who make working with a publishing company an absolute dream and utterly stress-free.

Finishing the edits on this one was bittersweet, as it was my last book with my longtime editor, Lynda Sandoval. I will miss her knowledge, her wit, and her tendency to make me a better writer with every book. My copy editor, Stacia Seaman, has the sharpest eyes of anybody I know, and I am eternally grateful that she helps make me look like I actually know what I'm doing.

Thank you to my friends: Melissa, Carsen, Rachel, Nikki, Kris, and more, who get me, hold me accountable on word counts, help me with titles, talk me up when I need it or off the ledge when I need that. Writing can be super lonely, even for an introvert like me, and having my peeps close by makes me feel supported and lucky to have them in my corner.

Finally, and always, I am eternally grateful to my incredible readers whose emails and messages give me confidence when I need it and haul me out of the mire when I feel stuck. Thank you never seems like enough, so I'll keep writing.

CHAPTER ONE

"Oh, my God, I love the first snowfall!"

It didn't matter that there was nobody around to hear her. Olivia Santini threw her arms out to the sides and turned in a slow circle with her face toward the sky. Big, fat, fluffy flakes of snow landed softly on her cheeks and eyelashes, and she stuck her tongue out to catch a couple. While she knew that in another two months, she'd be ready for the snow and the cold to silently slip away, leaving spring in its place, the first snowfall of the season really did hold a special place in her heart.

Her dog, Walter, obviously thought this spinning in a circle thing was a fun new game and that the appropriate course of action was for him to jump on his person, barking happily. Which he did.

Olivia fell to the ground laughing, grabbing at her dog with mittened hands, kissing his furry black-and-white head. Walter rolled on his back in the snow, and she patted his white belly as he squirmed with that level of joy reserved for dogs and toddlers.

"Okay, buddy," she said, with a final pat. "Let's get moving."

She never leashed Walter on their morning walks, as they'd only run into other people maybe twice and Walter didn't have a mean bone in his body. He wanted to be friends with everybody. It was early: barely seven in the morning, light enough to see, but no sun yet, thanks to the recent time change, which Olivia hated. Their walks in the summer were much brighter and sunnier, but there was something about this particular morning. The impending sunrise had tinted things a calm, serene blue. The snow, the trees, the sky. Everything had this veil of peace, and Olivia realized it was more of a feeling than an actual sight. She inhaled and held the fresh morning air in her lungs for a few seconds before letting it out.

It was going to be a good day.

Walter sprinted ahead, bounding through the new fallen snow like a small child. There wasn't a lot of it—an inch or two—but enough to enamor her dog, who seemed to live for walks and the outdoors and winter.

"Walter. Don't go too far ahead." She could see his furry butt bouncing along the trail about twenty yards in front of her, trotting happily and not looking back.

Olivia picked up her pace to a jog, following Walter's tracks, which veered off the path to the right. Probably a squirrel had caught his eye. She never got terribly worried. Walter was part Australian shepherd, and even when he left her behind, he never went far, and he always came back. She was his herd, and a good herding dog always stays close to his herd.

But it wasn't a squirrel. Surprisingly, Walter had found another person in the woods. A new friend. One with a camera. Olivia's initial panic—not everybody loved dogs, especially ones that ran up on you in the trees—eased almost instantly as the stranger, back to her, dropped to a squat and pulled off a glove in order to pet Walter. Olivia could hear the low rumble of a voice as she approached.

"I'm so sorry," she said to the stranger, who was dressed in a red parka, the fur-lined hood up. Jeans and low boots were all Olivia could see as she pulled Walter's leash from her pocket, preparing to clip it to his collar. "He's really friendly. He just wants to say hi to everybody. We've had many discussions about him not being pushy, but…" She indicated her dog, whose entire body was now between the knees of the stranger, his tailless rear end waggling with the happiness of finding a new friend. "As you can see, he's not big on retaining that information."

"Oh, no worries at all." The stranger chuckled, and the voice was decidedly female, soft and friendly. She pushed the hood off her head so she could see Olivia and held up her camera. "He's really beautiful. I took a couple of shots. I hope that's okay."

Weird things happened to Olivia in that moment. Her heart rate picked up speed. Her palms began to sweat inside her gloves. Her voice seemed to catch in her throat, and she swallowed hard. *He's* beautiful, she thought, as she looked at one of the most stunningly gorgeous faces she'd ever seen in her life. Large eyes the color of spring grass and lined with super-dark lashes focused on her. They were set into a face made of the smoothest-looking skin Olivia had ever seen, almost porcelain in its perfection. When the stranger smiled, high, defined cheekbones became more obvious, and her light brown brows matched the tousled hair on her head.

"Or not?" The stranger tilted her head, waiting for Olivia to respond. "I mean, I can delete them."

Olivia shook herself free of the weird spell she suddenly felt like she was under. "No. No, it's fine. Sorry." She smiled as she reached down to grab Walter's face in her hands. He looked at her with his big, soft brown eyes and she swore to God she could see a human in there sometimes. Then she stood and clipped his leash on. Evergreen Hills was a fairly small town and Olivia had never laid eyes on this woman before, which was a definite pity, because laying eyes on her was a lot of fun. A lot. Trying to yank herself back to being a normal human rather than an ogling creeper, she indicated the camera. "You getting some good shots?"

"I am. It's *so* beautiful out here." Those green eyes scanned the woods as if they were something brand new, never before seen. "The snow on the bare branches. All the evergreens mixed in. The slow brightening of the sky. The blanket of white that hasn't been walked on."

"Sounds like you've never been here before."

"I haven't. I'm also new to this time of day." They both laughed at that. "I didn't sleep well last night and was up way too early. Then I saw the snow and just got this urge to walk." The stranger turned her face so those eyes locked with Olivia's. "Which is very unlike me, believe me." She shrugged as if she didn't understand it herself.

"Walter and I walk here every morning."

"Every morning? This early?"

Olivia smiled as the two of them trudged back to the trail and began walking together by unspoken understanding. "Walter doesn't know what it means to sleep in. He's always gotten breakfast by six, so he's usually up around then. He eats, we walk."

"The order of things," the stranger said, with a nod. "I get that. I'm Hayley, by the way." She pulled a glove off and stuck out her hand.

"Olivia." They shook. Hayley's hand was warm and soft and Olivia tried not to hold on for too long, even though she wanted to.

"So, you walk here every day," Hayley said. "I'm going to go out on a limb and guess that you live here."

"Your powers of deduction are stunning," Olivia teased. "Yes. All my life. I'm an Evergreener."

"An Evergreener, huh?"

"That's what they call us." Olivia had stopped walking so Walter could sniff a tree, then lift his leg on it. Out of the corner of her eye, she saw Hayley lift her camera and aim it their way, then heard her snap a few shots of Walter, she assumed. Then she waited until Olivia caught back up to her. "What about you?"

"Oh, I'm a New Yorker," Hayley said.

"Well, so am I, if we're getting technical." Olivia bumped Hayley with a shoulder.

"Ah, a girl who needs specifics. I see. All right, let me amend that. I am a Manhattanite."

Olivia's eyes went wide. "Really? Like, you live there?"

"All my life," Hayley said, borrowing Olivia's words.

"I've never been to New York City," Olivia said, her voice probably a little dreamy.

"Seriously? That's a shame. It's the most amazing city in the world. So much to see and do."

"The city that never sleeps."

"A totally accurate description. You should definitely come some time. I could show you around."

"You'd do that?"

"I would." Hayley nodded, and something passed between them. Something almost tangible. Olivia wondered if Hayley felt it, too, or if she was just being a silly, fantasy-prone romantic.

"Are you here for long?" Olivia felt a small surge of disappointment at the thought of never seeing Hayley again, which she didn't understand. At all. In her line of work, people came and went all the time. It never bothered her; it was the nature of her job. But she felt a very odd…"connection" was the only word she could come up with to describe how she was feeling. She felt a very odd connection to Hayley. Something she'd never felt before. It had her off-balance.

"I'm not sure yet." Hayley squinted at the sky as if searching for the answer.

They reached the end of the path, which spat them out into the parking lot, where only two cars were parked. Oddly, they both seemed to stutter a bit in their forward momentum, taking what felt to Olivia like somewhat hesitant steps, as if not wanting the walk to end. Which, she knew, *she* didn't. As she turned to try to put words to her thoughts, Hayley must've hit a small patch of ice.

It seemed to happen super fast and also in slow motion. Hayley's arms flailed, Olivia reached out to catch her, and in the next moment, she was holding Hayley. Very tightly. Really close. Their faces were barely an inch apart as she stared into those eyes. Hayley's skin was even more flawless this close up, her bottom lip full and pink. She smelled like cinnamon somehow.

Time seemed to stand still.

Hearts raced. Olivia could hear her own in her head and was pretty sure she could feel Hayley's even through their winter gear.

A beat went by. Another.

Finally, they each slowly shifted, standing upright and putting a smidge more space between them. *Probably for the best*, Olivia thought, even though the rest of her body was crying out at the loss.

Hayley cleared her throat. "Thanks."

"Sure. Falling's no good." Olivia cringed inside. *Falling's no good? Seriously, Liv?*

"Well. I should probably get back." Hayley jerked a thumb over her shoulder in the direction of her car.

"Yeah. Me too." Olivia reached down to pet Walter, who had, surprisingly, sat quietly through the whole stumbling/catching event.

With a nod, Hayley turned toward the BMW, but then looked back at Olivia. "Maybe we could grab a drink or some coffee some time?"

Olivia pulled the back door of her SUV open so Walter could hop in. She didn't turn around right away so Hayley wouldn't see the goofy grin that had spread across her face. "I'd like that." She pulled out her cell, then turned to face Hayley, who was now a good fifteen feet away, and that was too far, in Olivia's opinion. "What's your number?" Hayley rattled it off from her safe distance, and Olivia punched it into her phone. A few seconds later, Hayley's phone pinged in her pocket. "There. Now you have mine, too."

"Excellent." Hayley smiled at her, and Olivia felt like it lit up her entire face. God, the woman was gorgeous. "I'll text you."

"I look forward to it."

They got in their cars and Olivia waited until Hayley had pulled back and out of the lot before allowing the goofy grin to come back, grow, and spread out over her face.

"Did you catch all that, Wally? Did you? Were you even paying attention?" She looked over her shoulder at her dog. Walter was lying on his blanket across the back seat, pink tongue lolling out, doggy smile on his face. "I hope you were. Because she was *hot*. My God. And she asked me out. *And*, did I mention how hot she was?"

Walter continued on with his doggy smile.

Before she could shift the car, her phone rang. Seeing it was Tessa, she picked up. "You're not going to believe what just happened to me," she said, forgoing any greeting.

"Good morning to you, too," Tessa said, her tone laced with amusement. "I was going to see how you're doing this morning, but your stuff sounds way more interesting. Tell me."

As her car warmed up, Olivia told the story of meeting Hayley, of walking together with her, of the chemistry she'd felt and the catch and of the invitation out.

"So, she felt it, too," Tessa commented.

"Right? I spent much of the walk wondering if it was just me, but then when she slipped and I caught her and we had this…moment… it was pretty clear. And then she asked me out, so…" A glance in the rearview mirror told Olivia she looked as giddy as she felt.

"I can't believe you managed to find a date in the middle of the damn woods at seven o'clock in the morning." Olivia could almost see the scowl on her best friend's face. "I can't even get one through an online dating service, and *that's their only job*."

Olivia laughed. "You'll find one. You just have to be patient."

"Yeah, yeah. At this point, you just sound like the teacher in the Peanuts cartoons." Tessa did an impression of the "wah-wah" voice to punctuate her statement. "That's all I hear." They laughed together and then Tessa asked, "How're you doing? You ready for today?"

Olivia took a deep breath and blew it out. "As ready as I can be, right? Not a lot I can do about it but smile and push forward."

"Good girl. It's all going to be fine. Don't worry. Okay?"

Olivia forced a smile onto her face and gave one nod, even though Tessa couldn't see it. "Okay."

"I'll see you there for the staff meeting."

They signed off and Olivia finally put the car in gear and backed out. Walter'd put his head down and was now close to napping. A good sign, since she had a busy day ahead and probably wouldn't have a chance to stop home at lunchtime like normal. Luckily, her mother was going to drop in on Walter.

Pulling out of the parking lot, Olivia headed for her small bungalow three miles away. There she'd shower, change into her work clothes, and head to the Evergreen Resort and Spa where she'd meet the new manager…the person who'd gotten the job that Olivia not only wanted but richly deserved, given how much work she'd done over the past six months.

In her driveway, she turned off the ignition and sat there in the silence for a moment. Walter had apparently grown used to her "thinking moments" and sat patiently as his person stared out the windshield at the door of her small garage.

Finally, Olivia took a deep breath and let it raspberry out, then pulled on the door handle. "All right, Wally. Let's do this."

❖

The snow had stopped falling and whatever had stuck earlier that morning would most likely melt by midafternoon, judging from the bright blue sky and not-quite-warm sunshine. Olivia admitted to herself that she'd be sad to see the snow go, though it was only just past the middle of November and still a bit early for feet of it. But once it arrived in full force, this was the kind of day she loved. The contrast of the electric blue of the sky and the clean white of the snow with the joy of the sun shining down on it all was something to behold. A thing of beauty that she'd been unable to find anywhere else, and a big reason she'd never moved away from Evergreen Hills.

Well, that and her mother would kill her.

Not officially expected to start work until 9:00 a.m., Olivia glanced at her watch as she entered through the employee door at the back of the building, happy to see that it read 8:25. She wanted to be in her office and ready to meet the new manager, show her the ropes, introduce her around, as well as get a feel for her competence (or lack thereof). She absently wondered how much slack she'd have to pick up the way she had with Roger, the previous—hopeless—manager.

"Nope. Not going there," she muttered to herself as she walked down the hall, her heels clicking on the granite. Every time she thought about how hard she'd worked cleaning up after Roger Stiles, she got more upset that she hadn't been given his job when he'd left, and she did not want that resentment showing when she met the person who did get the job. No, Olivia was nothing if not a team player and an asset as an employee. Plus, she loved the Evergreen. She wanted it to be the best resort it could be, and frankly, she had ideas. Lots of them. Ideas for improvement. Ideas for bringing in more profit. Lots and lots of ideas.

Maybe she'd get to share them. Finally.

"Good morning, Stephanie," she said to the woman behind the front desk.

"Good morning, Olivia. How is my boyfriend, Walter, this morning? Did he get a walk in the fresh snow?" Stephanie had worked the front desk of the Evergreen for more than a decade. Since before Olivia had worked there full-time. She was in her fifties but looked several years younger. She was a petite blonde who perpetually smiled, even when faced with the most difficult customers imaginable. Her shift began at 7:00, and she was never later than 6:30.

"He did. You know him. Ran like a rabbit through it. Stuck his nose in it. Rolled a little bit. The usual." Olivia walked around to the doorway on the side and joined Stephanie as the phone rang. Dropping her voice to a whisper, she asked, "Is she here yet?"

Stephanie shook her head as she put the phone's handset to her ear and said, "Front desk, this is Stephanie." She waited a beat, then, "Good morning, Mrs. Jorgensen. How can I help you on this beautiful morning?"

Olivia gave her a wave and entered the office that was situated behind the front desk area. Actually, there were two offices there. You had to walk through Olivia's small one to get to the larger one in the back that belonged to the manager. While the size of her office wasn't of huge importance to Olivia—she did a lot of walking around the resort, attending meetings, putting out fires—it sure would've been nice to move into the big one. She stood in the doorway of it, leaning against the doorjamb with her arms folded across her chest. All of Roger's things were gone now. No framed photos, no personal items on the desk. With the exception of a phone, a computer, and a lamp, the desktop was completely cleared. And shining. Mabel from housekeeping had done a fabulous job getting the room ready for the new manager. Olivia made a mental note to tell her so.

Resigned to being as cheerful and competent as she could, Olivia took a seat at her own desk, woke up her computer, and did some work. Reservations were looking good next week for the Thanksgiving holiday, one of their busiest times. They were close to completely booked, and people were already checking in for the week. She made a note to talk to Tessa—who was the head chef at Split Rail, the Evergreen's restaurant—about the menu for next Thursday, make sure she had everything she needed.

Scanning through the reservations, she saw names she recognized—regulars who stayed with them every year over the holiday—and a few new names. She knew there was still one penthouse suite on the top floor that was available.

Wait.

No, she was wrong. All four suites were booked.

"Well, that's good news," Olivia said to her empty office. The last suite had been booked and occupied last night by somebody named H. Boyd. "Thank you, Mr. Boyd, for taking the last of our most expensive suites through the holiday. Corporate will be happy."

Closing up the reservations app, she settled in to answer some email until the new manager arrived at nine. When she checked the clock to see that it was now 9:05, she gave a slight eye roll. *Late on your first day. Impressive.* Her phone rang, breaking into her thoughts, and she answered it.

Another phone call and three emails later, it was 9:35.

Olivia wandered out to the front desk where Stephanie was checking a couple out of their room. She put on a smile and asked if their stay had been to their satisfaction.

"Oh, my God," the woman said, pressing a manicured hand to

her chest, an enormous diamond ring sparkling in the sunlight that came through the skylights in the lobby. "It was wonderful. The spa. The food. The room. We'll definitely be back." She laid a hand on her husband's arm as he signed.

"Fantastic," Olivia said. "We look forward to it." She waved as they headed toward the exit to their waiting car. Once they were out of earshot, she murmured to Stephanie, "Any word on the new manager? I thought she'd be here by nine."

Stephanie shrugged and shook her head just as they heard the ping of the elevator doors from around the corner.

"Great," Olivia said. She had just decided she should probably give Corporate a call and see if they'd gotten any word about the new manager when the person who must've been on the elevator came around the corner.

Olivia's breath caught in her throat.

There was no red parka. No camera. No fur-lined hood to obstruct the view this time. But those green eyes were still just as engaging. They still sucked Olivia right in like some kind of weird vortex. Hayley from the woods did a small stutter step when she saw Olivia, seemed to falter for just a second before recovering and walking up to the desk.

"It's you," she said cheerfully. "Hi again. No Walter?"

Olivia felt herself blush, felt the heat start at her chest and rise up her throat, felt it bloom on her cheeks. *Act like a professional, for God's sake.* She cleared her throat. "No, I'm afraid Walter is home. Probably in the throes of a deep morning sleep."

"Well, that's too bad." Hayley wore black jeans, black knee-high boots, a black-and-white striped T-shirt, and a black blazer that might have been designer the way it was so perfectly cut for her. Her sleeves were pushed up to reveal her forearms, and Olivia took a moment to look at her hands. Soft looking. Feminine. Pretty. The light brown hair was pulled back and clipped at the nape of her neck, and Olivia could see blond highlights she hadn't noticed on their walk. Unlike earlier that morning, Hayley wore makeup now. Subtle, but there, dark mascara doing nothing but further accenting the green of her eyes. She was a little shorter than Olivia—maybe five five?—but her smile and presence made her seem bigger. "So, tell me, Olivia, where can a girl get a good cup of coffee around here?" Those eyes shifted their focus from Olivia to Stephanie and back to Olivia again as she waited expectantly.

"Well, the café is open." Olivia pointed to Hayley's right. "Or there's a Starbucks down that hallway on the way to the spa wing."

"Oh, okay. I thought maybe there was a lounge or something." When Olivia squinted at her, she clarified, "Like, designated for employees or something, you know? Though I do love Starbucks, which you can tell by the fact that I drank the stuff that was in my room already."

Olivia blinked at her. "I'm sorry...I'm a little confused."

A beat went by as the two of them looked at each other, both seeming slightly puzzled, before Hayley snapped her fingers and made a face that said she'd forgotten something important.

"Oh, my God, I'm such an idiot," she said with a chuckle. "You have no idea who I am, do you?"

Olivia's brow furrowed in yet more confusion as she shook her head slowly.

Hayley stuck out her hand, even though they'd already shaken hands in the woods. "Hayley Boyd. I'm your new manager."

CHAPTER TWO

Holy shit, what are the chances?

That was the first thought that ran through Hayley's head when she'd turned the corner and her gaze had landed on the stunningly beautiful girl from the woods that morning.

"Oh. Oh!" That was what she'd said when Hayley had introduced herself. The shock was clear on her face as she slowly put her hand in Hayley's. "Olivia Santini. Assistant manager."

Olivia Santini. Assistant manager. Hayley's right hand in this job. *Seriously, what are the fucking chances?*

Olivia hadn't left Hayley's thoughts all morning. Which was so weird as they'd spent, like, twenty minutes together and had exchanged what? Fifteen words? Twenty? Maybe? But something about her eyes— large and the richest, deepest brown Hayley had ever seen—captivated Hayley's attention. And Olivia had been wearing a hat earlier, so all that gorgeous, wavy dark hair that now hung past her shoulders was… unexpected. Hayley's fingers itched to dig into it.

"So, no Walter behind the front desk. Bummer," Hayley joked, hoping to erase that expression of…was it disappointment? Dejection? Irritation? It was one of those things. Maybe all of them. But they were all over Olivia's face. Hayley was used to being looked at that way, but something about it coming from Olivia made it sting more than usual. She had no idea why.

"I was expecting you by nine." Olivia was all business now. Her clipped tone of voice, the way she seemed to stand a little bit taller— which was unnecessary as far as Hayley was concerned, since Olivia was the taller of the two of them anyway—lifted her chin slightly.

"Oh. Right. Sorry about that. I lost track of time. Good thing I'm right upstairs." She grinned as she pointed upward.

Olivia furrowed that beautiful brow of hers. "What do you mean, you're right upstairs?"

"My room. It's on the seventh floor."

"You're staying here." It wasn't a question, and Olivia didn't look at all happy about it.

"Well, not for free, if that's what you're worried about. I'm paying for it." Not the whole truth, but not a lie either. Hayley swallowed, not liking what was turning out to be a continually disapproving expression on Olivia's face. *Hell, it's not like I don't see* that *look every day of my life.* She managed to keep from rolling her eyes. Not an easy feat, as that was her go-to when somebody expressed their disappointment in her.

Olivia seemed to have thoughts she didn't want to share as she stood there and just looked at Hayley for a good ten seconds. Finally, she turned and introduced Hayley to Stephanie. "She's our front desk manager. She knows pretty much everything about each guest, so if you have questions about special requirements or complaints or anything related to keeping our guests happy, you ask her."

Hayley shook Stephanie's hand. There was something comforting about her demeanor, her friendly smile, the firm-but-not-too-firm handshake. Hayley liked her instantly.

Olivia turned and went through a hidden door that took them behind the front desk and through another door. An office, nicely appointed for such a small space, led to another, much larger office. Olivia stopped in the doorway and held out an arm in half-hearted presentation.

"This is your office."

"Wow," Hayley said before she could stop herself. "This is nice." She walked in, absorbing the size of it, the shelves that lined one wall, the huge desk that must have been cherry or mahogany or some other expensive wood. The surface was so polished, she could see her reflection in it. The chair was one of those black, ergonomically correct ones, and Hayley dropped into it with a happy exhale. "I could get used to this," she muttered, locking her fingers behind her head and lifting her feet. She crossed her legs at the ankles and set them on the surface of the desk.

Olivia's eyes widened slightly before her face set back into that disapproving expression once again. She took a deep breath—Hayley could tell by the way her breasts rose, not that she was looking…okay, she totally was—and said, "I've scheduled a meeting for ten with all the department heads."

"How many departments are there?"

The question seemed to surprise Olivia, who blinked several times before ticking her responses off on her fingers. "Front desk, kitchen, bar, housekeeping, grounds, maintenance and custodial, spa. We're a small resort, but we run smoothly because of our staff. It'd be good for you to familiarize yourself." Those gorgeous brown eyes ran over Hayley, and for a minute, she let herself think Olivia was checking her out. That joy was fleeting, though, once Olivia added, "You might want to take notes or something. I'll come get you in a few minutes and we'll head to the conference room."

With that, Olivia left her alone. She didn't go far; Hayley could hear her milling about in the small office they'd walked through. Must be hers.

Hayley took her feet off the desk and used them to slowly turn her chair in circles. The massive window behind her looked out over what must be the side of the building, a long expanse of lightly snow-covered land that led to some trees in the distance. To the left, she could make out some wrought iron fencing, the solid black of it popping against the white on the ground. Must be where the pool was. To the right, she could see part of the drive that led under the outdoor canopy where guests unloaded their cars and left them for the valet to deal with. She watched as a dark green Land Rover pulled up, then inched out of her sight.

A ping sounded, announcing a text message. Hayley took her phone out of her pocket and glanced at the screen to see Guinevere's name. With a sigh, she clicked the screen off and put the phone back in her pocket without responding.

"God, what am I doing here?" she whispered to nobody. It wasn't that she was clueless. Her family had owned and run more than a dozen resorts and hotels her entire life. Some were super high-end and only catered to the very rich. Others, like the Evergreen, were a bit lower on the wealthy guests scale but still considered part of the upper crust of hotels. So Hayley had a pretty good handle on how it all worked. She'd grown up in and out of these places. She could manage one. Run it. Of course she could. Right? She was pretty sure...

It's time for you to grow up, Hayley.

Her father's voice, annoyed with her as usual, echoed in her head.

This is how you earn your money. You're thirty years old now. I'm not going to just hand it over to you anymore. You need to work for it, just like your brothers.

Ugh. Her half brothers. Her father would never in a million years consider himself sexist, but he was. All he talked about were her brothers. How successful they were. How proud he was of them. His boys! And they were good guys, Hayley had to admit. Jason was forty-five and Max was forty-seven, so there was a large age gap, but they were good guys, respectful men who loved her and she loved them.

But she'd never measure up.

Not the way her father wanted her to. It wasn't that she didn't have a head for business like her half brothers. She did, if she forced herself. But she didn't love business the way her father and siblings did. She found it tedious and hard—not difficult hard but unmoving hard—and not at all how she wanted to spend her life.

A knock on the doorjamb startled Hayley back to the present. "Ready?" Olivia stood there, looking slightly less disapproving, her expression now one of resignation.

"Oh, um..." Hayley hadn't done a thing but daydream for the—she glanced at her watch—past fifteen minutes. She hadn't even bothered with the computer. She yanked a drawer open, then another, until she found a legal-size pad of paper and a pen, grabbed them triumphantly. "Yes!" she said with more exuberance than necessary. "Ready. Lead the way."

Olivia turned away, obviously unimpressed with her, and headed out of the offices.

Hayley followed, feeling like she was being led to her execution.

❖

Oh, my God, I can't do this.

Those words ran through Hayley's head over and over again as the meeting wrapped up. She'd taken a crazy amount of notes, trying hard not to look as if she'd been scribbling feverishly like a madwoman in an attempt to learn everybody's name, what department they ran, and what issues they were having—God, did *everybody* have an issue *all the time*?

Olivia sat next to her during the meeting and, if Hayley was going to be honest, pretty much ran the thing. She called on each person, introduced them, and was fairly obvious about watching Hayley take notes. She didn't seem at all surprised that Hayley was clearly in over her head.

Hayley felt like she was drowning.

Back in her office, Hayley dropped her pad onto the desk with a slap and collapsed into her chair as if it was impossible for her to stand up any longer. She glanced at the top sheet of the pad, which was filled with names and scribbles and sentence fragments and notes in the margins going up the sides of the paper. It was a mess. She tried to read through what she'd managed to jot down clearly enough to understand.

Maintenance needed to hire two new people.

Housekeeping needed three new vacuum cleaners, and one of the washing machines was on the fritz—and needed to be fixed by maintenance, which was shorthanded because it needed to hire two new people.

The kitchen had hired extra staff to help with Thanksgiving dinner—"Oh, God, that's next week," Hayley muttered when she realized it—and Olivia had managed to help them make a shared schedule so that nobody worked the entire day except for the head chef, whose name was…Hayley scanned her chicken scratch…Tess?

The front desk needed a new printer, and she had to fire a valet for stealing change out of people's cars.

The budget for next year was due the week before Christmas.

Hayley swallowed, rifled through the sheets of paper again, and swallowed some more. Then she sat back in her chair and tried to breathe, to relax.

Her father was pretty sure the Evergreen wasn't worth keeping open. It was making a profit, but not much of one, and Hayley knew that. Which meant she also knew that he'd sent her there fully expecting her to fail miserably so he could close or sell off the resort and prove his point about her.

Well. She wasn't about to let that happen.

"Hey, Olivia?" she called out to the smaller office.

She appeared a few seconds later, leaned against the doorframe, and folded her arms across her chest, which Hayley was starting to see as her regular stance when it came to her. "Your phone has an intercom, you know."

Hayley blinked at her, then looked at the phone for the very first time. "Oh. Okay. Sorry."

"Did you need something?"

"Yeah." Hayley cleared her throat, not liking the way Olivia made her nervous. "When did the previous manager leave?"

"Roger? About six months ago. Why?"

"Really? That long? Who's been doing his job while waiting for me to arrive?"

Olivia waited a beat before answering, which Hayley found interesting. "I have. Just like I did the whole time he was here." With that, she turned and went back to her own desk.

"Oh," Hayley said softly, drawing out the word as she stared at the now-empty doorway.

❖

At the front desk, Olivia typed in some information, then scanned the screen. There it was. H. Boyd had reserved the last remaining penthouse suite a week before and had checked in last night.

"Do you think Corporate knows she's taking up a room?" she said under her breath, but loudly enough for Stephanie to hear her. "Not just a room. A penthouse suite."

"No idea," Stephanie replied, her voice just as low. "But she did mention she was paying for it. And she did enter a credit card." She pointed to the screen.

"Yeah." Stephanie was right. While it wasn't cool that Hayley was taking up a room that could be sold to a customer, it was still being paid for, so there wasn't a lot Olivia could complain about. Aside from how unprofessional it was.

"Maybe she couldn't find a place in town." Stephanie was the kind of person who could see the bright side of anything, so her giving Hayley the benefit of the doubt wasn't surprising. And just because Olivia was bent out of shape about the whole thing, that didn't mean

Stephanie had to feel the same way. Still, Olivia inexplicably wanted to hold on to her irritation a while longer.

Customers entered through the front doors then, saving Olivia from letting loose with any snide responses she might have. She swallowed them down, put on a smile, and greeted the middle-aged couple crossing the lobby floor.

She was going to have to find a way to suck this up.

CHAPTER THREE

Hayley collapsed onto the king-size bed in the bedroom of her suite with a loud groan. She lay there, flat on her back, and let herself simply breathe. She couldn't remember the last time she'd been this tired.

The cell phone in her pocket rang, and she let it ring again before making a move to extricate and answer it. She knew it was Serena, right on time, as they'd texted only a few minutes ago. She hit the green button, put the phone on speaker, and stayed staring at the ceiling.

"Hey."

"Are you alive?" Serena Winship asked, her voice laced with sarcasm.

"Barely."

"Well, you're talking, so I'm going to take that as a good sign."

"I'm sprawled on the bed in my room, and I'm not sure I can get back up again. I might just stay like this and sleep in my clothes." The reality was, Hayley was only half-kidding.

"One full day's work did that to you? Oh, honey. You really are spoiled. Your father was right." Serena had known Hayley since they were kids, and she was the only person in the world—besides Hayley's dad—who didn't let her get away with anything.

Hayley gasped. "How dare you?"

Serena laughed, then said, "Please. Suck it up, buttercup."

"You don't understand," Hayley whined. And it was a definite whine; she heard it herself. "I think my father's trying to kill me."

"Sweetie, I think your father just wants you to step up."

Hayley let loose a huge sigh. "You're supposed to cheer me up, not make me feel worse. That's your job as the BFF."

"Another of my jobs as the BFF is to call you on your shit." When Hayley didn't argue, Serena went on. "Tell me about your day. Why are you so tired?"

With a groan, Hayley forced herself to sit upright. With effort, she pushed herself off the bed and went out into the living area to find the room service menu, which she flipped through as she relayed her day to Serena. "I'm not physically tired so much as mentally. There's so much to remember. I had a meeting with all my department heads this morning. First thing. How can there be so many departments in one place? I don't even remember their names."

"That's a piece of advice I'm happy to pass along: Learn their names. It's important. They work for you. You need to know who they are. Plus, it makes it look like you give a damn."

More groaning from Hayley. "Everybody needs something in their department. And each thing costs money. And apparently, I have to come up with a budget. My assistant manager hates me, which we will come back to." She dropped her chin to her chest and muttered, "Pretty sure my father wants me to fail."

"Then don't." Serena's voice was firm. "I personally *don't* think he wants you to fail—he loves you—but if that's what you think, then prove him wrong."

"Easy to say. So much harder to do."

"Tell me why your assistant manager hates you. Which, by the way, I doubt is the case."

Hayley told Serena about the walk in the woods, meeting Olivia, the instant attraction, and the invitation to coffee. Then she told her how she'd shown up late and was pretty sure she'd taken a job Olivia thought might be hers.

"I stand corrected," Serena said with a chuckle. "She probably does hate you."

"Awesome. Thanks."

"Doesn't matter. You're not there to charm the mountain women. You're there to show your father you deserve your money."

Hayley snorted a laugh. "The *mountain women*? Have I time traveled back to 1873?"

"Hey, I'm a city girl," Serena said with a chuckle. "I don't know what people outside of that are called."

"They're called people, you dumbass."

The laughter was good. It helped. A little.

They chatted easily for a few more minutes, then hung up. Serena always put Hayley's mind at ease, but tonight, she'd fallen a bit short. Not her fault, Hayley knew. She just couldn't remember ever feeling this out of her element. It wasn't a feeling she was used to. She could usually fake her way through something unfamiliar, but this? This was different.

Her stomach rumbled loudly then, reminding her she hadn't had anything but coffee all day, and she picked up the phone to order a cheeseburger, fries, and a beer.

Olivia had her running around constantly. All day long. Meeting this person. Touring the entire resort. Checking out this room or that room. Pointing out guests. If Hayley had to guess, she'd say it was around 3:00 that afternoon when her brain had completely closed to any and all new information. Walls went up. Doors slammed shut. She simply could not absorb any more.

Olivia seemed to understand, though she wasn't happy about it.

"Yeah, nothing about me made her happy," Hayley whispered. "At least nothing after the walk." Against her better judgment, she let herself remember how easy it had been to walk through the quiet of the woods and talk to Olivia about nothing in particular. How natural it had felt.

The camera on the table caught her eye and she picked it up. Scrolling through the shots she'd taken that morning seemed to relax her just a bit. As a city girl, she wasn't terribly familiar with the kind of natural peace she'd discovered that morning in the woods even before Olivia had come along. The stillness. The lack of car horns and motors and constant hum of conversation. There'd been nothing but the birdsong and the gentle movement of branches. Hayley took so many photos, some quite good. She kept scrolling until she came to the shots of Walter, Olivia's dog. His black-and-white coloring and mismatched eyes—one blue, one brown—made him look like he belonged right there in the woods. He blended, looked like a natural part of his surroundings. She'd taken four or five shots, and after those came the ones she'd taken of Olivia without her knowledge. The first one when she'd taken Walter's face in her hands. Then she'd been stopped with Walter, letting him sniff, and Hayley was a few yards ahead. She hadn't even thought about it, just lifted the camera and snapped a few shots. She couldn't resist.

The photos couldn't have been more gorgeous, and one in particular made Hayley stop and stare at it, take it in. Olivia's hair was all tucked up in her white hat, and that was unfortunate. At the same time, it gave the contours of her face center stage. And she had a *beautiful* face. Even now, looking at the photograph, Hayley swallowed hard. Olivia's skin was olive-toned; she looked almost tan in the middle of November in the Northeast. Her eyes were big, slightly almond-shaped, and Hayley had never thought of brown eyes as having the possibility to be rich or deep or sensual, but Olivia's were all three of those things. She was looking down at her dog, his face in her hands, but her eyes were still visible. Still breathtaking. Her lips were full, especially the bottom one, and very pink. Hayley wondered what they'd feel like against hers, then immediately shook herself free of the spell cast by the photo.

"Jesus, Hayley, get your shit together," she said aloud, and set the camera back down on the table. "Just because you haven't had sex in…" She glanced up toward the ceiling as she tried to do math. "A really long time, that doesn't mean it's okay to fantasize about your assistant manager."

Although now that she thought about it, fantasizing was allowed, right? It wasn't hurting anybody, and she was pretty sure that coffee date was now off the table. Olivia was certainly fun to look at, there was no denying that. She sighed as a knock on the door sounded and somebody called, "Room service." She wished she could revisit Walking in the Woods Olivia instead of being a constant disappointment to Hates My Guts Olivia. As Hayley signed for her food, she wondered if she'd ever get to see that first version of Olivia again. The one in the woods. The one she'd asked out. The one who'd said yes.

Probably not. Wasn't the first time Hayley hadn't made the best of first impressions. No, that was a regular occurrence in her life, only this time, it was the second impression that had done her in.

The melancholy began to settle over her again, and she didn't bother to fight it. She was used to it. She sat down at the tall dining table near the small kitchen and took a bite of her burger—which was so frigging delicious, she moaned with pleasure. A glance at the far corner of the living room reminded her that she'd brought enough of her equipment to take her mind off her day, off the panic and the incessant feeling of being inadequate.

Might be just the thing she needed.

❖

"She has no clue what she's doing." Olivia took a sip of her gin and tonic, grimaced because it was stronger than expected, then shook her head in dismay. "Not a clue. She looked like the proverbial deer in headlights all day long."

"How did she get the job, I wonder," Tessa said, swigging from her beer.

The two friends sat side by side in Rosie's, a bar that had been in business in Evergreen Hills since before Olivia was born. And the bartender who waited on them looked like he'd been there since day one, all grizzled face and graying beard. But his eyes were kind, he knew Olivia's and Tessa's drinks by heart, and he was generous with his pour. Rosie's was where they went when they needed to talk about work but didn't want their discussion being overheard by other employees.

"I have no idea, but I'd sure like to find out." Olivia scowled into her cocktail.

"It was only her first day. Benefit of the doubt?" Tessa's voice was hopeful. "I mean, the girl did ask you out this morning." Tessa rolled her lips in and bit down on them.

"God, right? What's with that? Does God hate me? Because that was just mean."

Tessa let her laughter go, took another sip of beer. "Nah. He's just messing with you. I'm pretty sure he's got a sense of humor. Have you ever seen a platypus?"

"Well, I don't think he's funny." Olivia sipped, then shook her head. "That job should've been mine. I don't understand." This time, her anger had evaporated and only sadness came through in her tone. She was pretty sure Tessa could hear it.

"I know, babe." Tessa closed a hand over Olivia's forearm. After a moment passed, she said, "Maybe you need to start looking at other places? The Marquez is big. Maybe they're looking for somebody. Or Mountain View?"

Olivia shrugged in a noncommittal way. She appreciated Tessa's attempts to help, but the truth was, she didn't want to get a job someplace else. She'd been at the Evergreen for seven years as assistant manager. Before that, she'd worked summers and holiday weekends at the front desk. When she'd gone to college and studied hotel management, it was with the Evergreen in mind. There was something about the place. It was part of her. It was in her heart, in her blood, and she had no desire to leave. Evergreen Hills was her home. Unlike many of her friends, she had no wanderlust, no need to leave and see the world or live in a big city. She loved it here. Her mother was here. She had a house, a dog, and a job she loved. No, Olivia couldn't imagine being anywhere else.

"I'm good at my job."

Tessa made a humming sound. "You rock at your job."

"I do." And Olivia knew it.

They were saved from further discussion about it when the door opened and Mike Keller walked in. Tessa quickly ordered him a beer as he spotted them and crossed to take the stool next to her.

"Ladies," he said, getting comfortable. He nodded at the bartender when his beer was delivered. "Sorry I'm late. The newbie didn't know how to make a martini." Mike indicated how he felt about that by rolling his eyes. Mike was the head bartender at the Evergreen and, like Olivia, was a lifelong Evergreener. They'd known each other since the third grade.

"I noticed your not-so-secret admirer, Mrs. Graves, is here for the holiday," Tessa said, a teasing note in her voice. She leaned against Mike.

"Jealous?" Mike teased back.

"Maybe," Tessa said, then sat back up.

"She's the one who only drinks Manhattans and only if you make them, right?" Olivia asked.

"That's her." Mike took a pull from his bottle.

Tessa scratched at the side of Mike's face, then ran a finger along the hair at his jawline. "And you cleaned your beard up." Turning to Olivia, she explained. "Mrs. Graves made a comment about Mike's beard being too…what was the word?"

"Scrappy," Mike supplied with a laugh.

"Scrappy. Yes. So he obviously listened."

With a shrug, Mike said, "Hey, she's a really good tipper."

"Mm-hmm." Tessa finished off her beer and ordered another.

"What do you guys think of the new manager?" Mike asked.

Olivia groaned and Tessa laughed.

"We were just talking about that," Tessa said, then filled him in on the discussion so far.

"Wait, she asked you out?" Mike's eyes went wide as he turned to regard Olivia.

She drained her drink in response and ordered a second. "Yep."

"At least she's got good taste," he said, and Olivia turned to him, her entire demeanor softening.

"Aww, thank you, Mike." She picked up her fresh drink.

Mike shrugged, held out his drink in front of Tessa so Olivia could touch her glass to his bottle. "I just call 'em like I see 'em." They clinked. "So, she was less than impressive, huh?"

"Ugh," was all Olivia could manage.

"Maybe she just needs time to settle in. Get her shit together, you know?"

Tessa scoffed. "You're just saying that because she's pretty."

"She's not pretty," Mike said, clarifying. "She's *hot*. Big difference." He leaned forward so he could see Olivia. "Right, Livvy?"

Tessa tipped her head from one side to the other. "The man has a point."

Olivia blew out a frustrated breath. "Fine. She's hot. If only she was also competent…"

"Hey, benefit of the doubt, remember?" Tessa raised her eyebrows expectantly.

Olivia gave a reluctant nod. "Yeah, okay."

She could do that. Everybody deserved the benefit of the doubt until they proved that they didn't. Right? Even if that somebody took the job that was rightfully hers. It was fine. She could do this.

Couldn't she?

CHAPTER FOUR

Hayley's plan had been to take another walk in the woods before work. The way it had relaxed her the previous day…it was a feeling she'd like to have again, would be a nice way to start her Tuesday. And she wasn't going to lie to herself: She also remembered Olivia saying she and Walter walked there every morning. Maybe she'd run into them again, in a place where Olivia didn't hate her. Maybe…

But she'd stayed up late the night before. Much later than intended. So, when her alarm went off at 5:00 a.m., she very nearly threw the phone across the room. Instead, she managed to reset it to give her another hour of sleep.

Or so she'd thought.

When she opened her eyes again and the sun was shooting through the window onto her face, she growled in irritation and disbelief, knowing she'd overslept *again*. As usual. A glance at her phone had her swearing as she rolled onto her back and threw her arm over her eyes. She started to doze again, but caught herself and sat up. With a stretch and a yawn, she managed to pry her eyes open wide enough to navigate to the bathroom and turn on the shower.

That's what I get for staying up until after two. She shook her head as she squeezed shampoo into her hand and washed her hair. She'd gotten so lost in her work that she'd lost track of time, which wasn't unusual. Hurrying was probably the best course of action, but knowing she was already late and her father would probably hear about it eventually, she figured what was the point?

Interestingly, it wasn't thoughts of her father finding out she couldn't seem to get to her job on time, even from the same damn building, that had her feeling slightly dejected. It wasn't concern about disappointing him—some more—with her irresponsibility or proving him right that she was flighty and spoiled. No, that wasn't what sat on her chest like the lead vest you wear when getting X-rays at the dentist. No, it was the idea of putting that disapproving expression on Olivia's face for a second day in a row that had Hayley taking her time. She should've been downstairs and in her office twenty minutes ago, but it might as well have been an hour.

Once dried off, Hayley quickly brushed her teeth, dried her hair and pulled it back into a ponytail, and pulled on clothes. A coat of mascara and a bit of gloss on her lips, and she stared at her reflection.

"Ready to go disappoint the world?"

She pumped her fist in the air, grabbed her things, and headed out the door.

It was 9:43.

Hayley closed her eyes as the elevator doors slid shut.

"Damn it," she whispered, realizing she hadn't made herself any coffee. Detouring once she hit the lobby level, she headed to the Starbucks and waited in the fairly short line.

"Right on time again, I see." The voice was soft and came from behind her, and Hayley recognized it immediately.

Hayley turned to face Olivia, and those dark, dark eyes seemed to suck her right in. Make her knees a little weak. Make her palms sweat. She cleared her throat. "I'm sorry. I was up late, and I thought I set my alarm. My phone is new and…" She let her voice trail off because it was obvious by the expression on Olivia's face that not only did she not believe Hayley, she'd actually expected this. Expected Hayley to show up late. Hayley waved a hand. "You know what? Never mind. I'm sorry I'm late. Let me just grab some caffeine and we can get started."

With a nod, Olivia clicked off toward the front of the hotel, smiling and waving to various guests she passed. Hayley tried not to watch for too long, the sway of her hips, the smile that seemed so readily available. She stirred things in Hayley…

The winter season. Hayley blew out a breath. That was how long she had to stay here and do this job. Through the winter season, her father had said. That was the busy time of year for the Evergreen. So that meant once March was over, Hayley could get the hell out of this godforsaken place and go back to the city.

She counted the months on her fingers. The rest of November, December, January, February, March. A little more than four months.

Her groan had the barista looking at her quizzically. Hayley gave her a sheepish grin. "So much to choose from," she said with a shrug.

Pumpkin spice latte in hand, Hayley headed for the lobby and the front desk where Stephanie smiled at her while on a call. A younger woman was at the desk next to her, checking in a family of four. Another group was coming in the front door, and a car was pulling up in the circle outside. Things were bustling at the Evergreen Resort and Spa. Hayley headed to her office, passing Olivia's empty one as she did, and shut the door with relief. She flopped down into her chair, sipped her coffee, and used her feet to spin her chair so she could look out the window.

It really was beautiful here. Hayley could admit that, even being a city girl at heart. The trees that weren't lush evergreens were all bare of leaves, but snow still covered many of the branches, and the combination of brown trunks and green branches and white snow made for some gorgeous contrast. She bet it was even more striking to look out this window in the summer when everything was green and lush... two things she did not get in the city.

The knock on her door startled her back to the present.

"Come on in."

The door opened and Olivia stood there, a thick manila folder pressed to her chest. "You ready to go over a few things?"

"I am." Hayley gestured to the two chairs across from her desk. "Have a seat."

Olivia set the folder on the still-empty desktop and opened it. Pausing, she looked up at Hayley with those eyes and said, "You can bring personal items in here, you know. Photos or knickknacks. It's your office."

Hayley nodded, knowing she'd brought none of those things. "Okay. Cool. Thanks."

For the next two hours, they went over the pile Olivia had brought with her, and she'd forgotten nothing. From a list of all the staff and their departments to the profit report for the year so far to the menu for

Thanksgiving dinner, it was all there. Olivia went over each thing in painstaking detail, as if she knew Hayley needed it explained that way. Just when she was pretty sure her eyes had crossed in her head, Olivia closed the folder and sat back.

"That's probably good for now. It's lunchtime. Why don't we meet back here at 1:30 and I'll give you the basics on the computer you have yet to touch." Her half-grin took out much of the sarcasm in her words, and Hayley felt a small wash of relief.

"Sounds great."

Olivia patted the folder as she stood. "I'll leave this here for you."

"Thanks." Again, she watched Olivia walk away. Becoming a regular thing, apparently. Hayley told herself it had nothing to do with Olivia's amazing ass. Nothing at all.

❖

"Hi, Mama." Olivia put the phone on speaker and set it on the counter of her kitchen while she pulled ingredients for a turkey sandwich out of her fridge. "What's new? How are all the teeth?"

Angela Santini chuckled at the question, as Olivia asked it every time she called her at work. Olivia could picture her behind the horseshoe-shaped desk of the dentist's office where she'd been the admin for nearly thirty years. "So far, everybody has kept them in their head today."

"Then it's a good day."

"It is. How's my Walnut?"

Olivia peeked out the window into her small, fenced-in backyard. "Your Walnut is currently rolling in the snow, which he will then track all over my nice hardwood." She smiled, though, as not much made her happier than seeing her dog happy.

"And the new manager?" Her mother knew all about the work situation.

"Ugh," Olivia said with a groan, spreading mayo on bread. "Utterly incompetent. She's been late two days in a row. She looks at me blankly half the time when I'm explaining something to her. I swear, she's never done anything like this before. I can't understand how she got hired. Over me."

"Are you being nice, Olivia?" Angela's voice held a subtle undercurrent of scolding. "She's probably nervous being in a new job and all."

"Yes, Mama, I'm being nice." Was she? Furrowing her brow as she constructed the sandwich, she tried to be honest with herself. With a resigned sigh, she said, "You're right. I could probably be a little nicer."

"Mm-hmm," her mother said, as if expecting exactly that answer.

"It's so frustrating, though."

"I know. But this is life. You can't control anything anybody else does, only your own reactions to it."

It was advice her mother was famous for; Olivia had heard it more times than she could count in her life. And like now, it pretty much always fit. "I know. I'll try to be a little more empathetic."

"That's my girl."

They talked for another minute or two, then said their good-byes. Olivia took a bite of her sandwich while watching Walter run around the yard in the snow, which was melting in the above-freezing temperatures and turning into a wet, sloppy mess. Which was exactly what Walter would be when he came in.

She let her gaze wander to the trees that separated her house from the house behind hers, and her mind took her back to the previous morning, walking in the woods as she did every day and running into Hayley. There had been something oddly tangible about those—how long did they walk? Twenty minutes? Half an hour? Whatever the amount of time, there'd been something about it that Olivia couldn't shake. Something good that had stayed with her. Something palpable. She couldn't explain it, but she wished she could go back, relive that short span of time, before she'd actually understood who Hayley was in the grand scheme of her life.

Olivia was lonely. She could admit that. There was no shame in it. Her last relationship had ended over a year ago and she'd definitely needed some time on her own. Now, though? She'd had enough of time on her own. In a small town like Evergreen Hills, finding a date was a task in and of itself, but finding a gay date? Exponentially harder.

She finished her sandwich and checked her watch. There was time for a quick run before she had to meet back up with Hayley and explain more stuff to her that she should already know but probably didn't.

With a roll of her eyes, she opened the back door and called Walter inside.

❖

Hayley took a sip from her can of Diet Coke, which she was using to wash down the Snickers bar she'd had for lunch, as she wandered the different floors of the Evergreen. She'd reached the sports bar and grill—which was different from the fancy restaurant downstairs—and was peering through the open double doorway when her phone rang. She pulled it from her pocket and smiled as she saw her brother Jason's name on the screen.

"Hey, dickhead," she said joyfully, but lowered her voice as she caught the look of disapproval on the face of the older woman walking past. "Sorry," Hayley said, on a whisper.

"I decided to wait until day two before I called to harass you," Jason said. "How's it going? Why are you whispering? Should I be whispering, too?"

"I was walking past a guest just as I called you a dickhead, and she was not impressed with my vocabulary." Hayley continued to wander as she talked.

"Oh, yeah, you gotta be careful of that kind of thing. Managing 101. Are you wearing your name tag?"

"I don't have it yet."

"Then you're home free. This time. Once you have it on, you've got to watch the language. And smile. And say hi. To everybody."

"Okay." Hayley suppressed the groan she wanted to let loose and instead headed for the elevator so she could check out the rooftop bar.

Jason softened his tone. "You hanging in there, kiddo?"

"I'm trying," she said honestly. Jason was one of the few people in the world who Hayley felt she could be real with. "It's a lot, and I'm pretty sure Dad already thinks I'm going to screw it up."

"I disagree. I think he has more faith in you than you realize. That's why he doesn't want you to tell anybody who you are."

"But it would be so much easier just to tell people my last name is Markham." Hayley sounded like a petulant child and she knew it. All that was missing was a foot stomp.

The elevator doors slid open and Hayley found herself in a gorgeous, glassed-in lounge area with freestanding heaters to keep things warm. The 180-degree view of the grounds was stunning, even with the snow melting to reveal patches of matted-down grass. To her left was a well-stocked bar, and a brunette of about thirty that Hayley hadn't met yet smiled at her as she wiped the surface with a white rag. Hayley gave her a wave, then reentered the elevator.

"Exactly. And then everybody treats you differently and steps carefully around you. Dad wants you to actually do the work, not just coast along on your name." Their father had said very similar words to her when explaining her new job, but for some reason, when Jason said it, it didn't sting quite as much.

"What, running up a seven-hundred-dollar tab at a nightclub is coasting along on my name?" she teased.

"When the tab was actually closer to fifteen hundred, it is."

He had a point. "Fine."

"Come on, Hayley." Jason's voice was even gentler now. "You know it's all true." He didn't come right out and say she'd been spoiled her whole life and acted like it, but it was there. That the nightclub tab had simply been the straw that broke the camel's back for their father. The words weren't necessary—she could hear them in his tone.

"Yeah. I know." She tried not to whine as she reminded him, "He cut off my allowance, though."

"I know. I think he was at the end of his rope."

"If I want to buy anything, I have to ask." The humiliation she'd felt when her father had informed her of this decision reared back up, and she felt the heat in her face.

There was a beat of silence on the phone. Then, "Look, I'm here to help." Jason perked up, and Hayley could picture him sitting up straighter in his chair, looking all businessy in his suit and tie, his hair—much blonder than hers—cut close to his scalp, his face clean-shaven. "I've been doing this for a while, and I can answer pretty much any questions you have. The Evergreen is small compared to our other resorts, so this shouldn't be awful."

"I know you and Dad keep saying it's small, but it doesn't feel small. I've been wandering around for almost an hour and haven't seen everything yet."

"Didn't somebody show you around?" Jason seemed surprised.

"Yeah, the assistant manager did, but I wanted to stroll on my own. It's hard to remember where things are or how to get to them when somebody else is leading the way."

"That's a good point." There were muffled voices on Jason's end and then he said, "I gotta run. You hang in there. You're doing great. Call me if you need me."

"I will. Thanks, Jay."

"Any time. Love you."

They hung up and Hayley stepped out of the elevator and followed the signs for the indoor pool and fitness center. Many people were out and about, and she did her best to smile at each of them, remembering Jason's advice.

The indoor pool was good-sized. Not as big as the outdoor one, but still ample and, like the rooftop bar, enclosed in glass so the grounds could be seen. Hayley peeked through the glass doors, smiled as three kids were playing Marco Polo in the shallow end. Turning to her right, she saw the fitness center, also enclosed in glass. It, too, was generous in size and boasted quite a bit of equipment, albeit mostly older models. She scanned the ellipticals and stationary bikes—noting two had large pieces of white paper taped to them that she guessed said they were out of order—until her eyes stopped on one of the three treadmills.

Her heart rate kicked up.

Olivia didn't have her back to Hayley, but she was at enough of an angle where she'd have to make an effort to see Hayley where she stood. Her dark hair was in a ponytail, bouncing from one shoulder blade to the other as she ran. Her long, lean body was clad in capri-length black workout pants and a bright green racer-back tank top, black trainers with neon green accents on her feet. Her phone was strapped to her left arm and a purple cord led to the earbuds tucked snugly in her ears. Her arms and neck glistened with perspiration, her cheeks flushed a rosy pink as she pushed herself, and Hayley could do nothing but stand there and stare.

A flash came to her. From yesterday morning. Olivia catching her before she could fall, her arms tightening, her gorgeous face mere inches away…

"Gah," Hayley said, and shook her head vigorously as she turned away from the fitness center. She headed toward the bank of elevators so they could take her back down to the lobby and her office, where she could hide and hope nobody noticed her flushed cheeks and rapid breathing.

Yeah, that'd be better.

At least that's what she thought until she remembered that after lunch, Olivia was going to instruct her on the computer.

Hayley stepped into the elevator, which was blessedly empty. When the doors slid shut, she simply let her head fall forward against them and groaned loudly.

CHAPTER FIVE

"Okay? You understand?" Olivia waited for Hayley's response. Since she'd sat down and begun her tour of their network three hours ago, she'd been hoping the bewildered look that had pasted itself on Hayley's face the very first second would fade away. Into anything that said she had at least some understanding of what Olivia was showing her. "Hayley?"

Hayley blinked, and it seemed to take a significant effort to pull her attention from the screen and shift it to her assistant. "Oh, yeah. I'm good." She sounded anything but.

Olivia stared at her for a moment, then slapped her hands on her thighs and pushed herself to her feet. "All right. Here." She crossed the office—God, she wished she'd never decorated it in her head because now, that just hurt—and opened the top drawer of the filing cabinet in the corner. "Everything is online, but Roger was funny about printing things out." She pulled a folder and took it back to the desk where she'd moved a chair around so she could sit next to Hayley. "This is this year's budget." She opened the folder and smoothed her palm over the paper. "It should give you some guidance as you create next year's."

Hayley studied the sheets. At least, it seemed like that was what she was doing. Then she began to slowly nod. "Okay. Okay."

Olivia let another beat or two or seven of silence go by before she couldn't stand it anymore. "I could go over it with you tomorrow, if you'd like. Help you out a little bit. I pretty much did this one." She tapped a finger on the paper.

"Oh, my God, that'd be great. You don't mind?" Hayley looked so hopefully relieved that Olivia felt her irritation draining away.

"It's not a problem. I'm your assistant. My job is to assist you." She was reasonably sure she'd kept the snark out of her voice. Reasonably. "I would so appreciate that. Seriously." That look again.

"Not a problem. Want to meet at nine? Oh, wait." Olivia gazed off into the middle distance. "Maybe we should make it ten."

Hayley rolled her lips in and bit down on them. Nodded as if she completely understood. "Ten's probably safer," she said, but she didn't look happy about saying it. Which was interesting.

"Cool. I'll see you at ten tomorrow." Olivia escaped to her own desk. And that was the most accurate word: escaped. Sitting that close to Hayley had been…uncomfortable. In so many ways. In an annoyed way. In a confusing way. In a frustrating way. In a sexually tense way.

She exhaled slowly, letting herself accept that the sexual tension was exactly the problem and she needed to find a way to slide that to the side. It bummed her out that she had to do it, though, because the walk in the woods was still very much with her. The conversation, the subtle flirting, the way Hayley felt in her arms when Olivia kept her from falling.

Yeah.

She tipped her head from side to side, stretching out her neck, hoping to loosen the tightness that had intensified the longer she sat next to Hayley. She technically worked for Hayley now, so that sexual tension couldn't be there. It needed to go.

Problem was, she was pretty sure Hayley felt it, too.

An idea surfaced then. What if she simply did her best to focus on how much Hayley didn't know about this job? It would piss her off more often than not, absolutely, but at least she wouldn't be struggling with this not unpleasant discomfort. Because *that* needed to go away.

There was another hour of the workday left, but Olivia had zero desire to stay in her office, in danger of Hayley coming to ask her a question. Leaning close. In her space.

"Damn it." She slammed her desk drawer shut, grabbed her cell and slid it into her blazer pocket, and left her office, heading for Split Rail. Along the way, she waved to a couple of guests, then noticed Gary Shields heading her way.

"Hi there, Mr. Shields," she said with a smile.

"Olivia. How many times have I told you to call me Gary?" His voice was kind, as were his blue eyes. He was a regular guest at the

Evergreen and had been with them over Thanksgiving for the past two years, this being his third.

"Sorry." Olivia bowed her head in recognition. "Gary." She took in his ski jacket and boots, gloves and hat, the rosy color in his cheeks. "Were you snowshoeing?"

He pulled the ski hat off his head, revealing a mess of curly salt-and-pepper hair that seemed to do whatever it wanted. "That was the plan. It's kind of messy out. Didn't need the snowshoes after all. It was muddier than I like, but still nice."

"Nothing like that fresh November air, huh?"

"Nothing." He smiled as he moved past her. "How are you? Hanging in there?"

Olivia turned to face him as she walked backward. "Busy but good, thanks for asking."

With a wave, he was off and Olivia continued toward the restaurant.

Dinner prep was in full swing in the kitchen, Tessa shouting orders, and Olivia loved to stand in an out-of-the-way corner and watch. Tessa was loud, but she was never mean. Never disrespectful. She was a kind boss and wanted her underlings to succeed, not cower in her presence.

"Joey, keep those mushrooms in a single layer or they won't brown." She stood over one of her sous chefs as he shook a frying pan filled with sizzling mushrooms. "Single. Layer. Got it?" Joey nodded as Tessa looked up and saw Olivia. She smiled widely.

She always looked so amazing in her chef's coat and hat. Olivia loved the whole look. Tessa was gorgeous anyway, with her deep complexion and her big, brown eyes that saw *everything*, and the white uniform just elevated her presence somehow. She was the one in charge, no matter where she was. When she walked into a room, you just knew that. It was a little intimidating at first, but it eventually became awe-inspiring. At least, that was how it had been for Olivia when they'd first met a few years ago.

Tessa approached her, wiping her hands on a white rag. "Hey, how's it going?"

Olivia simply gave her a look.

"Ah, that well, huh?"

Olivia simply shook her head.

"Come with me. I need halibut."

Olivia furrowed her brow but followed Tessa until they reached the walk-in cooler where the fresh items that were delivered each day were stored. Once inside, Tessa turned to her and folded her arms so her bare hands were tucked into her armpits.

"Tell me quick before we both freeze to death."

Olivia mirrored Tessa's position, then shrugged. "I'm honestly kind of shocked by how little she knows about the business. I don't think she's an idiot by any means, but she just seems so…" She looked around the cooler, as if the word was propped on one of the metal shelves. "New. She seems really new to the running of a hotel, and I don't understand it."

Tessa made a sound somewhere between a grunt and a groan. "What can you do, though? Right?"

"Right. I'm doing my best to show her the things she doesn't get, and she's a good listener and a quick study, so there's that. But I'm starting to worry a little bit about this place. You know?"

"Yeah," Tessa said, but it was clear she wasn't sure what to say.

Olivia shrugged again. "Oh, well. All I can do is the best I can, right?" When Tessa nodded, she went on. "How are things looking for next Thursday? You have everything you need?"

By unspoken agreement, they exited the cooler, and Olivia was happy to be back in the heat of the bustling kitchen.

"We've got a few more deliveries coming, but aside from those, we're good. I'm proud of the menu." And Tessa looked it. She was notoriously hard on herself, so to see her looking content and satisfied made Olivia's heart happy.

"Great. I look forward to it."

Tessa scanned the kitchen, watching over her staff, which—as far as Olivia's non-cooking eyes could tell—was moving like a well-oiled machine. Chefs had their heads bowed over blue-flaming burners with pans on them. Waitstaff came in through the swinging doors, grabbed plates, left again. The air was filled with so many delicious smells, Olivia could only pinpoint a few: onions, garlic, beef. "Your mom coming to Thanksgiving dinner?" Tessa asked, pulling Olivia's focus back to her.

"She's talked about little else lately."

"Tony and Ann Marie, too?" Tessa asked, referring to Olivia's younger siblings.

Olivia nodded. "And Tony's bringing Priya."

"He's still with her, huh? That's new for him."

"I know, right? I don't think my mom knows what to do with it." They stood quietly for another moment, watching the show before them. Finally, Olivia said, "Okay, go work. I just needed a break. I'm going to go wander a bit, make sure things are running smoothly."

"It's what you do," Tessa said. "Thanks for checking in. Go." Tessa waved her away as she dove back into the action of the kitchen.

Olivia watched for a few more minutes before leaving the kitchen. She waved to Mike behind the bar and headed out into the open lobby area of the Evergreen, which was humming with activity. This was good. She could throw herself into the mix, chat up the guests, make sure everybody had what they needed.

Anything to keep her from going back to the office.

She'd had enough of Hayley today.

❖

Hayley's brain hurt. Literally hurt. She had this crazy image of it as a bag of some sort, and she'd just crammed it way too full of computer instruction and tidbits about the resort and rules about the staff and the intricacies of the budget, and now the brain bag was bulging at the seams—which culminated in a pounding headache for her.

Olivia had been beyond annoyed with her, but Hayley had to give her kudos for her patience. She'd been pretty good at masking her annoyance. It was only because Hayley was used to ticking people off, used to the irritated expression she'd become a pro at causing to appear on people's faces, the closed-up body language, that she'd had any clue. Olivia really was a consummate professional.

A consummate professional who smelled incredible.

With a literal shake of her head, Hayley pushed herself to her feet. "Enough of that," she muttered.

Her body needed a good stretch, and she reached over her head and did just that: stretched as high as she could, hands over her head, then she tipped from one side to the other, working out the kinks that had formed in her back over the past few hours. She squeezed her eyes shut—they were burning a bit from staring at both the computer screen and the small numbers on the budget printout—and wanted to rub them fiercely. She avoided doing that but blinked several times until they felt better.

A glance at her cell told her it was after five—and also that she'd missed texts from both Serena and Guin. She had no energy to deal with either woman, so she ignored them for now. She opened the door to her office and was surprised to see not Olivia but a young girl, maybe eighteen, sitting at Olivia's desk, nose in what looked like a textbook. She glanced up at Hayley, then tugged one earbud out.

"Hey," she said, in that tone all teenagers had that said they were completely bored with life. And you.

"Hey," Hayley said back.

The girl put the earbud back in and returned her attention to her book while Hayley squinted at her. When it was clear that was all she was going to get, she headed out to the front desk where Stephanie and another girl were busily working.

Stephanie tapped away at her keyboard while an older, extremely well-dressed gentleman stood at the counter and waited. Hayley inched up behind her and said quietly, "Who's that girl in Olivia's office?"

Stephanie jumped and Hayley laid a hand on her shoulder.

"Oh, my God, I'm so sorry. I didn't mean to scare you." She grimaced as Stephanie turned to her, that same subtle look of irritation Olivia had sported clear on her face.

"That's my daughter, Maddie. She comes to pick me up at the end of my shift and always does her homework at Olivia's desk." She turned back to the gentleman and apologized.

"Oh. Okay." Trying hard not to feel dismissed—but feeling exactly that—Hayley decided she'd had enough for today and headed toward the elevators. She was starving and, after looking at numbers for much of the day, was seized with a burning need to do something creative rather than logical.

How the hell was she going to survive this for four months?

CHAPTER SIX

Thanksgiving fell later in the month than it had in a few years, and the snow that had fallen overnight gave the world the fresh, clean look that was one of the things Olivia loved most about winter. It also muffled the sound of life a little bit, so when she and Walter were strolling through the woods, everything felt peaceful and quiet. The sun was just breaking over the trees, making the snow sparkle like glitter had been sprinkled all over it. The only sound was that of Olivia's footsteps as she walked along after her dog.

This was as close to meditation as she'd ever get, and she relished it.

Another thing she loved was making the first tracks along the path she and Walter walked every morning and sometimes at night. It might be a weird thing for her to derive pleasure from, but there was something about it, about being the very first human to walk through the fluffy white that made her feel grounded. She glanced down as she came to a fork in the path and furrowed her brow.

There was another set of footprints ahead of hers.

Her consternation annoyed her because she obviously knew she didn't own the woods, and it was a silly thing to get annoyed about, but still. It took a little bit of the spring from her step. She picked up her pace as she couldn't see Walter, who'd gone over the little berm ahead, and she followed his tracks—which followed the other ones.

As she crested the small rise in the path and her eyes found Walter, she was hit with a major sense of déjà vu. There was her dog, his butt wiggling with happiness.

And there was the red parka.

"Damn it," Olivia muttered.

Hayley turned around then, as if she'd heard, and stood up from the squat she'd been in while petting Walter. "Fancy meeting you here," she said, her smile a bit hesitant and much dimmer than the first time they'd met here. *God, was that only last week?*

"Hi." As she approached, Olivia gestured to the camera that once again hung from Hayley's neck, resigned to making at least a little bit of small talk. "Getting anything good?"

Hayley's expression seemed to brighten a bit. "I am. The sun coming up over the horizon is just breathtaking. Here, check it out."

Olivia stepped closer and tried not to be affected by the proximity.

Hayley wore gloves with no fingers, presumably so she could snap away on the camera, and she pushed a few buttons, then scrolled so Olivia could see the photos she'd taken.

"Wow," Olivia said softly, unable to hide her surprise. They were gorgeous. The way Hayley framed the peeks of sunlight that seemed to drop over the branches, the way the combination of colors—from the brown and green of the evergreens to the white of the snow to the soft yellow of the rays of sun—evoked a mood of peace and tranquility. "These are beautiful." Olivia meant it. She admired a couple more before asking, "What do you do with them? Frame them? Sell them?"

"I paint them." Hayley said the words as if they embarrassed her, as if she was ashamed, and she looked down at her feet.

"Really? Like, on a canvas and everything?"

That seemed to amuse her, and Hayley's smile grew a bit wider and seemed less tentative. "Yes, on canvas. Usually with pastels, but I've been experimenting with oil paints."

Olivia wasn't sure why she was so surprised—and intrigued— by this unexpected tidbit of new information. "Maybe you could show me some of your work some time?" *What? What? God, did I actually say that out loud? Am I in a cheesy romantic comedy with that line?* She quickly turned her focus to Walter, who could not get enough of Hayley, apparently, and was pushing his snout at her for more attention. "Wally, enough."

"He's okay," Hayley said, and lowered her hand so the dog could sniff and lick at her fingers. "He's such a sweet boy. Has he always been like that?"

As if by unspoken agreement, they fell into step together and headed down the path in the direction of the parking lot, Walter on his leash now, just like they had the first time they'd met. It was as if they did it all the time, this walk, and again, Olivia had to force herself not to dwell on those thoughts.

"He has. Not a mean bone in his body. He's the gentlest creature I've ever known."

"I always wanted a dog." Hayley's voice held a wistful quality to it, and when Olivia glanced at her, she was gazing off into the distance.

"You've never had one?"

"My brother was allergic. He's quite a bit older, so once he moved out, I started to torment my dad to get me one."

"No luck?"

"He's a tough nut to crack, my father."

"What about when you moved out?" Olivia lowered her voice and teased, "I assume you don't live in your parents' basement."

Hayley's chuckle held a musical quality. "No. I have my own place. I promise. I just never got around to seriously considering a dog once I got older." Something crossed her face then, quickly, but Olivia couldn't pinpoint what it was. "I travel a lot and stuff."

Olivia nodded as if she totally got it. "Are you seeing family today for dinner?"

"Dinner?" Hayley's light brow furrowed and she glanced at Olivia, clearly puzzled.

"It's Thanksgiving. Remember?" Honestly, they'd just discussed this yesterday.

"Oh! Right. We set up a schedule and everything. Totally slipped my mind." She spun a finger near her temple and widened her eyes. "No. No, I'm not seeing any family. I'll just be here. I know you said you usually hang here, but are you sure you don't want to take the afternoon? I'm sure I can handle things."

Olivia stopped in her tracks, every gene she'd inherited from her mother screaming in protest. "Wait. You're not going anywhere for Thanksgiving?"

Hayley had gone four steps ahead before apparently realizing Olivia had stopped. She turned and blinked at her. "No?"

"You're not spending it with your family?"

"No?"

"It's just you? All by yourself?"

"Yes?"

Olivia smiled at how all Hayley's responses sounded like questions. But then she grew serious again. This would not do. Her mother would kill her. "You're eating with us, then."

Hayley's eyes went wide. "Um, what?"

Olivia started walking again. She heard Hayley scramble to catch up. "My family comes to Split Rail because Roger"—she glanced at Hayley—"the guy who had the job before you, always had me work the holidays. My mom got fed up and decided that she and my brother and sister would come to the Evergreen instead of waiting for me to get home—which always ended up being way past dinnertime—and it's been great. We're all together, she doesn't have to cook, and I'm nearby if something happens and I'm needed."

"He made you work holidays? Plural?"

Olivia nodded.

"Well, that's some bullshit right there."

The factual manner in which Hayley said the words made Olivia burst out laughing. "It is, right?"

"Absolutely. What a prick. I assume *he* went home?"

"He did. Every holiday. Except for Halloween. Because he hated Halloween."

"Who hates Halloween? I repeat, what a prick." They walked a bit farther and finally reached the parking lot. Hayley turned to her, all humor gone from her face. "Listen, Olivia, I really appreciate the invitation, but it's not necessary."

"I know. But my mom will ask about you, and when I tell her you're alone, she will march herself right up to your room if she has to and drag you to dinner by your ear. So you might as well save her the trip."

They stood quietly in the parking lot then, Walter between them, looking up and turning his head from one of them back to the other.

"Okay," Hayley finally said quietly.

Olivia felt the grin spread across her face without her permission. "Good. Tessa has dinner being served at seven, as you know, but my family always comes a little early for drinks. So we'll see you there."

Hayley's cheeks were flushed and her smile was beautiful as she walked backward toward her car. "Thank you, Olivia."

Olivia nodded, forced herself to turn away and lead Walter to her own vehicle. Once inside—and sure Hayley had pulled out of the lot—she dropped her forehead to the steering wheel and groaned loudly.

What had she just done?

❖

"What the hell have I done?" Hayley asked her reflection in the bathroom mirror later that day. And why was she so nervous?

The day had been a long one, though the atmosphere around the Evergreen had been light and fun. Folks were in a good mood, laughing and joking, and Hayley had to admit it had been the best day so far, no lie.

Now she fussed with her hair, trying to tame the one hunk that liked to do its own thing, especially when she was trying to look presentable. She gave up on the errant locks and went out into the suite to stand in front of the full-length mirror. Thank God she'd packed her little black dress, because she hadn't packed much more that was beyond pants and shirts for her managing position—though if she asked Olivia, they weren't suitable for that.

No, she told herself. *Don't do that. Don't be snotty about her. She invited you to dinner with her family so you wouldn't be alone. That was nice.*

And it was. Hayley had a feeling it was more to satisfy Olivia's mom than anything else, but whatever. It wasn't until Hayley started to dress for dinner that, despite her nervousness, she found herself happy to not be spending Thanksgiving by herself.

Yeah. She didn't want to give too much time to that thought.

Serena had called her that morning to wish her a happy Thanksgiving, adding, "Guinevere keeps asking me where you are. You seriously didn't even tell her?"

"I was afraid she'd follow me," Hayley said, expressing a legitimate fear. "I just needed to get away from her."

"Yeah." Serena knew Guin could be pushy and demanding, so Hayley was pretty sure she got it.

Hayley shook any thoughts of Guinevere from her head, smoothed her hands down her sides, added a chunky necklace, and stepped into her black shoes with the slight heel. Serena was always trying to get her to wear higher heels, but Hayley couldn't get the horrifying image of rolling an ankle and falling on her ass in the middle of a crowd of people out of her head, so she tended to play it safe. Two inches, max.

Maybe she could look Olivia in the eye then.

Pretending she didn't just have *that* thought, she gave her hair one last fluff, glanced at her phone, which told her it was almost 6:30, and hurried out the door and into the hall.

Guests were dressed to the nines, Hayley noticed, as she did her best to fly under the radar. She nodded and smiled, but being new—and without her name tag—most people didn't know she was the hotel manager, and she kind of liked it like that. Way less pressure to impress, which she sucked at, so tended to avoid. In the back of the elevator, she smiled as she listened to a young boy of maybe seven telling his parents everything he was about to eat for Thanksgiving dinner, including "corn berries."

"Cranberries, honey." The woman holding his hand corrected him gently.

"That's what I *said*," the boy replied, obviously annoyed by his mother's inability to hear him correctly.

To Hayley's left was a beautiful woman with shining silver hair. Her red dress was by a designer Hayley recognized, and it probably cost a couple grand. A visible shiver went through the woman's body as the man next to her put his arm around her.

"Still cold?" he asked softly.

The woman nodded. "The hot water ran out so fast."

"I'm sorry I took such a long shower."

"You really didn't," the woman said, and shivered again. "I'm warming up. Some hot food will help."

"So will a martini," the man said with a chuckle, as the doors slid open again.

The elevator proceeded to stop at every floor, and by the time it was headed for the lobby, Hayley was flattened against the back wall by well-dressed, hungry hotel guests.

In the lobby, the riders spilled out of the elevator and moved in the same direction—toward Split Rail—like a school of fish. The hum of conversation mixed with the clicking of heels on the granite floor mixed with the scents of various pricey perfumes and colognes. Hayley observed it all from the back of the crowd, taking it all in, as she kept her pace leisurely so she didn't arrive at the restaurant with them. At the front desk, she stopped, rested her forearms on it, and waited for the guests to disappear around the corner.

Stephanie had worked the early shift and had since gone home to make dinner for her family, so a young man Hayley had met earlier, Jacob, stood behind the desk. If she remembered correctly what Olivia had said when they'd been introduced, Jacob was a college student who picked up hours at the Evergreen over the summer and when he was home for a holiday. When he glanced up and saw her, his eyes widened and he straightened his relaxed posture as if he were a soldier and Hayley, his commanding officer. She noticed him subtly (or not so subtly, really) slide his phone into his back pocket.

Hayley looked at him, keeping her expression dead serious for a beat, before she burst out in a laugh. "Relax, Jake. It's Thanksgiving."

"Yes, ma'am." His eyes darted around nervously.

"Ma'am?" Hayley echoed and put on her best horrified face. "Dude, I'm thirty, not fifty."

Jacob nodded, and his Adam's apple bobbed as he swallowed. His cheeks slowly began to redden.

Hayley shook her head with a grin and reached across the counter to pat his shoulder. "Seriously, take a breath. You're fine."

She hoped she'd calmed Jacob's nerves a bit, but meanwhile, hers hadn't settled. Hayley noticed, as she walked toward Split Rail, the butterflies in her stomach and the way she couldn't seem to stop clenching and unclenching her fists.

She'd never been good at first impressions.

A small group of people waited at the hostess podium while reservations were found and folks were led to their tables. Hayley scooted past everybody and made her way in, then stood and scanned the room.

Split Rail was classy, there was no arguing that. All dark wood and dim lighting and white tablecloths, it evoked a mood of richness. Of warmth. Of elegance. Hayley fit right into this kind of place, having practically grown up in them, and she felt some of her nerves slide away...until she located Olivia leaning on the bar and chatting with a handful of other people. Somebody said something funny, and she threw her head back and let go of a laugh Hayley had never heard from her before. It was gorgeous and sexy, and when she saw Hayley and their eyes locked, all those nerves came screeching right back into Hayley's body. Multiplied by about a million.

"Oh, what the hell was I thinking?" she muttered to herself, as Olivia waved her toward the group and she headed in her direction.

She was gorgeous, Olivia was. Hayley tried to take her in while not looking like that was what she was doing. Olivia's dress was a deep ivory—a bold choice for this time of year, but it worked wonders. It was the perfect combination of classy and goddamn sexy, and Hayley swallowed hard. All that dark hair was down, pin straight and sleek, and Hayley could easily picture Olivia on the catwalk during Fashion Week in New York.

The woman who was talking to Olivia and had her back to Hayley turned as Hayley stepped into their group. She was shorter than Olivia, but her smile was definitely bigger than Olivia's. She didn't have that slightly reserved, probably irritated veil that Olivia always seemed to have around Hayley. But it was more than obvious this was Olivia's mom.

"You must be Hayley," the woman said, closing her hand over Hayley's forearm. Her smile reached her eyes, also unlike Olivia, and crinkled them at the corners adorably. "I'm so happy to meet you. I'm Angela." And before Hayley knew it was happening, Angela Santini wrapped her in a warm hug.

Hayley looked over Angela's shoulder at Olivia, eyes wide. Olivia simply smiled in amusement, shrugged, and sipped her red wine.

The difference between Morning Walk Olivia and Work Olivia was marked, but Hayley realized quickly that there was more to the repertoire: With Her Family Olivia was the one at the dinner table that night, and she was different from the other two. While Morning Walk Olivia was quiet and kind, With Her Family Olivia was a little louder, a little bossy—though in a different way than at work. Very big sistery. Which made sense, as that was exactly what she was. Hayley watched the dynamic between Olivia, her brother Tony—who'd brought his girlfriend, Priya, who seemed to be fairly new, given the way Olivia and Angela were watching every move she made and asking her nine thousand questions—and her sister Ann Marie.

"What's this?" Ann Marie asked as she pointed to the orange pile on her plate.

"Squash. You'll like it," Olivia said, before Angela could chime in.

"I don't like squash," Ann Marie said with a grimace.

"You'll like this. Tessa made it different this year. Just give it a try."

Ann Marie studied Olivia for a moment, then pointed at her with her fork. "You did good with the flatiron." She took a bite of the squash.

Olivia colored slightly, cleared her throat, and thanked her sister. With a quick glance at Hayley, then back down to her plate, she said, "Ann Marie does hair."

"Olivia has so much to work with," Ann Marie said, as her face lit up. She was obviously excited to be talking about a subject she knew. "Her hair is gorgeous. But she wears it two ways: down or in a ponytail. I'm trying to get her to branch out."

"It's ha-a-ard," Olivia said, making the word into three syllables.

Ann Marie grinned and shook her head. "You're ridiculous."

Hayley put a forkful of potatoes into her mouth as she observed these two sisters who were grown adults but obviously fell back into childhood roles with minimal effort. The exchange about the squash told Hayley that Angela had worked a lot and Olivia helped to raise her siblings. The back-and-forth about the hair was just kind of sweet to watch, and not for the first time, Hayley wished she'd had a sibling closer to her own age.

"Where are your parents today, Hayley?" Angela's question caught Hayley off guard, and she used the act of sipping from her water glass to collect herself.

"Um...my dad is traveling for work." She wasn't actually sure if that was true, but since it was more often than not, she went with it. "And my mom passed away a couple years ago."

"Oh, no. I'm so sorry to hear that." Angela gave Hayley's upper arm a gentle rub.

"I didn't know that. I'm sorry, too."

Hayley turned her head to meet Olivia's dark, dark gaze and found genuine sympathy there. "Yeah. Thanks."

"You have other family?" Angela asked. "Siblings?"

"I do, yes." Hayley nodded, reminding herself there was no reason to be nervous. She could tell the truth about her family without actually letting on who they were. "I have two older half brothers. My mother was my father's second marriage."

"Oh, I see. And, where are they today?"

"Mama. Can you stop with the inquisition?" Olivia's voice was gentle but held a tone of firmness. She didn't look at Hayley. "It's Thanksgiving."

A flash of shame zipped across Angela's face super fast, but she recovered. "You're right." Turning to Hayley, she apologized. "I'm sorry. I'm just making conversation."

Despite the slight edge of relief at having the focus taken off her, Hayley now felt bad, Angela's regret was so apparent. "It's absolutely okay. Really." When it seemed like everything was good again, she asked, "What about you?" hoping to shift the focus. "What do you do?"

Dinner went on and Hayley, surprisingly, found herself enjoying it as long as she didn't look at Olivia for more than a second or two. Olivia wasn't thrilled to have her there. Her displeasure wasn't overt, but there was just something in her demeanor that Hayley could see. She was pretty sure Angela could see it, too, though nobody addressed it. She didn't really talk directly to Hayley at all, just added a line to the conversation here and there. Hayley let it roll off her as best she could. Maybe having Olivia's family at the table buffered everything, Hayley wasn't sure. All she knew was that sharing Thanksgiving dinner with the Santinis was mostly pretty okay, and as time passed, Olivia did seem to relax. Not a lot, but a little. The wine? Maybe. Initially, Hayley had thought being alone in her suite painting was the way she was going to spend the evening, and she was okay with that. But this was…nice. Nicer. Nicer than being alone.

And the food!

"My God, Tessa can *cook*, huh?" she said, as she wiped up every last trace of dinner from her plate with her final bite of bread.

"Is this your first meal here?" Tony asked, his plate as clean as Hayley's.

Hayley nodded. "I only arrived last week. I mean, I've had room service, but nothing more than a burger. This." She waved her hand over the table. "Listen, I'm from New York City. We have the best restaurants in the country there, on every street. But this was amazing."

"You should tell her." It was Olivia, and her voice was quiet. Matter-of-fact.

"Who?" Hayley furrowed her brow.

"Tessa. It's always nice to hear you did a good job from the boss." So much for the wine relaxing her.

There was something about the way Olivia said the word "boss." She didn't sneer it. She wasn't sarcastic. But her tone soured it just enough for Hayley to catch the dig. She let it sting for just a second before deciding maybe she'd stayed long enough. "You know what? That's a great idea. I'll do that." She wiped her mouth with her linen napkin and tucked it under the side of her plate. "Thank you so much for letting me crash your holiday dinner, Mrs. Santini." With a smile at Angela, then the others—carefully avoiding Olivia—she excused herself.

❖

Angela glanced around the table. Tony and Priya were deep in conversation and Ann Marie was scrolling on her phone. Pointing to Hayley's abandoned chair next to her, Angela gestured for Olivia to come sit next to her.

"Well, I hope you're happy," Angela said, when Olivia had scooted into the chair. She kept her voice low, but her eyes were narrowed and it was very clear to Olivia that she was not happy with her.

"What? What did I do?" Olivia feigned innocence, something that had never, ever in her life worked on her mother, so she had no idea why she continued to try it at thirty-two years old.

"You were rude, and you know it."

Olivia opened her mouth to respond, but knew better.

"I raised you better than that."

Her mother was right. "I know." She grimaced and shook her head. "I'm sorry. I can't seem to help it with her sometimes." She nibbled on the inside of her cheek. "The whole thing just makes me so mad." She reached back to her old seat to grab her almost-empty wineglass. "I don't understand it, Mama."

"Maybe it's not for you to understand."

They were words Angela Santini had learned to accept and live by, and Olivia knew that. But she was not ready to embrace them in this instance. All she wanted was for the evening to be over. And something stronger than wine.

"Maybe," she said. Then she made a show of glancing over her shoulder toward the bar. "I'm going to go chat with Mike for a bit."

Her mother nodded but said nothing more, and Olivia made her escape.

Mike was the head of the bar in Split Rail, so he delegated more often than he actually tended bar. Tonight was busy, though, and he jumped in every so often to mix up a drink or shake a martini to perfection. As all the waitstaff did, he wore black pants, a white oxford, a black vest, and a bow tie—which sounded really lame when described in those terms, but Mike looked nothing short of handsome, his dark hair combed back and his beard neatly trimmed again. Olivia found an empty stool at the far end and took a seat.

"Hey, Liv, happy Thanksgiving." He leaned over the bar to kiss her on the cheek. "Been so busy today I haven't had a chance to see you."

Olivia didn't need to order and Mike didn't need to ask. In under a minute, he slid a gin and tonic her way. She grinned at him.

With a half shrug, he said, "I saw you had her at your dinner table and thought maybe the wine wasn't doing the trick." He craned his neck. "She's gone?"

Olivia grit her teeth in an "oops" type of grimace. "I wasn't exactly welcoming, I'm told by my mother."

Mike's thick brows met in a V above his nose. "But you invited her."

"I did. Yeah." She hoped the face she made conveyed to Mike what a dumb decision she thought that had been.

Mike scooted out of the way to let one of his bartenders pass. Then he put his forearms on the bar in front of Olivia and looked her in the eye. "Okay, I'm going to say something and you can't get mad."

Olivia arched a brow, but said nothing.

"Because I'm just stating a fact here." His face was expectant and Olivia finally gave him one nod of permission to continue. "It's not her fault that she got the job you wanted."

Olivia looked down into the clear liquid of her drink, studied the lime, turned the glass in her hands. He was right. Mike was absolutely right. And Olivia wasn't a stupid woman; she knew what he was saying. Had known from the beginning. She scratched her head and looked up at him as guests bustled around her. With a frustrated, resigned sigh, she admitted, "I want somebody to blame."

It was the most honest thing she'd said in a long time.

"I know." Mike twisted a piece of lemon rind over the glass he was working on. "Not her fault," he repeated.

"Ugh. Okay. Fine." She added a little extra-sarcastic snark so Mike would know she was okay with what he'd said. She sipped her drink and looked around the restaurant. Most tables had finished up their desserts, and there was less boisterous excitement and more of a hum of conversation. Things were settling down. "Tessa must be relieved," she said, and as if on cue, Tessa appeared, all white chef's coat and respected authority. Olivia got up and offered her stool, which Tessa took immediately and with great relief, judging by her long exhalation of breath.

"I am officially off the clock, Mikey. Hit me."

Again, Mike didn't need to be told. He slid a clear shot glass in front of her and filled it with Absolut. Tessa downed it, indicated to Mike that she wanted a refill, then turned to Olivia.

"I hope that was okay."

Olivia shrugged. "You're off the clock. Dinner was spectacular, by the way. I thought you should hear it from your assistant manager."

"Well, I heard it from my manager as well, so here's to a kick-ass day of work for me." Tessa held up her shot glass.

"You did?" Olivia touched her glass to Tessa's, who sipped the vodka this time.

"Yep. She came back into the kitchen—did a good job of staying out of the way this time—and congratulated the whole line on a job well done. I don't think Roger ever bothered with that. Not once. It was nice."

Olivia didn't tell either of them that she'd assumed Hayley had used talking to Tessa simply as an excuse to leave…that she hadn't thought Hayley would *really* compliment Tessa on dinner, let alone the entire line of cooks. Instead, she sat quietly.

"Hot date tonight?" Mike asked as Tessa sipped.

"Nope. You?"

Mike shook his head. "How's that dating app been working for you?"

Tessa rolled her eyes with a groan. "It's brutal. They're all brutal."

"Been there, done that. I completely hear you."

Olivia nursed what remained of her gin and tonic, wanting another but knowing she had to drive home.

"I just feel like it'd be so much better to meet somebody in person, you know?" Tessa shrugged, looked from Mike to Olivia. "Like, then you know if there's chemistry. You can't really judge that by words on a screen. Or even a photo."

Mike nodded as Tessa spoke, his eyes never leaving hers. Olivia hid a grin behind her now-empty glass.

"I'm going to go back to my table. I left my mom alone with the two lovebirds and the girl in love with her phone. She's probably bored out of her skull by now." She left her glass on the bar, bid good-bye to her friends—kissing each on the cheek—and went back to her family.

Her head was full and racing. So many thoughts and so many conflicting emotions. Not what she'd expected from her Thanksgiving a couple of days ago.

Her mother stood as she approached. "You ready? I think I'm going to head out."

"Yeah, I'll walk out with you." Turning to her siblings, she said, "Mama's ready to go, you guys." They'd all driven together except for Olivia.

Tony jumped up as if poked with a cattle prod and offered to get the coats from the coat check. Priya watched him go. Ann Marie slid her phone into her purse and stood.

Hayley was nowhere to be seen, and part of Olivia was relieved by that. Another larger part felt guilty, as she knew she could've been a little warmer. She was quiet as she walked out with her family, knowing she had to make a shift in her attitude around Hayley and around her job.

She just wasn't sure how.

CHAPTER SEVEN

It was the middle of her third week, and Hayley had never felt so stressed out in her life. The number of things she was in charge of as manager was flabbergasting. She'd done her research—okay, a small amount, but at least she'd done some—when her father had first dropped this ridiculous punishment on her. She had a business degree. She wasn't completely clueless. But good God, there was so much.

It was going on eight on the Wednesday night after Thanksgiving, and Hayley was still in her office behind the front desk staring at things on her computer screen that she needed to deal with. The Evergreen was mostly quiet, though she could hear music coming from the bar at Split Rail through the side wall, which butted up to the restaurant.

Digging her knuckles into her eyelids, she rubbed hard, no longer concerned about smearing what was left of her makeup. That ship had sailed. She let go of a long, slow breath and took in the office. Olivia's suggestion to bring in a few personal items had been a good one. The framed photo of Hayley and Serena made her smile. The one of Hayley and her mother warmed her heart. She turned to look at the painting she'd hung on the wall, the only one of hers she'd decided to display. It always made her smile, made her heart happy, took her back to some of the best days of her life.

Some of her stress slid off as she sat there with her memories, but her cell phone rang, yanking her rudely back to the present. She looked at the screen and the sliding-away stress reversed direction and slid right back on, settled itself firmly on her shoulders.

"Hi, Dad," she said.

"Hayley." Her father's voice was deep. Authoritative. There was a beat of silence, something Hayley'd grown used to as a child. Benton Markham was always working on other things when on the phone. You never had his full attention. Hayley waited him out. "How are things?" he asked, after a moment.

"Things are great. Things are going really well." No way was she going to tell him she was drowning. And prove him right? Not a chance.

"That's good to hear. I assume you'll have a budget for us before long? I see four resorts still haven't turned theirs in, and the Evergreen is one."

"I'm working on it." Not a lie. "But…" She racked her brain to remember what Olivia had said. "It's not due until the end of the year, correct?"

"That's correct. I've just found that with December being so busy for folks and the holidays taking up so much time, most of my people tend to get their budgets in early."

"I see. Okay. Well, I'm on it."

"Good. Thanksgiving went well, I assume? The numbers are decent, which is a nice change."

Hayley's brain was scrambling to speak the same language as her father. For a split second, she thought he was asking about her Thanksgiving. But no, he was all business. She shook her head, wondering why she'd even allow herself to think otherwise. "It did. We were completely booked. And dinner was fabulous."

"Good news. Anything else?" He was ready to move on to the next thing on his list, Hayley knew, ready to check her off.

"Actually…" She let it dangle in the air while she gathered her words. "Can you take the freeze off my credit card? I need some things."

The silence on the other end of the phone was nearly deafening. Finally, her father said, "What is it you need?"

Hayley could lie. She could make up something necessary. God knew she'd done it before. But she knew she was already on thin ice with her father, and he did not take it lightly when he was misled. She cleared her throat. "There are a few art supplies I'm low on. Canvases. Green paint. A couple brushes."

More silence.

Just when Hayley was about to say, "never mind," her father spoke.

"Fine. I'll take the hold off. But, I'll be watching, Hayley.

If I see any charges that are exorbitant, I'll shut it right back down. Understood?"

"Yes, sir." Hayley hoped the relief she felt wasn't noticeable. "Thank you."

"I'll check in with you in a few days. Get me your budget."

"I will."

"Good." The call ended.

Hayley pushed the red button to disconnect. "Bye, Dad," she whispered. She set the phone down and picked up the photo of her and her mother. They'd been sitting on their favorite bench in Central Park, looking at the trees and also people-watching. Making up stories about the folks who passed by. It sounded silly, but it was her favorite thing to do with her mother. With a sad sigh, she set the frame back down. "I miss you, Mom," she whispered into the empty office.

Her father was certain she'd fail at this job; Hayley could feel it. In fact, he'd kind of stacked the deck against her from the beginning, throwing her in the way he had. She was pretty sure he'd already written the Evergreen off as a loss, and installing her as manager was just a way to prove his point about what a screwup she was.

"Well, fuck that," she whispered, turning to her computer. She called up a few things she'd seen earlier and began typing.

❖

Benton Markham hung up the phone and slowly let out a breath. He suddenly felt deflated, exhausted, a hundred years old.

It only took a slight turn of his head to see the incredible view from his corner office on the forty-seventh floor. Manhattan in December was stunning. Nothing compared. It was stunning when it wasn't December as well, but the addition of multicolored Christmas lights and holiday decorations just made everything that much more impressive.

Benton used to love the holidays. All of them: Christmas, Thanksgiving, Easter, the Fourth of July, even Halloween. He loved them all because Kerry loved them all. She'd been a huge decorator, decking their house out for any and all occasions, and he would just shake his head and smile, enjoying how much she enjoyed it.

Now, boxes upon boxes of decorations for various holidays remained untouched in the attic, not having seen the light of day in the two years since Kerry had been gone. Christmas was only a few weeks away, but the idea of putting up a tree crippled him into inaction.

Kerry had been the love of his life, which had understandably surprised his friends at first. She was everything he was not: playful, artistic, approachable, bighearted. Yes, he'd been married once before, and he wouldn't change that for the world, because Ellen had given him his two sons, good boys that he was exceedingly proud of. But Kerry... she opened up parts of him he didn't know were there. She dug and dug until she found his inner child and tugged him by the hand out into the light to play. She saw the good in everything and everybody, something Benton struggled with to this day. She was his heart, his light.

And then she got cancer.

It had been better for Kerry that the disease tore through her as quickly as it had. Four months from diagnosis to the end. Much less suffering for her than for many cancer victims he knew or had heard of. So that was a blessing. But he hadn't been prepared. Hadn't had time. No, that wasn't true. He hadn't *taken* the time. He'd naïvely assumed she'd beat it. When that seemed less and less likely, he'd stupidly assumed there'd be more time.

God, he'd been a fool.

Kerry was gone and she'd taken his heart with her. It had been more than two years now and he still missed her every single day, so intensely, it made his chest ache.

This would be his second Christmas without her and Benton had learned that the only thing he could do was hold on until January 2. Once that date showed up on his calendar, he would breathe easier. Until the next holiday. Which was Valentine's Day. He groaned.

Turning back to face his computer, he saw the numbers for the Evergreen were still there, and they tugged his attention right back to Hayley.

She was so much like her mother, it frightened him. He literally had trouble looking at her, as she was the spitting image. Light brown hair that would get even lighter in the sun. Green eyes so intense you couldn't look away. Playful disposition. Insane artistic talent. Not much of a head for business, but the willingness to try.

They'd pushed each other away after Kerry had passed. He knew it, and he was pretty sure Hayley knew it, too. She frustrated the hell out of him with what he considered her flightiness. Her irresponsibility.

Kerry had spoiled Hayley, that was indisputable. But so had he. His youngest by a lot of years and his only daughter. Of course he'd spoiled her. Paid her bills—her rent, her car, her credit card—but she'd been a good kid. A good girl. Respectful.

Until Kerry's death.

After that, Hayley had done a one-eighty. Spent hours, days in the extra bedroom in her apartment that she called her studio, painting things he never got to see—mostly because he never asked to see them—talking to nobody, barely leaving her apartment. Then that had changed, but not in a good way. She began clubbing. Partying until all hours. Spending exorbitant amounts of money at high-end clubs, on clothes and shoes she didn't need, on fancy restaurants where she'd pay for all of her friends' meals as well as her own. It wasn't that Benton didn't have the money to cover her credit card charges, it was the utter lack of responsibility and respect he had a tough time with.

And then he'd gotten the credit card statement from her last night out: $1,457.68. He'd hardly been able to believe it. He was so flabbergasted, he'd called the club, asked for a breakdown of her charges, and oh, he'd gotten one. Bottles and bottles of expensive champagne. Top-shelf liquor. Pricey hors d'oeuvres. Hayley had apparently lost her mind while there.

That was it for Benton. The straw that broke the camel's back. He'd had enough, and he wanted to punish her. For acting like a child. For pushing him away. For reminding him so very much of her mother that it made him want to cry every time he laid eyes on her. Yes, he'd wanted to punish her. He wasn't proud of it, but he could admit it. He wanted to teach her a lesson, show her that his wealth was not handed to him. That he'd worked his ass off for decades so that she could frivolously spend $1,500 at a nightclub without batting an eye. He wanted her to understand that the business of resorts was not a simple one, and she shouldn't take it for granted that it was.

So he'd sent her to the Evergreen, and he'd set her up to fail.

Yeah, he could admit that now. He could also admit that he felt bad about it. The Evergreen had been losing money almost steadily for the past two years. Benton knew it was because of that idiot Roger Stiles—the manager he should've fired ages ago. And Benton had already pretty much made up his mind that he'd close the Evergreen down next summer and sell it unless it could be shown that it was possible to improve the bottom line. Which he didn't think it was. He wasn't proud of himself for sending his daughter into a virtually unfixable situation and expecting her to fix it, especially given she had little to no business experience. He just hoped maybe she'd get to a point where she had more respect and understanding of where her privilege came from.

It had been a terrible idea.

He ran a hand through his salt-and-pepper hair and groaned again. What the hell was he doing?

"Ben?" A gentle rap on his doorframe snagged his attention, and Susan, his secretary and the woman who kept his schedule—and thereby, his life—somewhat manageable, stood there. "You've got a meeting in fifteen minutes in the conference room, I moved your dinner from tonight to next Thursday, and Keith Harper is on line three."

Benton nodded his thanks.

"Have you eaten?" she asked, before he could punch the right button.

He glanced up at her and she tipped her head to one side, seeing the answer. She sighed quietly, smiled tenderly.

"I'll order you a sandwich."

He nodded again and reached for the phone.

Anything to stop him from thinking about the impossible situation he'd tossed his daughter into.

❖

Friday was payday, and Olivia always brought the paychecks to her staff personally. There was something about handing over the envelope, about looking that individual in the eye, about thanking them for their hard work, that Olivia loved. So that Friday, just before lunch, she got the mail, sorted the checks, and headed to the back of the building where the staff break rooms, lockers, and mailboxes were.

Olivia loved the holiday season. She loved decorating. She loved baking cookies with her mother. She loved giving gifts to the people important to her. She loved the lighter, friendlier attitude that most people had at this time of year. There was a little extra spring in her step as her heels clicked down the back hallway as she approached the break room.

Straight ahead was the loading dock, a big, brown UPS van backed up to it, and Lenny, the head of maintenance, helping the driver stack the day's deliveries. Olivia smiled and waved at the men, took two steps into the break room, and stopped. Brow furrowed over what she thought she saw, she took those two steps backward so she was in the hall again, squinting in Lenny's direction.

"Hey, Lenny, how's life?" she asked, as she approached.

"Not bad, Ms. Santini," he replied, signing his name on the computer the UPS guy handed him.

"Are these new vacuum cleaners?" Olivia ran her hand over one of the large boxes.

"Yup. Finally." Lenny grinned. "Mabel's gonna be thrilled."

Olivia nodded slowly. "I bet." She handed Lenny his check as two of his guys walked by with a red toolbox. She followed them with her gaze, then turned back to Lenny, eyebrows raised in expectation.

"There's a hot water problem in 506," he said, as if Olivia knew exactly what he was talking about.

She nodded, then hurried around distributing checks to those she could find and putting the rest in mailboxes.

Half an hour later, she dropped into her chair in her small office and tapped several keys on her computer, scanning the screen, then tapping some more. Five minutes after that, she burst into Hayley's office like somebody had shoved her. "What did you do?" she asked with a bit more force than she'd intended. At Hayley's wide-eyed look, Olivia took a deep breath, counted to five in her head, then asked again, calmly this time, "Two new vacuum cleaners were just delivered. And there's a problem with the hot water on the fifth floor?"

Hayley smiled and looked very pleased with herself. "You are correct on both counts."

"But, there's no paperwork for either thing."

Hayley's smile dimmed a watt or two. "What do you mean?"

"I mean there's no purchase order for the vacuum cleaners. There's no work order for the guys who are fixing the hot water."

"I don't understand what you're upset about. Some things needed to be done, and I got them done. I thought you'd be happy about it."

"How are we paying for the vacuum cleaners?"

This time, Hayley looked at her with vague impatience. "We're going to get a bill and send them money," she said slowly. The "duh" was unspoken, but it was there.

"But they weren't budgeted for this year."

"Then we'll write them into next year's budget."

It wasn't the right way to do things, at all, but she couldn't really argue. "What about the hot water thing?"

Hayley tipped her head to one side. "I overheard a guest mention that her shower got cold really fast, so I asked Lenny to have somebody take a look." She glanced down and then back up. "I didn't think about a work order. I'm sorry about that."

The wind taken out of her sails, Olivia stood there for a beat before saying lamely, "Oh." Now she felt...she wasn't sure. A little silly for flying off the handle? Embarrassed that she'd busted in like an obnoxious child? Annoyed that she didn't know these things were happening in her hotel?

Yeah. That last one. It was definitely that last one.

She stood there, feeling awkward, and looked around to avoid eye contact. For the first time, she noticed Hayley had brought in some personal items. Like the painting that hung on the wall.

It was beautifully serene, a scene from a park in the summer, and it drew Olivia closer. Big brown tree trunks and lush green leaves. Black metal benches and many people milling around, some with dogs on leashes. Peeks of bright blue sky appeared through the leaves, rays of sunlight casting the scene in a warm, golden glow. "This is beautiful," she said quietly, almost not realizing she'd said it aloud.

"Yeah?" Hayley asked.

"Absolutely. It evokes so much. Peace, tranquility, comfort, nature, humanity..." Olivia scanned the whole picture again. "Where'd you get it?"

"I painted it."

Olivia whipped her head around in disbelief. "Get out. You did not."

"I did." Hayley's smile was filled with pride as she moved to stand next to Olivia. "This is the scene from my favorite bench in Central Park. My mom and I used to meet there and just people-watch."

Olivia pressed a hand to her chest, her heart filling with warmth. "Really?"

"Mm-hmm." Hayley pointed to a well-dressed older gentleman in a fedora on the right side of the painting. "That's Jeeves. Mom and I named him that and decided that he was somebody's butler, because he was always dressed so nicely and carried himself all stiff and proper." Olivia watched Hayley's hand as she moved it to point at one of the dogs. "This Scottie is Angus. I know this because he would come right up to us to say hi. Not long after the first time, my mom started putting a handful of dog treats in her pocket." Hayley turned to Olivia, and the expression on her face was completely different than Olivia had ever seen. Filled with joy and happiness at the memory she was sharing. "Needless to say, Angus came by every single time after that. As did many of the other dogs."

They stood quietly for a moment.

"I can't believe you painted this," Olivia said. She was truly awed. The colors, the level of detail. "It really is impressive."

"Thank you." This time when Hayley said it, her voice was soft. "It's my favorite piece I've ever done. Goes with me everywhere."

Olivia was so curious now as to the process. "I don't have a creative bone in my body, so I have no idea about painting and art. Do you paint from a photograph? Is that why you always have your camera when you're outside?"

Hayley nodded and moved back to her chair, took a seat. "Yeah. If I see something I might like to paint, I snap some shots from different angles."

Before they could get into any further detail, Olivia heard the phone on her desk ringing. Gesturing to Hayley's phone, she said, "Do you mind?"

With a shake of her head, Hayley turned her phone around so Olivia had better access.

"That was Nancy down in the spa," Olivia said as she hung up. "She's the head of that department." At Hayley's blank stare, Olivia suppressed a sigh. "You met her at the first staff meeting."

Hayley did sigh. "Yeah, that entire day was a blur."

"Well, she needs help."

"With?"

"Don't get me wrong, Nancy's an amazing massage therapist. I've had her work on me and she's got incredible hands." Olivia stood. "What she does not have is any kind of sense when it comes to scheduling her people. With Christmas right around the corner, everybody wants time off, and she's having trouble picking and choosing. Never mind she should have already had this taken care of." Olivia headed for the door, then had an idea. "You should come with me."

"I should?" Hayley's eyes went wide.

Olivia shrugged. "You're the manager."

❖

Walking through the glass double doors and into the spa area of the Evergreen was like walking into a different world with a different atmosphere. It was suddenly much quieter, as if a white noise machine had been running constantly and somebody finally turned it off. The scent was something Hayley couldn't identify, but it was nice. Mild and lovely. The lights were pleasantly dim and the temperature was a bit warmer. Even if you didn't come there to relax, Hayley thought you'd have trouble fighting it.

"This is our spa," Olivia said, and Hayley noticed she'd adjusted the volume of her voice to match the quiet of the lobby. She watched as Olivia looked around, hands on her hips. "It really needs updating. Maybe a little expansion."

"It does feel a bit...dated," Hayley agreed as Olivia headed toward a small hallway and she followed.

"These are the massage rooms. We have six. If we had a few more, I think we could use that to book more guests on the off-seasons, when the ski runs are closed for the summer or it's too early in the fall to ski yet."

"That sounds like a good plan."

"Those are the times we have trouble booking rooms and our profits plummet. If you're not a nature lover or somebody who wants to lie around the pool all day, there's not much to draw you here. But if we had a state-of-the-art spa, we could advertise that, focus on it, and bring in more guests for things like Couples Weekends or a Girls' Spa Weekend, you know?"

Hayley nodded, finding herself enjoying this side of Olivia.

Olivia pushed her arm out in a gesture of doing the same to the wall she was aimed at. "We could expand from here. Enlarge the current rooms and add another three or four." She continued walking until they came to a locker room. It was nice, though also a bit dated. The lockers were a classy wood, but a bit faded and clunky. The décor was also a little bit…eighties. Pinks that should have been mauves. A green carpet that looked clean, but also around when Hayley was a toddler.

Two women were changing, big, fluffy white robes draped nearby. Olivia greeted them each by name, which was astounding to Hayley, as she could barely remember her own name.

Beyond the lockers were a few more doors. Olivia pushed one open once she'd checked to make sure it was unoccupied. "Sauna," she said by way of explanation. "Kinda small." She let the door shut and they moved on.

"Have you brought this stuff up to—" Hayley cleared her throat—she'd almost said *my father*—and continued. "Corporate?"

"At Markham?" Olivia sighed. "I used to send them all my ideas. I've probably sent them fifty or sixty of them in the time I've been in management. I always get the same reply. *Thanks for your suggestions. We'll take them under advisement.* And then I never hear from them again."

"That doesn't seem like very good business."

"Right?" Olivia shook her head. "I was in Boston a couple years ago for my birthday, and my friend and I had a spa day. The place was gorgeous. You got these super-thick robes to put on and the waiting area had overstuffed chairs and a fireplace, and champagne was delivered to you. I was truly pampered." She stopped walking and turned to face Hayley. Pointing at her, she said, "*That* is something people will pay for. They do at the Marquez."

They passed a small bank of windows through which the pools—indoor and outdoor—were visible. Then Olivia pushed through another door and they were back in the lobby at the front desk. This time, a tall blond woman was behind it.

"Oh, hey, Liv." Hayley knew this was Nancy by the name tag fastened to her top. When her gaze landed on Hayley, she looked momentarily surprised. "Ms. Boyd," she said, with a nod.

"Let's see the schedule," Olivia said and the next minute, they had their heads together, looking at the screen of an iPad.

Hayley watched and listened but also looked around, envisioning all the things Olivia had mentioned, all the changes.

"There," Olivia said. "Is that better? I mean, it's not perfect and not everybody gets what they want, but they get *most* of what they want."

Nancy nodded, and her relief was so obvious it made Hayley smile. "Yes. Yes, absolutely. This will work. Thank you so much."

"No problem. Come to me sooner next time, okay?" Olivia smiled that smile of hers, the one that Hayley was starting to realize made everybody feel a bit more at ease.

The smile that had never been aimed at her.

"Ready?" Olivia was looking at her expectantly.

"Oh. Yes. Ready."

They left the warm, quiet cocoon of the spa and plunged back into the day.

CHAPTER EIGHT

Early December had arrived cold and snowy—as early December apparently did in this part of the state. The glittering decorations around the Evergreen were beautiful and festive, but they didn't keep Hayley from missing New York City. Nothing pulled out her holiday spirit more than the Christmas tree and the angels in Rockefeller Center, the lights and decorations dangling and sparkling all over Manhattan.

She was going to need to plan a weekend getaway, and soon. She missed her loft on the Upper East Side. She missed the coffee shop next door and the art galleries she frequented. She missed Fifth Avenue at Christmas. She missed warm pretzels from the guy with the cart at the entrance of Central Park.

But she'd only just started her job here. She couldn't bail yet.

Hayley lay in the king-size bed and stared at the ceiling. It was Saturday, and while she needed to check in to make sure everything was okay at the front desk, she didn't really need to work today. Olivia had today covered, and Hayley would work tomorrow so Olivia could have the day off. Apparently, that's how weekends were done in the hotel business. If they needed a day off during the week, they could work that out together.

"Lotta hours," Hayley said quietly to the empty room, then pushed herself out of bed.

Forty-five minutes later, the elevator doors opened and Hayley exited onto the first-floor lobby level. She could hear the noise before she even turned the corner: the sound of a very busy front desk. Hayley stopped in her tracks. Should she go help? Olivia was working, she knew, and probably had things under control. She toggled between two thoughts in her head.

One: *You're the manager. Go help.*

Two: *It's your day off, and they do better without you screwing things up.*

Surprising no one, she went with number two and turned on her heel to find the back door.

The town of Evergreen Hills looked shockingly like the set of a Hallmark Christmas movie, and Hayley's eyes went wide. She drove down the main drag and took note of all the small shops, stores, restaurants. Hell, there was even an art gallery and an art supply store. She'd ordered a few things online last week because she'd assumed there was no way such a tiny town would have such a place.

"Huh," she said to nobody, as she found a parking spot and slid her white BMW into it.

It was still very cold, much colder than it ever got at home, and Hayley pulled her hat down a bit and zipped her coat higher. But the clouds had drifted away, and blue sky had begun to show, the sun peeking out here and there and leaving the pavement wet while making the snow that had fallen last night sparkle. Hayley grabbed her bag and got out of the car, looking one way, then the other, deciding where to start and which way to stroll. Storefronts were decorated for the holiday and the sidewalks were surprisingly busy. Maybe not such a small town after all?

The Cinnamon Bun across the street looked promising, a coffee and pastry shop in one, so she made her way to it and opened the door to the most delicious smell of warm cinnamon, so enticing, she stopped in her tracks just inside and simply inhaled.

"You might as well just order one," a man said with a smile as he moved around her. "It's almost impossible to leave until you do." He was probably in his sixties, almost completely bald, and wore wire-rimmed glasses. He was tall and lanky, his smile kind as he aimed it toward Hayley, then went to the counter and greeted the girl there by name.

Ten minutes later, she was seated at a small table by the window, sipping a latte and eating the most succulent, fluffy, delicious cinnamon roll she'd ever had the pleasure of experiencing. It was all she could do not to hum in pleasure with every bite.

By the time she finished, the sun was shining full force in invitation and the street of shops was bustling, which was good, because a large part of Hayley wanted to stay where she was forever and live in the Cinnamon Bun.

Strolling along what she'd dubbed the "street of shops" turned out to be much more fun and relaxing than she'd even hoped. Every storefront was decked out with lights and garland and big, red bows and menorahs and festive window displays. Christmas music played from what must have been a sort of outdoor public announcement system, as it was the same song from storefront to storefront. She wandered in and around and out of a craft store, a pet supply store—where she looked at toys for Walter, but bought nothing—and a bookstore. Next up was the art supply store, Brushstrokes. She didn't expect much from such a small place, but she pushed through the door anyway, the smell of paints and canvas wrapping around her like a blanket, comforting her like it always had, and she instantly loved the place.

"Well, hello there again." The man behind the counter was the bald, lanky guy from the coffee shop. "Tell me you had a cinnamon roll."

"I did." Hayley smiled. "Thanks for the advice. Do you get a cut of commission for every one they sell?"

"Oh, I can't talk about that. I signed a nondisclosure agreement." He winked at her, then pushed his glasses up his nose with his forefinger. "Help you find something?"

"I'm just going to wander a bit, if that's okay."

"Absolutely. Let me know if you have questions. I'm Ross Edwards. Owner."

"Thanks, Ross. I'm Hayley."

He gave her a wave and a nod and went back to doing whatever he'd been doing before she arrived. Three other customers were browsing, one with several brushes in her hand, another picking up tubes of paint and setting them back down, and a third was looking at charcoal pencils of different widths.

Hayley had been painting seriously since her teens, but aside from the art history courses she'd taken in college for her minor, she'd never actually studied painting. She watched videos all the time on YouTube or other sites where people who weren't teachers tried to share their knowledge. Mostly, though, she just followed whatever vision was in her head and did her best to duplicate it. She was by no means great, but she wasn't bad, and she knew that.

She pulled a couple of canvases off the shelf, three different sizes, then strolled over to the large display of tubes that contained oil paints. Hayley had tried working with different paint types—watercolors, acrylics—but once she'd started to play with oil paint, she doubted she'd go back. There was something about the way it spread on the canvas, the way it felt under her brush, that she just hadn't found with any other type. She scanned through the tubes, looked at the seven different shades of green, and chose three, then moved on to other colors.

Ross approached her as she stood in front of the alarming number of brush options. He pointed to a cylinder containing one brand, pulled out a small, angled brush, and said, "May I suggest these if you're using oils? It's a fairly new brand, but I've gotten a ton of great feedback from customers, and I've used them myself. I have to agree. Smooth strokes, no paint clumps, Taklon bristles." He handed the brush to Hayley.

She ran her finger over the soft bristles, moved the brush so she held it in her hand like she would if she were painting. Felt the weight of it, the smoothness of the handle, the comfort against her palm. "That's nice."

"No pressure," Ross said, holding up a hand. "Just a suggestion."

"I appreciate it."

"I haven't seen you around before. You visiting? Here to ski?"

"Oh, no. I like my legs to stay unbroken, thank you very much. I'm actually new in town. I work at the Evergreen Resort and Spa?" Hayley phrased it as a question, not sure Ross would know what she was talking about.

"The Evergreen? Love that place. Split Rail has the most amazing T-bone." Ross put his fingers to his lips, kissed them, then opened his hand, like an Italian chef giving a sauce his blessing. "That chef works magic."

Hayley grinned, feeling inexplicable pride from the compliment. "She does. Her Thanksgiving dinner was out of this world."

"Oh, I bet." Ross walked her over to the counter, then went around behind it to ring up her purchases. "You know, I have a workroom in the back for people who maybe don't have a lot of space in their house for their art supplies. And we have an artists' group that meets a couple times a week back there." He jerked a thumb over his shoulder. "Very informal. Different mediums. Just a nice group of like-minded folks." He pulled a sheet of paper from under the counter and handed it to her. "Here's this month's schedule."

Hayley took it from him, surprised to find herself actually considering attending. "Thanks," she said, holding up the paper. "I may pop by."

"Great." Ross bagged her purchases and Hayley let out a small sigh of relief when her credit card cleared. "We have quite a bit of space and some tabletop easels, cleaning materials, and the like. So just bring your basics."

"That sounds awesome." Ross held out his hand and Hayley shook it. "Thanks so much, Ross. I'll see you again soon."

Back at her car, Hayley stood and watched the hustle and bustle of the street...that really wasn't hustle and bustle at all, now that she looked more carefully. It was still busy, but people seemed relaxed. They didn't hurry places, they wandered. Strolled. Stopped to look in shop windows. Sipped from their cups of coffee or hot chocolate. The sun gave things just enough warmth to allow folks not to run inside to escape the frigid winter temps. And the overall atmosphere—the *feel* of the place—was one of comfort and invitation.

When she woke up that morning, Hayley had missed the city badly. Now? She tossed her bag into the car ahead of her and dropped into the driver's seat.

"I kinda like it here," she said quietly. "Huh."

❖

Saturdays were almost always crazy busy at the Evergreen, but Olivia didn't mind. Crazy busy kept *her* crazy busy, and that made the day go by much faster.

The lobby hummed with the buzz of conversation. Stephanie didn't work many weekends, so there were two part-timers manning the front desk, but they'd each worked there for a while now—Olivia had hired them herself—and things moved along smoothly. The 4:00 shuttle had just pulled up out front, spilling out the folks who'd spent the day skiing on nearby Clearpeak Mountain. They'd stomped in carrying bags and skis and smelling like snow and the outdoors. The fireplace in the lobby burned bright and warm and several people stopped there to warm up.

Tessa had sent one of her staff members out with a rolling cart and big silver insulated containers of coffee and hot chocolate, as she did every time a shuttle returned, and guests stood and chatted as they sipped. It looked like cocktail hour before a dinner party, except all the guests wore ski jackets and boots and had rosy, flushed cheeks.

Olivia oversaw all of it. She made sure the bellhops were taking care of bags of equipment, skis, and poles, that they got where they needed to be. Most folks owned their own stuff, but the Evergreen also had its own stockpile of equipment, and it was important that the two weren't mixed up. One bellhop went by carrying two pairs of Evergreen skis, and Olivia made a face at the fact that they were obviously not new. She made a mental note to add "new skis" to her list of things they needed to budget for in the coming year. She'd have to leave a note for Hayley.

As if she'd conjured her up by thinking about her, she caught sight of Hayley off to the side of the front door, eyes wide as she stood and watched guests and bellhops pushing wheeled carts of baggage for people just checking in. She looked…Olivia took in a big breath and blew it out. Yeah. She looked really good in her coat—not her red parka, but a very expensive black puffy one from North Face that Olivia had looked at herself online but knew she could never afford—fur-lined boots, and cute white hat. In her hand was a bag from Brushstrokes, the art supply store in town.

She just watched. So did Olivia.

When their eyes met across the lobby, it seemed to take a beat before they realized it, Olivia noticed. Their eye contact held for a second. Two seconds. Three. And then Olivia blinked; Hayley raised a hand and gave her a little wave and half-grin and started across the lobby toward her.

"Wow," she said, when she reached Olivia. "Busy today."

"Weekends tend to be like this. It won't be this bad tomorrow, but it will still be busy." Tomorrow was Olivia's day off, and she wanted Hayley to be prepared.

"Got it."

"I see you found Brushstrokes. Did you meet Mr. Edwards?" Ross

Edwards had taught art at Evergreen Hills High School when Olivia was there. "Super-nice guy."

"I did," Hayley said. "He was great." She pulled a sheet of paper out of the bag as she continued, "There's an art group that meets at his shop he told me about. I was surprised."

"How come?"

"Well, it's a pretty small town…" Hayley let the sentence dangle as if she wasn't sure where to go with it.

"Evergreen Hills is actually very popular with artists. Lots of them come here and use it as a sort of retreat so they can work. Painters, sculptors, writers. There are several different groups that get together."

"Really?" Hayley looked impressed. "I had no idea."

"Well, why would you? You come from the big city where you probably have everything you need within a block or two, am I right?"

Hayley nodded and somehow seemed to deflate just a bit. "You are."

They stood quietly side by side, a subtle sense of awkward floating around them.

"Well, okay. I'm headed up," Hayley said, turning away. She stopped suddenly and looked back at Olivia. "Unless you need my help?"

Olivia shook her head, weirdly wanting Hayley to stay but fighting it for reasons she didn't want to explore. "Nope. It's your day off. Enjoy."

Hayley nodded once and walked away.

Olivia watched for longer than necessary, then gave her head a shake when she realized she was doing it. With a quick glance around to make sure there were no impending crises, she pivoted on a heel and headed for Split Rail.

Tessa and Mike both worked on Saturdays, and maybe that was how the three of them ended up such close friends. Olivia had known Mike since they were kids, but they'd easily let Tessa in to form their threesome, and it felt like it had always been that way.

The kitchen was like a beehive, buzzing and filled with activity. The line cooks and sous chefs were working hard on prep work. While some guests would wander in this early for happy hour and appetizers, the real dinner rush wouldn't hit for another two hours or so. It was a good time to catch Tessa, and Olivia found her with no problem.

"Hey," Tessa said, approaching Olivia as she stood in a corner out of the way, leaning against the wall. Tessa leaned next to her and folded her arms.

"Hi. All set for dinner?"

"Am I ever not?"

"Not that I've ever seen, no. You are a consummate professional."

Tessa bumped her with a shoulder. "And don't you forget it."

"You busy tonight?"

Tessa gazed up at the ceiling for a moment, probably contemplating her social calendar. "Nope. I don't think so."

"Feel like dancing?" Olivia had felt, for several days now, that she really needed to burn off some energy, and going out dancing was her favorite way of doing so.

Tessa's eyes went wide. "Are you kidding me? Do I feel like dancing? Does Donald Trump have ridiculous hair? Is chocolate food of the gods? Has it been almost six months since I've had sex? Hell yes, I feel like dancing. Is that even a real question?"

Olivia laughed at her friend's excitement. "Good. Me too."

"Think you can keep up with me?"

Olivia snorted. "Not a chance. But I can bust my ass trying. Should I invite Mike?"

"The more the merrier." One of the sous chefs craned his neck and his gaze landed on Tessa. "Gotta go. Meet you there?"

"Text me when you're headed over. I'll Uber."

Olivia left the kitchen feeling much lighter. A night out with her closest friends was always a good way to right her world when she was feeling off-balance. And she'd been feeling *very* off-balance these past few weeks. She didn't want to analyze it. She didn't want to talk it through. No. She wanted to dance.

There was a little spring in her step as she walked back toward the lobby, smiling at guests.

Yeah. A night of dancing was just what she needed.

CHAPTER NINE

There had been a surprising number of bars and clubs in Evergreen Hills when Hayley did her internet search. She wasn't quite sure what she was looking for, but she needed to get out of her room and around other people. Wandering around the small town earlier had been nice. It had distracted her for a while. But it didn't make up for the fact that she missed New York terribly, missed the faster pace, the endless sound, the smells of the city. She wanted something loud. Something pumping. She also wanted to drink.

Club Glitter seemed out of place in the peaceful, slumbery town. Its name was lit up in swooping purple neon across the front of the building, and the music's bass line could be heard from the street as Hayley thanked her Uber driver and headed for the front door.

Glitter wasn't just a state of mind, apparently, it was reality. Everything in the club sparkled. Hayley paid the ridiculously inexpensive cover, got her hand stamped, and headed inside, her heels clicking on the glitter-covered floor. Upon a slightly closer inspection, she realized that everything that glittered did so under a coat of what she guessed was some kind of polyurethane. Thank God, she wouldn't be going home covered in the stuff and finding it in her clothing for the next five months.

It was a Saturday night, and it was busy. The dance floor was packed, bodies bopping up and down, arms flailing in the air as house music pumped out of the speakers. Hayley could feel it in the pit of her stomach as she sidled through the crowd and found a spot at the bar, where she asked the broad-shouldered bartender for a vodka tonic. The bar's surface was also covered in glitter with a clear coat over the top, and the lights from the ceiling made it seem almost as if it was moving, like the glitter was liquid. A very cool effect, though Hayley thought maybe not so cool if you'd had too much to drink. She handed over her credit card and told the bartender to keep her tab open.

Turning around, she leaned back against the bar and watched the crowd. Part of her wished she had her camera—though she was pretty sure these people wouldn't appreciate having their photo taken by some stranger lurking in a nightclub. But the colors of the lighting were kind of amazing. Very purple, but with blues and yellows thrown in as the lights in the ceiling tilted and rotated to the beat of the music.

"You a local or a tourist?" The guy next to her had to lean close to be heard. He had also turned his back to the bar and mimicked her stance. He was handsome, with sandy hair and a neatly trimmed goatee. Tall. Maybe thirty, thirty-five. He wore a white henley and jeans.

"A little of both, actually," Hayley replied. "You?"

"Local. Lived here all my life." He had what looked like a rum and Coke in his hand, and he used that hand to point toward the dance floor. "Mostly tourists out there right now. A few locals."

"What do you do?" Hayley asked. Unlike many of her friends back home, she liked to talk to new people. She didn't mind when a guy hit on her, as long as he wasn't disgusting about it. Talking to people was enjoyable. She liked to learn about them.

"I work over at the Marquez. You know it?"

Hayley racked her brain, feeling like she'd heard the name before, but couldn't place it and shook her head.

"It's a resort on the west end of town. Pretty high-end. Really nice. I'm surprised you haven't heard of us. This is our busy time and we're booked solid, so when I get a chance to cut loose and come out for a night, I do."

"Makes sense." Hayley sipped her drink and took a moment to absorb the fact that this guy was actually competition. "Are you the only resort around here? It's a pretty small town."

Hayley couldn't hear the guy's scoff, but she could see it. "No, there are two others. Mountain View, which does well because of its location and"—he leaned close—"its mountain view."

Hayley chuckled. "I see what you did there."

"The Evergreen is the other, but that's a nonissue."

"Oh? How come?" Hayley sidled a little closer to the guy so she'd be sure to hear him.

"Because they're old." The guy shrugged like it was the simplest answer around. "They're completely outdated. I mean, they've got some plusses—mainly the restaurant—but they're on their way out. No, Marquez is the place to be. We're completely booked through the beginning of January." He looked at her, pride on his face, and then something in his gaze shifted. "You should come by. I could work on you."

"Work on me?"

The guy grinned. "I'm a massage therapist." He flexed the fingers of the hand not holding his drink. Open, closed, open, closed. "I've got great hands."

Hayley wrinkled her nose. "I'm sure." She turned back toward the bar and ordered another drink.

"I'd give you a discount."

I wonder what I'd have to do for that discount. "That's very kind of you, but I'm good."

"You sure?" He flexed his hand again.

"Dude, now you're just being creepy." Hayley shook her head, took her drink, and walked away, looking for someplace—*anyplace*—else to hang. She noticed a group of women gathering their things, about to abandon a small, round, high-top table, and she swooped in, leaned her forearms on it, and claimed it as her own. She kept watch from her peripheral vision, but the guy made no attempt to approach her again. She'd probably bruised his ego, poor thing. She made a mental note to do some research on Marquez tomorrow, see what the guy was talking about, and with a shake of her head, she turned her focus to the dance floor.

Bodies were moving, swaying, bouncing. Arms in the air, hips rocking. Laughter could sometimes be heard over the music. Probably seventy percent women to thirty percent men out there dancing. Hayley smiled. She wasn't much of a dancer, but she loved to watch other people, and she envied the way some of them became one with the music. She was thinking exactly that about one woman in particular. She had her back to Hayley, but she was beautiful to watch. Wearing snug jeans, a sleeveless black top, and heels, she moved and swayed as if she'd written the music, as if she knew exactly where the next section was going, like it was created specifically for her body to enjoy. She moved her bare arms above her head, then reached back and lifted her oodles of dark hair up to bare her neck, which was long and sensuous, her hips continuing to sway the whole time.

She was mesmerizing.

Hayley forced herself to glance down at her drink before looking back up again, not wanting to come across as creepy as the massage guy had, but she couldn't help it. She stared. At one point, the sexy woman danced slightly to her right, revealing her dance partner. Who turned out to be Tessa, the chef from Split Rail.

"Oh, my God," Hayley said quietly, when she realized the sexy dancer was Olivia, and her body did weird things then. Her knees felt a little weak, her legs rubbery. Her palms began to sweat and her throat went dry. She swallowed hard, then took a sip of her drink to help.

Tessa saw her then. Made eye contact briefly. Hayley watched as Tessa leaned forward and said something to Olivia, who then turned to face Hayley, the expression on her face unreadable in the club lighting. She gave a tepid wave and they finished out the song before retrieving their drinks, coats, and purses from a nearby table and making their way to Hayley's.

"Hi," Olivia said, slightly out of breath. "I didn't expect to see you here." There was a gentle glow coming from her skin. Perspiration from working hard on the dance floor. Her cheeks were flushed; Hayley could see that even in the dim light.

"Yeah, I needed to get out. Be around people." She pointed at their near-empty glasses. "You guys need refills?"

Tessa nodded. "That'd be great. Cosmo for me, vodka cranberry for her."

"You got it." Hayley headed for the bar. When she returned, three drinks in hand, the girls were watching the dancers on the dance floor. She returned to leaning her forearms on the table and joined them in simply observing the crowd, which almost seemed to move as one giant, throbbing entity, waves rolling through it to the beat of the music. It was kind of crazy in a very cool way.

"Hey there, sexiest girls in the whole club." Mike, who Hayley remembered as one of the bartenders from the Evergreen, sidled up to their table. He smiled at Hayley, then seemed to realize who she was because his expression faltered. "Oh. Hey."

Hayley gave him a nod and what she hoped was a friendly grin. He looked slightly uncertain but returned the nod, then spoke to Tessa. "Sorry I'm late. It got busy."

"Well, that's a good thing." Tessa leaned her head closer to Mike's, and that made it hard to hear what they were saying—which Hayley decided maybe she wasn't supposed to hear anyway. A new song kicked in and the crowd got a little louder in its enthusiasm.

Hayley refocused her attention on the dance floor. Or tried to, rather, because it was hard with Olivia standing a mere foot away. Hayley watched as Olivia took a large gulp of her drink, then studied her as she looked ahead at the dancers. She had a great profile: straight nose, dark brows, strong chin, delicate throat. Hayley swallowed hard. She was so focused on Olivia that when Olivia turned to regard her, she almost jumped.

Olivia seemed to pause a moment, her eyes slightly glassy and making Hayley think she'd had quite a bit to drink. When she opened her mouth to speak, the words that came out weren't even close to what Hayley was expecting.

"Dance with me."

It wasn't a question or even an invitation. It was an order, a command, and Hayley, who didn't really like to dance, had no intention of not obeying. Olivia headed toward the throng of writhing, sweaty, intoxicated people. Hayley followed her without hesitation, tried not to stare at her ass as Olivia began to move to the beat of the song, arms over her head, eyes unfocused.

There was something surreal about this, about dancing with Olivia, bumping into her as the crowd moved and blended and absorbed them. Hayley felt like they were in slow motion, everything at half speed as she recalled the first time she'd seen Olivia. That morning in the woods—was it only a couple weeks ago?—and how instantly taken she'd been. That morning, that walk, had done something to her, but had there been a gun pointed at her head, Hayley couldn't pinpoint what. Just…something.

Olivia moved like she'd been born to dance, created for just that one activity. Her body was fluid, carefree. She let her head fall back as she raised her arms again, and moved them in tandem. Hayley did her best to imitate some sort of dance moves, to not stare.

She couldn't help it, though. Olivia was just too beautiful.

Luckily, Hayley was far behind Olivia in terms of alcohol consumed, and she was able to force her gaze away and concentrate on pretending to have some rhythm. Being so close to Olivia was intoxicating in its own way. She could smell her perfume—something with a hint of citrus—and she did her best to be subtle about inhaling deeply.

The next time she ventured a peek at Olivia's face, she noticed her tossing glances at their table where Tessa and Mike seemed deep in conversation, heads still close together, bodies almost touching.

"She's into him," Olivia said, as if making a random observation.

"Yeah? You okay with that?" Hayley knew Olivia and Tessa were tight. She didn't know much about Mike, though he seemed like a nice enough guy.

Olivia shrugged and made a face that said she was on the fence about it, but the song changed before Hayley could dig further, and Olivia announced she was thirsty. Hayley was both relieved to not have to pretend-dance any longer and bummed not be in such close proximity with Olivia any longer. She followed her off the dance floor and back to the table.

Olivia had had more to drink than she probably should have, but Hayley kept buying her refills. No, correction: Hayley kept buying everybody refills. She took a sip of her vodka cranberry and knew this was it for her. The cranberry juice was starting not to sit well in her stomach and the last thing she needed to do was puke her guts out in a nightclub restroom. She wasn't a college kid anymore. She was a grown-ass woman who knew when she was drunk, when she'd reached her limit.

She should've stopped two drinks ago, but she was feeling off-balance with Hayley causing her worlds to collide. She was drinking and dancing with her boss. That was the reality of the situation. It had been nothing more than a coincidence that they were both at Glitter, as Hayley had no way of knowing Olivia would be there, but it was still weird. *I mean, what are the odds? And why does she have to look that good?*

The thoughts shot through Olivia's alcohol-dulled brain, and she chewed on the inside of her cheek to keep from responding to them.

And Hayley did look good, that was for damn sure. The black jeans looked tailored to her body—especially her ass—the ankle boots with the slight heel were sexy as hell, and the white top showed much more cleavage than she needed to see. No. No, that was a lie. Olivia actually felt like she needed to see more cleavage. More skin in general. *Yeah, more skin, that would be great...*

"Right, Liv?" Tessa's voice yanked Olivia out of her steamy daydream and back to the cold harshness of reality—mainly that she was drunk and fantasizing about her boss. God, she was pathetic.

"I'm sorry." She squeezed her eyes shut and shook her head. "I missed it."

"Hayley was just saying that Alec over at Marquez was hitting on her."

Olivia took an extra couple of seconds to comprehend what Tessa had said, then was surprised to feel her lip curl, as if she were a lioness and was about to snarl. "Ugh, that guy. He's such a dick."

Hayley's eyes went wide, as Tessa and Mike both burst out laughing.

Olivia took a slug of her drink, then set the glass on the table too firmly. "I'll go talk to him."

Both Tessa and Hayley had a hold of her before she could take a second step. "No need," Hayley said. "I handled him." But there was a sexy little half-smile on her face that Olivia loved.

"How'd you get so drunk this early?" Tessa asked, looking at her watch in obvious disapproval.

"I drank too fast."

"Mm-hmm." Tessa sighed.

Tessa was annoyed with her. Even drunk, Olivia could tell. "All right. Fine." She began to gather her things.

"I can take her home," Hayley said.

Tessa stopped. Olivia looked from Hayley's open, friendly expression to Tessa's uncertain, hesitant one. "You can?"

"Sure." Hayley took out her phone. "I'll get us an Uber. What's the address?"

Tessa held eye contact with Hayley for a long beat, then turned to Olivia. "You okay with that?"

No words would form, for some reason, so Olivia nodded. Tessa rattled off Olivia's address.

"Done. Be right back." Hayley headed for the bar, presumably to close her tab.

"You sure you're okay with this?" Tessa asked. Mike looked on expectantly.

Olivia nodded again.

Tessa pointed at her then. "You keep your hands to yourself, understand me?"

Olivia was drunk, but not so drunk that the implication passed her by, and she felt her eyes go wide.

"Oh, please," Tessa said with a scoff. "Don't play all big-eyed innocent little girl with me. I've seen the way you've been looking at her."

Olivia had no time to respond—or come up with a response—because Hayley reappeared. "Uber's super close by," she said. "Ready?" She picked up Olivia's coat and held it open while Olivia put her arms in. Turning to Tessa, she said, "Thanks for coming over to hang with me so I didn't look like a friendless loser."

Tessa smiled reluctantly. She liked Hayley, Olivia could tell, and she couldn't really blame her. She gave Mike a hug, then Tessa.

"Advil and water before you go to bed, ya lush," Mike called to her as she followed Hayley through the patrons—having to inch by sideways in some instances—toward the door.

The Uber was waiting for them right out front, and within a minute, they were seated in the back seat. The car was a smaller model, and Hayley's thigh was pressed against Olivia's. "You ladies have a good time tonight?" the driver asked, as he pulled out into the sparse traffic.

"I don't know about this one," Hayley said, jerking a thumb in Olivia's direction. "But I did. That's a pretty cool club."

"Ah, so you're not from around here."

Olivia listened as Hayley chatted with the driver like he was an old friend. Between the easy banter and the warmth of Hayley's thigh against hers, there was something comforting about the whole situation. Olivia couldn't put her finger on why.

Evergreen Hills wasn't terribly big, and the driver pulled into Olivia's driveway within about twenty minutes. She sat there, looking out the window at her house, her brain a little bit foggy.

"Okay," Hayley said, as if she'd suddenly made a decision. "Let's get you inside." She got out of the car, went around to Olivia's side, and pulled her door open, helped her out of the car, then leaned back in to thank the driver.

Cold, fresh air was always a good tool in getting a person to sober up a little bit, and it started to work on Olivia. She threw her arms out to the side and inhaled deeply through her nose, then held the air in her lungs, savoring its sharpness. "God, I love it here," she said quietly as she exhaled. "I love the fresh air. Don't you?"

Hayley was watching her but also had her hands pushed deep into the pockets of her coat and was bouncing slightly on the balls of her feet. "I do, yes, but I'd like it to be a little less freezer-like."

Olivia chuckled and shook her head. "Wimp."

"Guilty as charged. I freely admit it. Where are your keys?"

Olivia arched one eyebrow as questions floated through her head. What was Hayley playing at here? Why hadn't she just taken the Uber back to the Evergreen? And why had Olivia chosen a black SUV? It looked so dirty in the winter. And whose dog was howling like a wild animal at this time of night?

"Um...isn't that Walter?" Hayley asked. "He must hear us out here."

Olivia squinted at her, letting the words roll around in her head.

"Look, I just want to make sure you get inside okay." Hayley held her hands up, palms facing Olivia. "You had a lot to drink, and I want to make sure you're safe. Okay?"

Well. That was nice, right? Olivia cleared her throat and handed her keys over to Hayley. "Okay."

Hayley took the keys and held out her arm. "Here, hold on to me. It might be slippery."

Olivia wanted that short walk to last longer, but she pretended she didn't. Hayley was shorter than her, but solid. Steady. She unlocked the door, then held it open for Olivia to enter. She started up the five steps that would lead into her kitchen.

Walter was his usual exuberant self at the top of the steps, so happy to see her, as if she'd been gone for days and days. He made little whining sounds as his entire body wiggled with joy and he spun in a circle, then another. Olivia's foot caught the top step and sent her pitching forward, but that motion was stopped suddenly by Hayley's grip.

"You okay?"

Olivia nodded and righted herself. She felt her face heat up. It was a good sign that she was sobering up a bit. Drunk people were rarely embarrassed, right?

"Does he need to go out?" Hayley asked as she squatted down to lavish attention on Olivia's dog.

Olivia pointed toward the back door.

"Fenced in?"

"Yes."

"Okay." Hayley toed off her shoes and called for Walter to follow her. The door opened and closed and the motion sensor light clicked on. Olivia could see her own backyard lit up. Hayley came back into the kitchen, walked straight to the fridge, and opened it. Which Olivia thought was a little bit obnoxious until Hayley handed her a bottle of water. "You should start drinking that now."

Oh. Yeah, okay, that was nice. Olivia did as she was told.

Hayley looked around, then stopped abruptly, as if she didn't want to seem like she was looking around. "I like your place."

"Thanks. Me too." Olivia took another long pull from the bottle.

They stood there, awkwardly enough that Olivia could feel it even in her still-slightly-inebriated state, until Walter saved them by barking at the door from outside. Hayley jumped to let him in. It's funny how an animal can alleviate uncomfortable situations, and Walter was no exception. The second he came bounding into the kitchen, spinning and grabbing various toys from his basket to bring to her, the awkwardness evaporated.

"Walter's awesome," Hayley commented as she watched his antics, a grin on her pretty face.

"Isn't he? I love him more than life." Olivia attempted to sit on the floor with her dog, but it was more of a drop. More comfortable than standing, that was for sure. Walter took the opportunity to kiss all over her face, which always made her laugh.

"You have Advil? Motrin? Something?"

Olivia tipped her head back. "You have amazing eyes." Then she furrowed her brow, trying to decide if she'd thought that or actually said it.

"Oh. Um. Thanks." They held one another's gaze for Olivia had no idea how long before Hayley spoke again. "Advil?"

Olivia pointed. "Cupboard to the right of the sink." She bent forward and placed loud kisses on Walter's head. Her butt was starting to hurt sitting on the tile floor, and her feet hurt from dancing in heels. She toed them off, then shrugged out of her coat and pushed herself to her feet. Her home wasn't large and it only took a handful of steps to get her to the living room and her couch, which looked more inviting than she could ever remember it looking. When Hayley, handful of Advil, a saucepan, and another water bottle in hand, found her, she was lying on her back on the overstuffed gray microfiber, Walter covering her like a blanket, his front paws on her chest.

"That looks cozy."

Olivia wrapped her arms around Walter in a hug. "He's warm."

Hayley opened her mouth, then closed it again, as if she couldn't decide whether or not to say what was on her mind. After a beat, she said, "Do you need help getting upstairs to bed?"

Olivia studied her. Squinted. Found everything about her face interesting. Magnetic. Sexy. She pulled her gaze away and said, "You know, I'm pretty comfortable. I might just stay here for a while."

With a nod and a slight grin, Hayley put the water on the table, and set the Advil next to it and the pan on the floor. "That sounds like a good plan." She pulled the blanket off the back of the couch and unfolded it. Walter hopped down and Hayley draped the blanket over Olivia, then perched on the edge of the coffee table.

Olivia snuggled in and was pretty sure she made some weird happy groaning sound that would make her want to hide the next day when she remembered.

Hayley checked her phone. "Okay, my Uber is almost here." Those green eyes met Olivia's, and there was a moment of quiet when they just looked at each other. "You sure you're okay right here?"

Olivia smiled at the veiled worry in Hayley's tone. "I've spent many a night on this couch. I'll be fine."

Again, the silent eye contact. It did things to Olivia. Warmed her from somewhere inside and...yep, she was sure. It turned her on.

Hayley placed her hands on her thighs and pushed herself to her feet. "Okay, then, as long as you're sure." Olivia nodded and Hayley buttoned her coat, saying, "You're off tomorrow, so I'll see you on Monday, yeah?"

Olivia pointed at her, then wondered what the hell she was doing pointing. "You will see me on Monday. Yes."

Hayley indicated the water with her chin. "Make sure you drink as much as you can. I put a pot on the floor. Just in case."

"Seems like you have experience with being overserved."

"You have no idea." Hayley's half a smile was sad somehow, and she turned to go.

"Hayley?"

"Hmm?" Hayley turned to her.

"Thank you."

This time, the smile was bigger, happier. "You're welcome."

The door clicked quietly shut behind her. A moment later, Olivia heard a car drive off, and she lay there, hand on Walter's head, staring at the ceiling and willing it to ease up just a touch on the twirling.

What a weird, wonderful night.

She had a good five or six seconds to bask in that thought before her stomach finally revolted and she clambered for the saucepan.

CHAPTER TEN

Hayley wouldn't go so far as to say she was getting the hang of her job, but she did feel like she was learning—sort of like being tossed into the deep end of the pool to force you into swimming. Her father had definitely tossed her into the deep end, but she was determined not to drown. At least not today.

There were only a couple weeks left until Christmas, and they were less than 60 percent booked. Hayley had checked yesterday, Sunday, when she had the office to herself because it was Olivia's day off. They were essentially a winter resort right now. If they couldn't book up through the holidays, what was the point? Unless...

She was doing her best to recall her conversation with the guy at the bar Saturday night, the things he said about his resort versus hers, when Olivia came into the outer office. Hayley saw a brief glimpse of her as she passed by the door, slipping out of her coat as she did.

"Morning," Hayley called out, and Olivia peeked her head in, apparently unable to hide the look of surprise on her face.

"You're here already." It wasn't a question, it was a statement, as if she was waiting for some sort of explanation as to why Hayley was in her office, sitting at her desk at seven a.m.

"I am," Hayley said, not at all offended. "Hi."

"Hi." Olivia studied her feet for a beat, then said, "I was going to hit the Starbucks this morning. Can I bring you back something?"

Hayley furrowed her brow, wondering if she had woken up in some parallel universe. "That would be fantastic."

With a nod, Olivia was gone and Hayley sat staring into space.

She'd texted Olivia yesterday to see how she was feeling. She'd gotten no response for over an hour—which made her wonder if Olivia was sleeping—and when an answer finally came, it was a simple *Much better. Thanks.* While she'd hoped for a little more, Hayley knew she wasn't *entitled* to more, so she'd left it alone and done her best to try to focus on her job. Or at least on the aspects of her job she understood.

Olivia returned shortly, a large cup in each hand. She entered Hayley's office, handed one to her, then sat in one of the two chairs in front of the desk.

"Thank you so much," Hayley said as she carefully removed the lid and took a cautious sip. The coffee was hot, sweet, and creamy. "God, is there anything quite like that first sip of coffee?"

Olivia's smile was small, hesitant.

"Everything okay?" Hayley asked.

Olivia took a deep breath, then blew it out. "Listen. I want to apologize for Saturday night."

"Why?"

Olivia's dark brows met at the top of her nose. "Why?"

Hayley lifted one shoulder in a half shrug. "Yeah. Why? What do you need to apologize for? Having a good time? Blowing off some steam with your friends and indulging a bit too much?"

Olivia blinked at her.

"Seriously, Olivia, you have nothing to apologize for. I've been in your shoes a million times. I was happy to help you get home, and I'm so glad you're feeling better today." Hayley had rehearsed that speech about a dozen times yesterday because she somehow had a feeling Olivia would be in here doing exactly what she was doing: apologizing for letting her guard down and being a person. Judging from the startled expression on Olivia's face that was slowly morphing into relief and maybe a little gratitude right in front of Hayley's eyes, she'd rehearsed it well and it landed exactly where she'd wanted it to.

A few seconds passed as they each sipped their coffee. Finally, Olivia said quietly, "Okay. Thank you."

"You're welcome."

"That looks cool." Olivia pointed at Hayley's chest. Momentarily puzzled, Hayley looked down and realized what Olivia meant.

"Oh. Yeah." She fingered the gold and green oval that was

magnetically attached to her blazer. "It came in Saturday's mail. This magnet thing is kind of awesome."

"Right? The last name tags we had attached with large pins, and people complained about the holes left in their clothes. I thought we'd better do something about it before management started getting people's bills for new shirts."

They chuckled together, then took tandem sips from their coffee cups, then chuckled some more.

"Well. See you at the staff meeting at ten?"

Hayley nodded. "I mean, I'll probably see you before that. Since you sit right outside my door and I can't really leave without seeing you, so…"

Olivia stood, still smiling. "You're hilarious."

"Yeah? Well, I'm glad to hear that because I do put forth a valiant effort. Takes a lot out of me."

Olivia shook her head. Then she took her coffee and headed to her own space.

Hayley took a moment. Maybe two. Just sat there, thinking and grinning. So, that had been a nice span of time, sitting there and having coffee. No tension—well, not as much as usual—no feeling inadequate. Yeah, that had been nice. Then she remembered Olivia's words, and her grin dimmed several watts. Staff meeting. So much for not feeling inadequate. This would be her fourth, and she was pretty sure she wasn't going to like it any better than the first three, and there wasn't much that would help, except…

"More coffee," she said softly.

❖

Olivia spent the walk from her office to the kitchen bracing herself. Tessa was going to kill her. Or at least smack her around a little bit. Deservedly so.

She'd barely made it through the kitchen door and Tessa was right there. She grabbed Olivia by the elbow, and Olivia had to almost jog to keep up. Tessa steered her through the kitchen, past the salad counter, past the stove where soup was simmering, and right into the walk-in freezer. It wasn't until they were safely ensconced in the bitter cold that Tessa looked at her, deep brown eyes flashing.

"So?" she said, arms folded across her chest.

"So…?" Olivia raised her eyebrows expectantly, even though she knew exactly what Tessa was asking.

"You're alive, I see. You apparently made it home in one piece, not that I would know because you didn't text me Saturday night."

"No, but I texted you yesterday."

"You did. With one-word answers that took twenty minutes to arrive."

Olivia grimaced because she realized Tessa wasn't so much angry as hurt. "I know. I'm sorry. I felt terrible and, frankly, I was a little bit embarrassed."

Tessa stood and regarded her silently for a moment. Olivia had to fight not to squirm under that disapproving gaze. Finally, after what felt like a day and a half, Tessa sighed and uncrossed her arms.

"Just…don't fucking worry me like that. Okay? Please?"

"I won't. I'm sorry."

"So?" Tessa waited expectantly.

"So…?" Olivia raised her eyebrows once again.

Tessa slapped playfully at her. "Oh, for God's sake, you're a pain in my ass. You make me spell everything out. So, *what happened*? With Hayley there?"

"Oh. Hayley. Yeah."

The freezer door opened and one of Tessa's staff members stood there, obviously surprised to see them and at a loss over what to do next.

"Five minutes," Tessa said to him. He nodded and shut the door again. "And?"

"I honestly don't remember a lot." Lies. She remembered every single moment of Hayley in her house. Taking care of Walter. Taking care of her. "Why did you let me drink so much?"

"What am I? Your mother? You're a grown-ass woman. One who apparently wanted to drink her face off."

With a shake of her head, Olivia said, "She got me home, set me up on the couch—where I spent the night—and took an Uber home."

Tessa blinked at her, then finally said, "Wow. Your life is just as boring as mine."

"Truth."

"Well, I can say that you two were doing a lot of looking at each other that night. It wasn't just you. It was her, too."

That was news to Olivia. Whether she'd purposely not paid attention to that or she'd been too inebriated to notice, she hadn't caught any looks from Hayley…wait.

Dancing.

The dancing.

They'd danced. Right?

"Did we dance together?" she asked Tessa, who snort-laughed.

"Did you ever."

Snippets of their time on the dance floor came back in shards of memory, and Olivia covered her eyes with a hand. "Oh, my God."

Tessa's warm hand on her upper arm made her feel the slightest bit better. "Sweetie, you were fine. I promise. Plus, you looked amazing." At Olivia's wide-eyed look, she added, "I've told you before what a good dancer you are when you've been drinking." She punctuated that with a wink.

Olivia groaned.

"I mean it in a good way. It's nice to see you loosen up a bit and have more fun, that's all."

Olivia mock-gasped. "Are you calling me rigid?" At Tessa's one arched brow, she gasped for real. "Oh, my God, you *are*."

"No." Tessa held up a hand. "No. I would never call you that. I do think it's good for you when you relax a little, that's all I'm saying."

Olivia wanted to argue. Wanted to defend herself and state her case…except she didn't really have one, and a shiver hit before she could come up with one. "Okay, I'm freezing."

"Me too."

They exited the freezer.

Any more conversation was interrupted by two of Tessa's chefs with questions, so Olivia told her she'd see her at the staff meeting and escaped. With an hour to kill, she couldn't bring herself to go back to her office and face Hayley. Not that there was anything to face. Olivia didn't remember every detail from that night, it was true, but she did remember how Hayley looked. How Hayley looked *at* her. How Hayley smelled when she was close and how surprisingly strong her small hands were when they'd kept Olivia from falling on her ass.

Yeah, she remembered a lot more than she'd let on with Tessa. And once a memory cleared in her head, it stayed.

She gave herself a mental shake and took the back way around to the elevators so she didn't pass the front desk. Putting on her happy work face, she smiled at several guests, stopped at the gift shop to chat with one who'd checked in yesterday, visited with Julie behind the cash register. She did all of this while still thinking about Saturday night. Still thinking about the dance, which, once she'd recalled it fully, had been playing on a loop in her head.

She needed to get a handle on this. Seriously. It had been a long time since she'd found herself so instantly attracted to somebody, and she hated that it was suddenly, obviously Hayley. Hayley really was off-limits. She needed to be. Olivia had to make sure she kept herself in check.

Heels clicking rhythmically as she walked down the hall, she glanced up at the large Evergreen logo displayed on the wall and gave it a glare.

"Why do you hate me?"

❖

If only there was a way to will yourself not to sweat. Hayley needed that right now. She stood at one end of the room and faced the people seated in chairs that were placed in no particular order or arrangement. There was the hum of conversation as people visited with their coworkers. The clock on the wall behind everyone said it was 10:05. She should probably get started, but Olivia wasn't there yet and, that made Hayley even more nervous.

She knew she needed to get things started.

She was also pretty sure she'd sweat right through her shirt and was well on her way to soaking her blazer as well.

"Okay, um." She cleared her throat as nobody stopped talking. "We should get started." Still nothing. The buzz continued. Hayley wet her lips. "Um…"

"Guys. Come on." Olivia was suddenly there, thank fucking God, and she didn't really have to raise her voice at all. She had a large box in her hands and she slid it to the center of the conference table. "Here, stuff these in your faces so you stop talking and listen to Hayley, all right?"

Chuckles went around the room as the Evergreen employees descended on the box of donuts like vultures on roadkill. The muttered thank yous quieted and, suddenly, all eyes were on Hayley. Which made her sweat more.

"Okay, um." She glanced down at her notes. Why was she freaking out? Actually, she knew why. Because this felt so much like public speaking, and public speaking was one of her worst fears. *Everything's written down. Just follow your notes.* She tried to talk herself through.

"Listen, I don't mean to be a pain in your ass…"

Hayley looked up and met the eyes of the head of maintenance… what the hell was his name again? She'd brought a cheat sheet with her and flipped to it. Scanned. Lenny! She looked back up at him, eyebrows raised.

"I still need to hire a couple of new people. My guys are working too many hours right now."

Crap. Hayley'd forgotten about that…because she hadn't looked at her notes from last week since she'd ordered the new vacuum cleaners without thinking. "Right," she said, nodding enthusiastically as if she'd been working on Lenny's request feverishly. "Right." She jotted down notes.

When she looked up, the head of the valet service, who was technically part of the front desk staff, had his hand raised. Hayley pointed to him.

"I thought you were going to fire Ronnie?"

Hayley blinked at him, lost.

Olivia leaning close enough for Hayley to smell her didn't help. But her words did. "Valet stealing change out of cars," she whispered quickly.

"Right!" Hayley said with relief. "Right. Yes. When is he in next?"

"This afternoon. His shift starts at two."

Hayley nodded. "Send him to the front desk when he gets here."

The man nodded once and was quiet.

Hayley's armpits were soaked and she could feel sweat trickle down her cleavage as four more hands raised. She swallowed hard, glanced down at her notes, at the visible tremor of the pad of paper, and closed her eyes. When she felt a gentle tug on the pad, she opened them and looked up into Olivia's deep brown ones.

"Are you coming down with something?" she asked, loudly enough for some to hear. "Why don't you sit down and rest, let me do this."

Hayley nodded mutely, swallowed again, and dropped into a nearby chair, equal parts relieved beyond belief and mortified that she was such a miserable failure at something as simple as a staff meeting.

The mixed emotions carried over as she watched Olivia. On the one hand, Hayley was frustrated with herself. Embarrassed that she apparently couldn't handle a simple meeting. She wasn't really a newbie any longer. She should have no trouble with such things. Instead, she'd stood there like a sixth grader giving her first presentation, shaking and sweating. Yeah, the shame she felt was intense. At the same time, though, she was mesmerized by Olivia. By the ease with which she stood in front of the staff and commanded their respect without raising her voice or asserting her authority. Just by being her casual, friendly, approachable self, she had the attention of every single person in the room. Some of them had smiles on their faces as Olivia addressed all questions, concerns, and items on Hayley's list. After about forty-five minutes, it was over. Olivia excused the staff and they filed out of the room until there was only the two of them left.

"I'm sorry," Hayley said, still in her chair.

Olivia shook her head as she handed back the pad of paper. "No reason to be."

"I don't do well in front of people. I never have." It wasn't something she liked to admit, but Hayley felt like she could tell Olivia and not feel like a pathetic loser. She was almost right.

Olivia's brows met above her nose as she headed for the door and waited for Hayley to follow. "You did okay the first few meetings."

Hayley scoffed. "The first one was just you introducing me. Still figuring things out for the second. Last week's was quick and painless because of Thanksgiving. This one was all me. Standing up in front of everybody and being the boss. Which I obviously suck at."

"You're really hard on yourself, you know that?" They were walking now, down the back hallway toward the public part of the resort, and Olivia didn't look at her as she spoke.

"I am?"

"Seems like it to me." Olivia didn't elaborate, just kept a brisk pace as they made it back to their offices and desks.

The remark stayed with Hayley for the rest of the day, in the back of her mind, put aside but not forgotten, as she went through email and fielded phone calls. An email popped through in the afternoon from her father. It said simply, "Budget?" With a groan, Hayley dropped her forehead onto the surface of her desk.

"Are you napping?" Olivia's voice held gentle ribbing, and as Hayley lifted her head, she was pretty sure she saw a ghost of a smile.

"Napping. Yes. That's exactly what I was doing. Not beating my head against my desk in frustrated confusion. Certainly not that."

Olivia squinted for a beat before jerking a thumb over her shoulder. "Ronnie is here to see you," she said quietly.

Hayley stared at her with what she was sure was a blank look on her face.

"The valet." Olivia lowered her voice as her expression changed. The subtle disapproval again.

"Oh. Oh! Oh, shit." She had to fire somebody. Yeah. That. "Shit," she said again.

Olivia pushed off the doorframe and stepped into the office. She shut the door behind her and said. "Ronnie Dean. He's worked here for a little over six months. I'm not at all sure why Roger hired him, because his work experience is minimal and he doesn't make a great impression. I question a lot of things Roger did." She waved a hand in front of her face. "Never mind that. Ronnie has been late at least once a week since he started. Last month, there were complaints from three different guests that change had been stolen from their cars. Ronnie was the only common denominator. Nothing even close to large sums of money, but it's the principle of it."

"Messes with our reputation," Hayley offered.

"Exactly."

"Okay. I understand. Send him in." Doing her best to ignore the explosion of nerves in her stomach, Hayley schooled her features, wiped any expression at all off her face, and folded her hands on her desk as the same sentence ricocheted through her head on repeat.

You can do this. You can do this. You can do this.

CHAPTER ELEVEN

The afternoon had been a blur for Olivia. She'd had a meeting with Lenny in maintenance to go over some of the applications he'd received for the empty positions he had to fill. Hayley should've been there, but she was dealing with Ronnie the valet, so Olivia had gone in her place. Then she'd made the rounds of the Evergreen, something she tried to do a couple times a week just to make sure things were running smoothly and no guests that she ran into along the way had complaints of any kind. She made a quick trip up to the rooftop bar, said hello to the staff there, and visited with a couple of guests, asked them about their stay—something she felt was important. Also, she loved the Christmas decorations they used up there, all the glass lined in white lights, garland along the front of the bar and lining the back shelves. The way the lights reflected off all the bottles gave the whole place a warm, welcoming feel and made Olivia want to order a glass of wine and make herself comfortable on one of the overstuffed couches. Maybe later...

Back behind the front desk, Stephanie was on the phone and computer, working on a reservation, from what Olivia could tell as she passed and entered her own office.

Where she was surprised to find both Maddie and Hayley, their heads close together, as Maddie sat at Olivia's desk and Hayley stood behind her, bent over so she could see Maddie's laptop. Hayley pointed at the screen. "See? I mean, you're not there, but it's pretty close." She glanced up, saw Olivia, and smiled.

"Hi, Liv," Maddie said, eyes bright. "Hayley was helping me

with my art history homework. Did you know a lot of museums have virtual tours? So you can actually look at the paintings and artwork just like you were there? Like, you can walk from room to room, check everything out at your own pace."

"I'm surprised you didn't know this already," Olivia said.

Maddie shrugged. "I never thought about it."

It was close to five, so Maddie started packing up her stuff as Hayley stood up.

"How'd everything go?" Olivia asked. "With Ronnie."

Hayley lifted one shoulder and tipped her head toward it. "Fine. He was rude and shocked and is going to sue us, but other than that, it went totally okay." She actually seemed amused by it rather than freaked—which would've been the reaction Olivia expected.

"We'll wait anxiously for the call from his lawyer," Olivia said, grinning.

"That's what I told him."

Stephanie came back to collect her daughter as the front desk changed hands, and they said their good-byes. Olivia reclaimed her desk and Hayley adjourned to her own. There was some paperwork to deal with and a few emails to respond to, but Olivia felt restless. She loved her job, and it was rare that she felt smothered at her desk, but she felt that now. Before she even realized what she was doing, she stood and popped her head into Hayley's office. When Hayley looked up from her computer and smiled at her, Olivia's insides went all warm and soft.

"What are you doing right now?"

Hayley looked back at her computer screen, as if to double-check. "I am working on this stupid budget that my—er—Corporate keeps bugging me about. Why?"

"Can you take a break from it?"

"Hell, yes."

"Feel like a cocktail?"

"Hell, yes again." Hayley was up and out of her chair so fast it made Olivia laugh. "Lead the way."

Less than ten minutes later, name tags removed and tucked into pockets, they each had a glass of wine and were reclining on an overstuffed couch in the rooftop bar, facing the windows so they could see the wide expanse of the Evergreen's front property. Lampposts and trees lined the drive. Each post had a wreath hanging from it. Each tree was wrapped in festive white lights.

"It looks like the proverbial winter wonderland from up here," Hayley said softly. "It's gorgeous."

"Thank you," Olivia said. At Hayley's furrowed brow, she explained. "Roger didn't want the lights out front. He said decorating the lobby and stuff was enough, that having lights outside wouldn't matter. I disagreed. Took me three years to change his mind, but when he did, I made sure we went all out. And we got compliments and comments almost immediately. Our Yelp reviews around the holidays consistently talk about how gorgeous our property looks, all decked out. That it makes them want to turn into our driveway just to see it."

"You were right. It's beautiful, and if I was looking for a place to stay for the holidays or to go skiing, this place would definitely catch my eye."

Olivia sipped her wine, feeling oddly satisfied at Hayley's words. "I don't do this often, drink among the guests. But it is after hours, and sometimes I just need this view, you know?"

"I can see why." They sat quietly for a moment before Hayley spoke again. "How come you're so good at this job?" It was an odd question, and the look on Hayley's face said she knew it. Still, she turned her head so she was facing Olivia, brows raised in expectation, and Olivia suddenly envisioned her helping Maddie with her homework, showing her something she was passionate about it. It had been lovely to watch.

Olivia shrugged. It might have been an odd question, but it was easy to answer. "Because I love it. Because it's what I've always wanted to do."

"Really?" This time, Hayley's expression said this was anything but what she wanted to do.

With a nod, Olivia went on. "The first time I came here, it was for Ski Club in high school. We met here and took one of the Evergreen shuttles up to Clearpeak. It was a very cold day and we had to wait for the shuttle to come back, so we all stood around in the lobby. And I was just taken with the place. I can't really pinpoint why. But I just watched. The folks at the front desk, the bellhops, the valets, the guests. It fascinated me." She looked to Hayley to see if she was bored to tears. Surprisingly, she sported a small smile and watched Olivia intently. She went on. "When I was old enough to get a job, I came here, and I kind of begged. The manager then was a really nice man. Mr. Klein. Super patient with me. When he gave me a job doing filing and data entry for him, I'm pretty sure it was just to get me to quit bugging him." Grinning at the memory, she said, "I went to college and majored in hospitality and hotel management, and I worked here on all holidays and vacations. Once I graduated, I worked in several different departments until the assistant manager job opened up. I was all over that."

"I bet you were." Hayley sipped her wine, her eyes still on Olivia. "You've told me how you got here, now tell me why you love it so much."

God, she was good at questions. Olivia scrunched up her nose and gave the inquiry honest thought. There was something about Hayley, about her being this close, about the intensity of her eye contact, that made Olivia feel exposed somehow. Almost naked. Not unpleasantly so. She shifted in her seat, and when their thighs ended up touching, she didn't readjust.

"I like seeing people happy. I like making their vacation or their weekend away or their holiday something they remember and want to revisit. It's why I constantly have new ideas to make us better. Not that Corporate ever listens to me." She sighed, knowing she was about to admit something to Hayley that she probably shouldn't. "To be honest, I'm a little worried about this place."

"How come? We were booked solid over Thanksgiving."

"We did well over Thanksgiving, true. But our smaller size hinders us a bit in the grand scheme of Markham Resorts. Corporate wants us to do better, needs us to do better in order to justify spending more money on us. But it's hard to do better when we're starting to appear dated. You know? There are two other big resorts in the area and we're losing to them because they're a bit more modern than we are."

"You don't think Corporate hears us?"

Olivia shrugged, finished off her wine. "They don't seem to. I have a file on my computer with scads of ideas on how to improve things. But like I said, we're so small, I think we just fall by the wayside. Have you *seen* some of the other Markham resorts?"

An odd…something…zipped across Hayley's face in that moment. Super fast. Olivia would've missed it if she hadn't been looking in her eyes. Unidentifiable.

"I know of them, yes." Hayley finished her wine and set her empty glass down on the table next to their couch.

"They're glamorous. Elegant. And huge." Olivia thought back on all the websites she'd visited, taken virtual tours of. "Not that we're not elegant. I believe we do a good job with that."

Hayley nodded her agreement. "Definitely."

Olivia blew out a breath and looked around. Several guests sat in clusters or pairs, laughing, drinking. The space was really beautiful, all the glass catching the reflections of the Christmas lights, and not for the first time, a sense of pride welled up in her. When she turned back to Hayley, she was still looking at her, still intently, but Olivia didn't think she was focused on anything to do with the hotel. Her eyes were dark, her lips sparkled, and Olivia's stomach fluttered. With a clear of her throat, she said, "Sorry about that. I get a little protective of this place."

"No reason to apologize. I get it."

Yeah, Olivia was pretty sure she didn't. "Anyway. I need to get home to Sir Walter, who awaits his dinner." As she stood, Hayley remained seated.

"I think I'm going to hang here for a little bit longer. It's the first time all day I haven't felt completely stressed out." She smiled softly. "Thank you for bringing me up here."

Their gazes held, Olivia looking down at this woman who was, undeniably, a gorgeous specimen of the female form. She swallowed down the lump of arousal that had settled in her throat, gave one nod, and fled.

Once in the elevator, she fell back against the wall and expelled all the air from her lungs in a long, frustrated groan.

Hayley sat on the couch and tried to focus. On the Christmas lights twinkling in the night. On the gentle hum of conversation around her. On the subtle tinkling of ice cubes against glasses. Not on the jelly-like feel of her legs or on the tightening in her stomach or on the dampness of her underwear. No. Not those things.

Olivia was gone, but Hayley could still smell her, as if she'd left something behind to remember her by, and Hayley inhaled slowly, deeply, wanting to take it in and hold on to it. Something natural, a little woodsy, maybe? Musk? She couldn't pinpoint it, only knew it was Olivia.

What are you doing to me? she asked silently of the universe. She hadn't been so attracted to somebody the way she was to Olivia in years. *Years.* Sure, she'd dated. She'd had a couple of relationships, though none lasted longer than a year or two. Guinevere was beautiful and successful, but she didn't do it for Hayley like Olivia did. Not even close. Hayley was *drawn* to Olivia. Yeah, that was the word. She was drawn to Olivia like she'd never been drawn to anybody before. In any other circumstances, she wouldn't hesitate. She'd have asked her out. Taken her to a fancy, expensive dinner. Maybe dancing, since she now knew what a beautiful sight that was. She'd have kissed her good night, taken her time with that, let her lips linger, leave them both wanting more.

Yeah, that wasn't going to happen. None of it. If her father was mad at her now, imagine how enraged he'd be if Hayley took her assistant manager to bed. She closed her eyes and shook her head slowly.

So unfair.

Olivia was warming to her. It was obvious. That constant look of disapproval had become…less constant. Bringing Hayley up here to this bar, sharing a drink and some personal information? That had definitely been a step toward warming, toward friendship. You didn't go to happy hour with people you couldn't stand, did you?

Hayley scrubbed her hands over her face, hoping to rub away all of these unproductive thoughts. She really wanted to go paint, but she still needed to finish up the budget and she knew without a doubt that was the best way to derail her train of thought from its current track.

Nothing like numbers and math to dampen your mood.

CHAPTER TWELVE

It was Friday and the week had gone surprisingly well. Hayley was still stressed out. Pretty highly stressed out, as anyone would expect to be when their job is nonstop and they're not terribly confident that they know what they're doing. But she'd managed not to insult any guests, piss off any employees, or skip over any necessary paperwork.

And it was Friday. Yeah, that was worth thinking about twice. She had the day off tomorrow and could do whatever she wanted. What she wanted was to paint. That was, if she could avoid being sought out by the weekend staff for minuscule things. She hadn't thought it through when she'd decided staying in one of the penthouse suites was the smartest thing to do. It made her far too accessible if somebody had a question or a guest became unruly.

She spun in her chair to look out the window. It had snowed quite a bit overnight, but her maintenance crew had worked hard—was still working hard—to clear it all off the driveway, parking lot, and sidewalks. Now the sun was shining, making the snow sparkle and the icicles drip like wet diamonds. She still missed the city terribly; that hadn't changed. But this view did not suck. That was the truth.

Things were going okay. Finally.

Hayley was so relaxed and lost in her own thoughts that when her cell phone rang, it startled her enough to make her flinch in her chair and press a hand to her chest, a muttered curse escaping her lips.

The screen said it was her father. *Probably calling to tell me he got the budget at last.* She'd sent that in last night after about fifty-seven revisions and her finger hovering over the Send button for a year and a half.

"Hey," she said as she answered. *I'm breezy. Casual. That's me.*

"Hayley." Such a personal greeting. Yeah, that was her dad lately.

"Did you get the budget?"

The question seemed to surprise him. "You sent it in?"

"Last night. Yep." Probably a bit too much satisfaction in her tone, but she didn't care.

"I haven't seen it yet, but I'll look for it." He cleared his throat, and Hayley got a weird sensation in the pit of her stomach. A bad feeling. "I'd like to discuss your credit card charges."

Her brow furrowed. "Okay." She braced, but she wasn't sure what she was bracing against.

"There's a charge from a place called Glitter."

Shit.

"I looked it up. It's a nightclub." Benton Markham's tone made it clear what he thought of that.

"Dad, I went out with some friends and I bought their drinks. It wasn't that much."

"That's not the point, Hayley. I told you I wanted you to focus on your work and stop screwing around."

"And I'm not allowed to go out at all? To have any fun at all?" Yeah, she probably should've counted to five before she spoke, but she was kind of shocked he was so mad.

"This is just another example of your irresponsibility. You asked me to release your credit so you could get art supplies. You get them, and in addition, you go out partying."

"I wasn't partying." Hayley's voice held a little bit too much of her indignation and she knew it. "And I'm not sixteen."

"That's right. You're not sixteen. You are a grown woman who should know better."

"Dad, I—"

"I don't want to hear it." Her father interrupted her, his tone getting firmer, which Hayley didn't think was possible. "I've had enough. No more charging. Understood?"

"Come on, Dad—" She tried not to sound too childish, but was pretty sure she failed when he cut her off again.

"Understood?" It was *that* tone. The I'm-the-boss-how-dare-you-argue-with-me tone. That one. The one he only used once in a great while before her mom had passed away. Since then, it seemed like it was one of the only two tones he used on her. That one and the you-continually-disappoint-me tone. She swallowed.

"Yes, sir," she said quietly. There was no way to win when he got like this, and she knew it. Fighting him only made it worse.

"Good. Now, show me you're taking some initiative over there and not just coasting. Do your job."

He hung up before she could say anything more, and Hayley sat there at her desk, staring at the smartphone in her hand. Sometimes her father stoked the anger fire within her until she thought the top of her head would blow off. Sometimes he made her so sad she wanted to curl up in a corner on the floor and rock herself to sleep. Sometimes it was a weird combination of the two. But today? Today she'd plowed through both of those emotions until she arrived at a new one. The current one.

Numbness.

She'd reached a point where she felt blank. Lost. Nothing.

"Hey, you okay?" Olivia's voice was soft, laced with concern.

Hayley looked up at her, at the sight for sore eyes standing in her doorway. Dressed in a smart gray pantsuit with a navy shell under the jacket, she looked both professional and a little bit sexy. Hayley gave a small nod. "Yeah. I am."

"You sure? 'Cause you look like somebody stole your puppy."

Slow breath in. Slow breath out. "Yeah." She held up the phone. "Family stuff."

"Drama?"

"I guess you could say that."

Olivia seemed to debate something in her head as she studied Hayley. After a moment, she glanced at her watch. "Okay, listen. It's lunchtime. I want to show you something." There was a glimmer in her dark eyes that Hayley could see even from the desk.

"Okay." She pushed herself to her feet.

"Run up to your room and change into something warmer. Boots. Bring your coat and gloves."

Hayley squinted at her. "Okay." This time, she drew the word out, uncertain.

Olivia grinned widely. "Trust me."

Hayley nodded because there really was no question.

"And bring your camera."

"Yes, ma'am."

"Meet me at the front door in fifteen?"

"I'll be there." Hayley watched her turn and leave, no idea what was in store, but absolutely on board with it. One hundred and fifty percent. She needed to be pulled out of the funk her father'd shoved her into, and she could think of nobody she'd rather follow, anywhere, than Olivia Santini.

She headed up to get her things.

❖

Hayley had sat in the passenger seat of Olivia's SUV like an excited child as they drove. It really was super cute, the way she sat up straight, looked out the window, and almost bounced with anticipation. It was so much better than the demeanor she'd had when Olivia had looked in on her less than half an hour ago. She'd looked so dejected. A little confused. But mostly just sad.

Olivia decided in that exact moment that Sad Hayley was something she wanted to see as little of as possible.

And what the hell was that about?

She'd tried not to dwell, not to think about that kind of thing—that kind of thing being how often Hayley was on her mind. Tried not to analyze it too much. Maybe taking her up to the rooftop bar on Monday evening had been a mistake, because Olivia hadn't been able to get Hayley out of her head since then, how comfortable she'd been opening up. Olivia didn't open up easily to other people. It had been a complaint leveled at her by more than one woman who'd tried to date her. Hayley, however, felt safe somehow, and that made Olivia nervous. At the same time, the thoughts she was having—many of them naughty—were fun. Of course they were. And wasn't it about time she had such things in her head? So what if nothing could happen between them? They were just thoughts. Fantasies. And it had been way too long since she'd had them.

"Where are we going?" Hayley asked for the third time.

"God, you're worse than a kid," Olivia said, but kept it playful and light. "We're almost there." A couple minutes later, she turned into a parking lot.

"Archer Nature Trails," Hayley read off the sign as they drove past.

It was the perfect weather for this. Snowy and crisp, but sunny. Olivia pulled into a nearly empty parking lot, which was what she'd hoped for. Not many tourists came here in the winter. It was more a summer attraction, but Olivia loved it on a day like this. Walking alone in the woods along the trails made her feel like she was the only person on the planet sometimes. The parking lot overlooked a small open space, and beyond that was a wall of trees. Several trailheads were visible, brown wooden signs at each one announcing the name, the length, and some history. To their left was a large building that Olivia knew housed the public restrooms and a gift shop. She turned off the ignition, then looked at Hayley. "Ready?"

With a nod, Hayley yanked her door open and jumped out.

Olivia did the same, then pulled on her hat and gloves. "Follow me."

The snow crunched under their feet. The folks at Archer were very good about keeping sidewalks and trails clear enough for walking, though if you came early enough, Olivia knew from experience that it might serve you well to bring snowshoes.

She led Hayley to the trailhead she wanted, then waited as Hayley read another brown wooden sign, this one smaller and on a post.

"Archer Nature Park Fairy Trail." She looked at Olivia with a furrowed brow. "Fairy Trail? What's that?"

"Let's find out." Olivia turned and walked farther into the woods for about twenty yards until they came across another small sign.

"Fairy Trail Rules," Hayley read dutifully. "One. Don't leave the trail. You don't want to step on a fairy or wander into poison ivy." She glanced at Olivia with a skeptical expression, then read rule number two. "Speak softly so as not to disturb fairies that might be sleeping."

Olivia said nothing and walked a few more yards to a third sign that had rules four, five, and six.

"Touch gently." Hayley was now more curious than doubtful. Olivia could tell by the slight change in her voice. "Fairy houses are fragile and not all the doors will open. Four, take pictures and leave everything else behind. Five, we love dogs as much as you do, but they scare the fairies and the wildlife, so leave them at home." She turned to Olivia. "That's why no Walter." Olivia nodded as Hayley's gaze traveled beyond her as if scanning the path ahead. "A fairy trail, huh?"

Olivia grinned. "It always makes me feel better to walk it, and you looked like you could use a nonstressful hour of life."

"You're not kidding about that." Hayley's entire face softened as she said, "Thank you."

Their eyes locked for what felt like a long time to Olivia, and she could feel those naughty thoughts she'd banished earlier surface low in her body once again. Hayley was an odd combination of cute and sexy in her red parka, white knit hat, and matching gloves. "Are you warm enough?" Olivia asked quietly.

Hayley nodded.

"Good. Shall we find the fairy houses?"

Hayley held up the camera that hung around her neck by a thick black strap. "Yes, please."

For the next forty-five minutes, they walked. Hayley's ever-growing smile of joy and wonder reminded Olivia of the very first time she'd walked the fairy trail several years ago. She'd had no idea what to expect but had been surprised and filled with warmth every time she discovered a new fairy house. Artists—local and visiting—used pieces and parts of nature. Tree trunks, branches, discarded deer antlers, anything they could find. Some fairy houses were freestanding, brought in from wherever the artist worked. Others were constructed right there in the park, built into existing trees or stumps or fallen logs too big to move. The houses were small and it seemed to be an accepted fact that the fairies "living" in them were maybe an inch or two tall. Some were at ground level, perched on rocks or the tops of stumps. Others, like the one Hayley was taking a photo of, were at eye level. The artist had found a tree with a large knothole in it. He or she had added a wooden V over the top of the hole, like an awning to a front door. The knothole was painted red, a tiny doorknob and mullions added in black. Beneath the "door" was a small wooden platform, like a tiny deck, and hanging next to it was a small sign that read in itty-bitty lettering, "Shh...fairies are napping."

Hayley snapped away, held the camera out to check the display screen, then snapped a few more shots from different angles. When she was seemingly satisfied, she turned to Olivia, and the smile on her face was one of the most beautiful things Olivia had ever seen. Joyful and genuine, it lit up her entire face with a childlike happiness. "This place is *amazing*," she said, her green eyes sparkling in the rays of sun that cut through the branches and made the entire trail feel almost like, well, a fairy tale. "I'm so glad you brought me here. This is just what I needed."

"You seemed pretty affected by whoever you talked to on the phone this morning."

"My father," Hayley said, but the happiness on her face only dimmed a little, and Olivia was beyond curious to know more about her, so she pressed a bit.

"You don't get along?"

Hayley sighed as they started walking again by unspoken agreement. "It's...complicated. He's always been kind of a tough guy. And I don't mean tough like boxer tough or mob boss tough." Olivia chuckled at that. "I mean tough to get to. Tough to impress. But I'm his only daughter, youngest child by a pretty good stretch, and he gave me more attention than most."

"I hear a 'but' coming."

"But...since my mom died, he's been..." Olivia could see Hayley's breath as she blew it out in obvious frustration. "I don't know. Distant. Stoic. Hard."

"Sad?"

Hayley looked at her like she'd never thought about that one. "Yeah, maybe."

"What were you talking about this morning that got you so upset?"

Something zipped across Hayley's face then, but she turned to face forward as they walked and Olivia couldn't pinpoint what it was. "It's not important. Really. Nothing I'm not used to."

Olivia saw the impending return of Sad Hayley and scrambled forward to the next fairy house, just before a small bridge that led over the creek running through the park. This house was one of her favorites. She squatted down and pointed. "See this one?" It was positioned against one of the bridge's wooden posts. Its door was purple and there was a small sign above it that read "Beware of Trolls."

Hayley let out a high-pitched, girlish squeal. "Oh, my God, that's adorable!" She backed away and took a couple snaps before looking around. Then she shrugged, lay down in the snow on her stomach, and took a few shots from the same level as the house, head-on.

Just like that, Sad Hayley was gone again.

Olivia gave herself a point and a mental pat on the back, and once Hayley was back on her feet, they walked some more.

The two were quiet, no sound but the crunching of snow under their feet as they moved through the woods. To Olivia's right, she heard the same sound—snow crunching under steps—and she grabbed Hayley's arm to stop her. When those green eyes met hers, Olivia held a hand to her lips, telling Hayley to keep quiet, then she pointed in the direction of the sound.

Three deer were meandering through the woods, stopping here and there to look for food to nibble. Maybe some stray vegetation poking through the snow. The errant crab apple.

Hayley let out a small gasp, and one of the deer raised her head and looked right at them. She couldn't have been more than twenty or thirty feet away and she was gorgeous, all smooth rust-colored coat and huge brown eyes. Her ears twitched as she listened. Deer were very, very common in the area, but Olivia never tired of seeing them. They were so graceful and beautiful, and she could simply watch them for a long while.

When she turned slowly to look at Hayley, a grin spread across her face because Hayley was totally in awe. Her eyes were wide. Her mouth was in the shape of a silent "O," and Olivia had a flash of what six-year-old Hayley might have looked like. Hayley blinked rapidly, those eyes sparkling when they met Olivia's, and something about the absolute wonder on her face made Olivia inexplicably happy they'd come.

Eventually, the deer wandered off into the woods, and Hayley finally blew out a breath and said quietly, "That was amazing!"

"I take it you don't have deer wandering around Manhattan?"

"God, no. That was just..." Hayley shook her head, her gaze still following the direction the deer went. "Magical. It was magical. I've never felt such...peace. I don't know how to explain it." Her voice was quietly excited, and the words came out in a rush. "I've never felt that before. Such beauty and grace. It makes everything else pale in comparison. I feel so...alive now, if that makes any sense at all and oh, my God, could I ramble more? I can't seem to stop talking. I just feel like my blood is pumping and my heart is happy and...and thank you. I don't know how to say it, but thank you." She wrapped her arms around Olivia's neck and hugged her tightly, whispered her thanks again with her lips tickling the skin there.

And that was when the air got suddenly heavy. Olivia could feel it, like it had become thicker and slowed movements down somehow. Hayley pulled away very, very slowly until her nose was mere millimeters from Olivia's lips, her hands still on Olivia's shoulders, and when she looked up, Olivia could see a million different things in those eyes, but every one of them said the same thing.

Kiss her.

Hayley's head must have been saying the same thing, because Olivia was pretty sure they moved at the same time, closed the tiny gap between them in tandem. Their lips met, tentatively at first, as if testing the waters, just a gentle kiss. They pulled back just slightly, and then there was eye contact. Eye contact that was the most sensual Olivia had ever experienced. She could feel it in the pit of her stomach. She could feel it lower. Those eyes, the deepness of the green, the darkness they suddenly had, they startled her with their intensity. They also aroused her like nothing ever had, and she realized belatedly that she really had no choice but to kiss Hayley again.

So she did.

Suddenly it wasn't cold at all. Suddenly it was warm. Very, very warm as the kiss went from gently testing the waters to full-on making out so fast, Olivia lost track. First they were softly pressing their lips together. In what felt like the next moment, mouths opened, tongues pressed in, and Olivia felt herself pulling at Hayley, trying to get her body closer. Not an easy feat given all the winter outdoor gear they were wearing, but she did her best because all she wanted was Hayley closer.

My God, this girl knows how to kiss!

The thought ran through Olivia's brain like a toddler on a sugar high, bouncing around in her head, ricocheting off her skull. Hayley's kiss wasn't forceful, but it felt erotically demanding. It wasn't selfish, but she took what she wanted. Olivia was used to being in control, but with this kiss? She so *was not.*

Time didn't exist for Olivia. Nothing did but Hayley's mouth. Hayley's tongue. The small, breathy sounds she made...or was that Olivia making them? She had no idea, but they were sexy as hell.

Were Hayley's hands in her hair? She wasn't sure, but Olivia grabbed Hayley's coat—being careful of the camera around her neck—walked her backward until she let out a soft *oof* as her back hit the tree trunk, and then Olivia's mouth was on hers again.

Somehow in that moment, Olivia realized this had been bound to happen, that it was somehow destined. From that first walk in the woods with her dog, from her first glimpse of the red parka and those ridiculously sexy eyes, it was all leading to this kiss, and Olivia absently wondered how she'd managed to fight it for so long.

When they finally wrenched apart and stood there, panting like sprinters, foreheads pressed together, Olivia had no idea how much time had passed.

As if reading her mind, Hayley said quietly, and with a tint of wonder in her voice, "Did we just make out for, like, a year? Or a minute?"

Olivia chuckled. "Right? I have no clue."

"That was…wow." Hayley shook her head slowly, as if she had no more words. Only awe.

Olivia smiled, stepped back, and felt something under her boot. She looked down to see Hayley's gloves on the ground. Her hands had been in Olivia's hair. She picked them up and handed them over. "We should probably get back," she said.

With a nod, Hayley agreed. "You're right." She pushed her hands into her gloves. Her answering smile seemed to have dimmed a couple of watts, but Olivia didn't want to think about that. Instead, she turned and headed down the path and toward the parking lot, so many mixed emotions in her head, she thought she could drown in them.

She would analyze this later.

Definitely.

Over and over and over.

❖

Hayley could've stayed on the fairy trail for the entire day. It was true that her fingers were slightly numb from all the picture taking, as she didn't like to do that with gloves on. It was true that the rest of her was pretty much frozen solid. But the simple joy of discovering the fairy houses—not all of them were in plain sight, but rather needed to be searched for—warmed her from the inside. And kissing Olivia? There was nothing warm about that. No, that was fucking hot.

They probably shouldn't have. But right now, Hayley didn't care. They had and it had been amazing and she wasn't ready to analyze it or dissect it or let it go. She would simply hang on to it and think about it later.

Because there was work. Unfortunately. It probably hadn't been a great idea for the manager *and* the assistant manager to leave the resort completely at the same time, but Hayley was beyond grateful that they had. Not just for the fairy houses, but for the company and the...rest of it. And they'd only been gone a little over an hour.

They trudged through the employee entrance at the back, Hayley and Olivia, stomping snow off their boots and greeting various staff—maintenance guys, cleaning folk—who were just starting or just finishing their lunch breaks. Hayley's inner train of thought went something like this: *Hi, staff! How was lunch? Everybody okay? It's us, your managers. Don't be silly. Everything is perfectly normal. Of course we weren't making out in the woods! Why would you say that?* Olivia's cheeks were a rosy pink as she pulled her hat off and unzipped her coat, and when she looked down at Hayley, it took everything in Hayley's being not to reach out and lay her hand against Olivia's skin, against her face, and pull her in for another scorching kiss.

Instead, she said simply, "Thank you so much, Olivia. I really, really needed that." And before she could second-guess herself, she reached out, wrapped her arms around Olivia, and hugged her. She let herself bask for just a moment in the feel of Olivia's form under the coat, in the scent of her, that same musk but with a hint of almond. She let her mind remember the softness of Olivia's mouth, the assertive way she'd trapped Hayley between the tree and her body, and it all forced her to swallow hard. She didn't look back as she let go and walked down the hall toward the elevators. She didn't want to see Olivia's expression then, because it was clear by her silence on the ride home that she maybe wasn't thrilled about what they'd done.

Or maybe not. Hayley allowed herself to hold on to one simple fact: Olivia had hugged her back. Tightly.

Once safely ensconced in the elevator she surprisingly had to herself, she fell against the back wall with a happy sigh. She wanted to bottle this feeling. Keep it somehow so she could take it out and spray it all over herself when she needed it.

As the earlier conversation with her father filtered back into her brain, she dropped her chin to her chest.

Because, yeah.

Sometimes she needed it.

CHAPTER THIRTEEN

Ever since the Fairy Trail Incident, as Olivia had taken to calling her ill-advised kiss with Hayley, she'd been reduced to doing one of two things. She either worked harder than a one-armed juggler or she stared off into space. Nothing else. No scintillating conversations. No hanging with friends—she'd been avoiding Tessa, who was most certainly going to kill her at some point in the very near future. She'd tried watching television but found that once she finally decided on a show, after twenty or thirty minutes, she had no idea what was happening. Reading posed a similar problem in that she'd read the same paragraph seventeen times before she retained any of it. She had managed to walk with Walter a few times, but she'd gone to a completely different park, afraid she'd run into Hayley if she went to her usual one.

The only person she'd told about the Fairy Trail Incident was her mother when she was at her house on Sunday, and she now wished *vehemently* that she hadn't. The conversation had been dizzying.

"You kissed? That's wonderful!" her mother had said, with enormous excitement, as she rolled meatballs and set them in the electric frying pan.

"It's not wonderful, Mama. It's not wonderful at all." Olivia shook her head as she used tongs to turn the meatballs that were already browning.

"Why not? Tell me why it's not wonderful."

"Because," Olivia stressed and sounded lame even to herself. "She's pretty." She set another meatball in the hot oil.

Olivia inhaled a big breath and let it out very slowly before nodding in reluctant agreement. "She definitely is that."

"She was lovely on Thanksgiving. Polite. A good conversationalist."

"Ma. Enough."

"I think it's wonderful. I like her."

And they'd gone around and around like that for what felt like days but was really only the time it took to finish the meatballs.

Thankfully, Hayley hadn't seemed to be trying to find her either. Olivia had worked Saturday, and Hayley had worked Sunday, and neither of them bothered the other. At all. More unusual for Hayley, as she lived upstairs, but still. Olivia was grateful.

And at the same time, a little bit annoyed.

Whiskey tango foxtrot, Liv? she'd chided herself more than once. She knew she had no right to be upset with Hayley's lack of contact if Olivia herself wasn't willing to make an effort either. Maybe Hayley was having the same issue? Olivia sighed. She had no freaking idea.

It was Monday now, the first day they'd have to be together all day, and so far, they'd managed to do exactly not that. It was almost funny, really, how strategically they'd avoided each other, Olivia finding a reason to go to another part of the resort within five minutes of Hayley coming into the office. Hayley doing the same.

With a sigh that was almost more of a groan, Olivia returned to her work, tried to focus on the list of emails she should have answered this morning. Now it was after noon.

She'd only been typing for a few moments before she heard cheerful greetings coming from the front desk, a voice she recognized instantly cutting through the air and coming closer.

"Hi, sweetie." Angela Santini breezed into the small outer office, bundled up in her thigh-length down coat and purple knit hat. She held out two Tupperware containers.

"Are you bringing me lunch?" Olivia hadn't expected the visit, and her heart warmed.

"I went by to see my granddog and let him out, so I thought I'd swing by here on my way back to the office and make sure you're eating."

"Mama, you didn't have to do that. Walter will be okay if he doesn't get let out at lunch every single day."

"Well, who wants to be cooped up for eight hours like that, hmm?" Angela craned her neck to get a better view of the doorway to Hayley's office. Olivia shook her head.

"She's not in there."

"Oh, no?"

"No, she's in the back with maintenance going over applications."

"She was, but she's back," Hayley said, as she walked through the door. "Mrs. Santini, what a nice surprise."

It was like they were old friends, and Olivia watched slightly wide-eyed as her mother held out a hand to Hayley and pulled her in for a kiss on the cheek. "It's so good to see you. How are things going? You getting the hang of it?"

Hayley grinned and Olivia tried not to stare, but she couldn't help herself. That stupid grin was gorgeous. Damn her. "I'm learning. Slowly but surely." Hayley's gaze shifted to Olivia and held for a beat before she added, "Your daughter's been amazing at helping me out, though. She's a good teacher. Very patient. I'm grateful."

"She's a catch, my Olivia, that's for sure."

She did not just say that. Oh, my God. Olivia closed her eyes and willed her mother to leave. She did not. Instead, she held out one of the Tupperware containers toward Hayley.

"Here you go. I brought you lunch."

Hayley's face lit up like a child who's just been given a toy she's wanted for ages. "You did not have to do that. You're so sweet."

"Sunday is sauce day, so there's rigatoni in there with sauce and a couple meatballs that Olivia helped me make." She turned and winked at her daughter.

Olivia poked the inside of her cheek with her tongue and said nothing. Only because she couldn't think of a thing to say.

"It just so happens that I'm starving," Hayley said. "So, thank you."

There was a moment when the three of them said nothing, Angela and Hayley smiling at each other, Olivia wishing she was anywhere else. Finally, Angela spoke again.

"You all ready for Christmas? Where do you go?"

Something flew across Hayley's face then. Olivia saw it, but only for the briefest second. "Oh," Hayley said, her gaze leaving Angela's face and moving toward the window. "I'll probably just stay here. No big deal. My father isn't a big Christmas guy, and my brothers are in different states. So. Yeah. I'll just be here."

Olivia knew what was coming before the gasp even left her mother's lungs.

"What?" Angela's face matched her voice in level of horror. "You'll be all alone on Christmas?"

Hayley shrugged and attempted a smile. "It's totally fine. It won't be the first time."

"What?" Angela said again. "No. No way. This is not okay with me."

Hayley, for the first time since she walked into the office, looked sincerely at Olivia, eyebrows raised in a silent *what do I do?*

Olivia gave a small shrug and shook her head subtly because there was nothing to be done but come to the Santinis' house for Christmas. That was where her mother was going with all the horrified faces, and she knew it. It followed instantly.

"You'll come to our house for Christmas Eve dinner. Right, Olivia?"

And that was how she did it. Olivia had to give kudos to her mother because there was no way she could say anything like, "Um, no, Mama, I'd rather my direct supervisor who I made out with three days ago not come to Christmas at our house." No way at all. Angela Santini was no dummy.

"Right," Olivia said, because what else could she say?

Angela pulled out her phone, did some scrolling and some tapping, then handed it over to Hayley. "Here, put your number in and I'll text you the details next week. I live right next door to Olivia, did you know that?"

"I did not know that." Hayley shot Olivia a cute little grin, then did as she was told and handed the phone back.

"Perfect. Oh, I'm so excited!" Angela pocketed her phone. "All right, girls. I need to get back to work. Eat your lunches." As she turned to go, walking past so Hayley was between her and Olivia, she shot a wink at her daughter.

Dammit.

Hayley turned to stare at the doorway for a beat before shifting her focus to Olivia and asking, "What just happened?"

With a sigh, Olivia said, "Congratulations. You've just borne witness to Hurricane Angela. There's nothing you can do. Just grab a tree or something and hold on tight."

❖

The pasta and meatballs Mrs. Santini had given Hayley for lunch were freaking delicious. And she lived in New York City, which meant she'd eaten at some of the best, most famous Italian restaurants in the country. Yeah, Olivia's mom knew what she was doing. Wow.

She forked the last bite into her mouth, despite the fact that she was full six bites ago, and absently thought about licking the bowl clean. Deciding against that, she sat back in her chair and blew out a huge breath, as if she'd been working really, really hard.

Olivia was avoiding her. Which was fair, because she'd been avoiding Olivia. She shook her head slowly. Were they twelve? Why couldn't they just talk about what had happened in the woods?

God...

And then her brain ran away with her, just like it did every time she reflected on that walk in the woods. Easily one of the best days of her life. The combination of the beauty of nature, the craftsmanship and creativity of the fairy houses, the thoughtfulness of Olivia actually taking her there.

And the kissing.

Can't forget the kissing because...dear God.

Hayley had tons to get done, but once again, she found herself staring off into space. It seemed to be her thing, what she did at the Evergreen. Stare off into space, or out the window, and wonder. Think. Reflect.

What was going on with Olivia? Was it simply a physical thing? Hayley was devastatingly attracted to her and that only increased a hundredfold after making out with her. Hayley had no doubt at all that they'd probably ignite the bed if they ever got that far.

Was it more than that, though?

Hayley had been with her share of women. Not a ton. She wasn't the type to just fall into bed with anyone who caught her eye. But she'd had a couple of experiences that were nothing more than that: physical experiences. And she was okay with that.

Maybe that's all this was with Olivia?

They didn't really know each other all that well…though Olivia had opened up a bit more lately, and Hayley was very interested in learning more about her. That said a lot. If this was a purely physical thing, would she care about Olivia's past? About her hopes and dreams? Because right now, she did. Hayley wanted to know everything.

But how did Olivia feel?

"Only one way to find out," she said aloud to her empty office, then pushed herself away from her desk and to her feet.

Yeah. They needed to talk.

But Olivia wasn't at her desk.

"Of course," Hayley said with a sigh, then headed out toward the front desk.

Stephanie Dunne was manning the front, as usual, her friendly demeanor and welcoming smile like sunshine on a cold winter's day as she typed away on her computer.

"Hey, Stephanie, have you seen Olivia?"

Stephanie turned to her as the phone rang and she picked it up. "Evergreen Resort and Spa, this is Stephanie, how may I help you?" She held up an arm and pointed Hayley toward her left.

Which could mean almost anything. Olivia went to Starbucks. She went to Split Rail. *She's decided she's had enough and left through the front door, never to return again.* Hayley stifled a sigh of frustration and started walking in that direction hoping she'd maybe just run right into her.

Olivia wasn't outside. Hayley had taken a few steps out there, glanced at the valet on duty. He shook his head when she asked if he'd seen Olivia, and that was enough for her because it was freezing out and she had no coat.

Starbucks was next and was also a bust, as Olivia was nowhere to be seen.

She wasn't at Split Rail either. Hayley hesitated entering the kitchen, given that she couldn't seem to get out of anybody's way when she did, but as luck would have it, Tessa came out just as Hayley was ready to leave. She was apparently looking for something and seemed surprised to see Hayley.

"Oh, hi, Hayley." Her smile was…odd, and there was a strange glimmer in her eyes. "Looking for Olivia?"

"I am, yes." Why did Tessa make her nervous? Hayley couldn't pinpoint what it was, but her stomach always did uncomfortable flip-flopping whenever Tessa looked at her. She always felt like Tessa was silently judging her, mentally scoring everything she did or said.

"She went to change, so she could run."

"Oh, okay. Thanks." Relieved to have a solid destination, Hayley left the restaurant quickly and wondered if Tessa noticed.

She should've asked where Olivia went to change her clothes, because she wasn't sure. Since Hayley lived in the Evergreen, she could just run upstairs if she needed something. So where would Olivia go? The ladies' room? The employee locker room in the back?

The other question was, should she continue to look for her? Olivia was obviously busy. Was she going to want Hayley interrupting her run? On her lunch hour? But there was one thing Hayley was sure of: If she didn't talk to Olivia now, she'd lose her nerve, because in reality, she was just a big scaredy-cat, especially when it came to this subject.

The entire time she had this internal debate, her feet kept moving, and it wasn't long before she found herself in the hallway that led to the indoor pool and had a view of the fitness center.

Her eyes landed on Olivia immediately, and they roamed over her body with little regard for what was appropriate. The skintight workout pants. The bright orange T-shirt. The same black and green trainers on her feet. But she wasn't running. Not yet. Rather, she was standing near an elliptical machine. There was a woman on it who looked rather confused.

Hayley moved around the corner to the door and tugged it open. Olivia didn't see her, but Hayley could hear them. Their backs were to her, but she could see their faces reflected in the wall of mirrors.

"So, if you just want something simple, you can push Quick Start and go." Olivia looked up at the woman with a gentle smile. "It will keep track of everything, and you set the pace right here. These arrows will increase the resistance if you want. But you don't have to. It's up to you."

"Okay." The woman nodded, but there was obvious worry on her face. "I don't want to go too fast."

Olivia's expression softened. Hayley watched it happen. "Are you nervous, Mrs. Dale?" Her voice was kind. Understanding.

The woman—Mrs. Dale—couldn't have been older than sixty, and she brought a hand to her chest, rubbed it. Her pale face colored a bit, her cheeks turning a light pink, visible even to Hayley. "A little. Yes."

Olivia reached up, laid her hand on Mrs. Dale's upper arm, and rubbed gently. "I remember after my uncle had a heart attack. He was terrified to do anything more than go for a walk, even though the doctors told him it was absolutely okay, that his heart had recovered and was strong. They told him it would be *good* for him to exercise, but he was still so scared."

"What did he do?"

Olivia shrugged with a chuckle and said, "He walked." When Mrs. Dale joined her with a smile, she went on. "It just took time for him to decide he was ready to take it up a notch, and then he started jogging again. It's the same for you. Only you know when you're ready, so listen to your body, and don't let anybody push you. Okay?"

Mrs. Dale nodded. "Thank you, Olivia. I needed to hear that." She took in a deep breath and hit a button on the machine, then began moving gently, keeping her pace slow and even. Her reflection showed relief on her face, even a slight smile and determination in her eyes.

Olivia stood nearby for a moment, as if watching to make sure Mrs. Dale was okay, before turning away. Her gaze landed on Hayley and she stopped, stared and—did she just swallow? Hayley was amused by the apparent case of nerves, although she had them, too. She waved Olivia toward her.

"Hey," Olivia said, when she got closer. Her purple earbuds were draped around her neck like a stethoscope, connected to her phone, which was strapped to her upper arm. A white gym towel dangled from her hand. Her dark eyes were wary. "Everything okay?"

"Yeah." Hayley looked around. "Can we talk for a sec?"

For a tiny instant, Olivia looked like she was going to say no, and Hayley had no backup plan for that. Instead, though, she looked around the gym, sighed quietly, and indicated they step out through the doors.

In the hallway, Hayley leaned a shoulder against the wall. She smiled; she couldn't help it. Being this close to Olivia—regardless of why—made her happy.

"Listen, first of all, I want to tell you that it's totally okay if you'd rather I didn't come to your mom's on Christmas. I don't want to make you uncomfortable, and you seemed a little less than thrilled when she asked me, but…I couldn't say no. Have you met your mom?"

That brought a gentle laugh out of Olivia. "Yeah, I have. She's pretty persuasive."

"Seriously, though. I don't want it to be awkward."

"Me, neither." Olivia let her body lean toward the wall until she mirrored Hayley's stance. She looked around and lowered her voice. "I guess the best way to prevent that is to talk about…" She let the sentence dangle, which pulled a small chuckle from Hayley.

"How we made out in the woods, likely traumatizing all of the woodland creatures for the rest of their little woodland lives?"

This time, Olivia's laugh was bold, louder, and Hayley loved the sound of it. "Yes. That."

"I agree. Let's talk."

And they stood there. Quietly. Looking around, then looking at each other until they both burst out laughing.

"Okay, well, that was productive," Hayley said.

"Good talk," Olivia agreed.

When the laughter died down, Hayley smiled at Olivia. "Look. I like you. I realize our situation isn't ideal, but…" She shrugged. "I like you."

Olivia nodded. "I like you, too."

"And we kiss really well. So, there's that."

Olivia's eyes went wide in agreement as she nodded. "No argument here."

Before either could say anything more, Olivia's phone lit up on her arm, and she stretched around to see the incoming text. "Stephanie's got an issue."

"I'll take care of it," Hayley told her. "You take your run."

"You're sure?" Olivia was obviously hesitant, and Hayley did her best not to be insulted by that.

"I'm sure. I've got it. Go." With a small wave, she turned and headed around the corner to the elevators.

With a smile at the handful of folks already in the car, she rode down to the lobby level, her mind full. They hadn't really talked, had they? Although…Olivia did admit to liking her. Which wasn't really a surprise, since she'd had her tongue in Hayley's mouth a few days ago. But Hayley was going to put it in the win column.

"We really love this place."

It took Hayley a beat to realize the statement, which came from a woman to her left, was directed at her. She blinked rapidly and turned to her, an attractive brunette in her forties. "I'm sorry?"

The woman pointed at Hayley's name tag. "I see you're the manager. I just wanted to tell you how much we love this place." She tightened her hold on the tall gentleman standing next to her.

"I'm so glad to hear that," Hayley said truthfully. "Is this your first visit with us?"

"Oh, no. It's our—" She looked up at the man. "How many holidays have we spent here now?"

"Four, I think." The man's voice was a deep baritone. "Maybe five."

"Wow," Hayley said. "That's amazing. Thank you so much." And then, as if hearing her father's concerns in her head, she ventured a question. "Is there anything we could do to make your stay better?" God, she sounded like a brochure. Or a robot.

"Some updates would be great," the man said, without hesitation. "Things are starting to feel a bit...dated. You know?"

Hayley nodded, listening as he listed various places he'd considered revamping, from the spa rooms to the pool area. She mentally listed them in her head.

"There are a lot of other places around here that are newer. Or... feel newer, if that makes sense."

"It does." Hayley nodded again as the elevator came to a stop and dinged to let them know. "Thank you so much for your input, Mr...."

"Kowalsky," the man said, and held out his hand.

Hayley shook it, then the woman's, and thanked them again as they stepped off the elevator and went on their way. Pulling out her phone, she jotted the things the Kowalskys had suggested into a notes app, along with their name, then headed toward the front desk to see what Stephanie needed.

As she walked, "I'll Be Home for Christmas" emanated softly from the hidden speakers in the lobby, and just like that, she was dragged back to the conversation she'd had with Olivia's mom. Then the one she'd had with Olivia. Christmas was almost here.

Olivia had a little less than a week to change her mind about Hayley joining her family for Christmas.

The problem, as Hayley saw it, was that she was already looking forward to it. If Olivia did change her mind, which she had every right to do, Hayley would be more let down than she cared to admit.

Yeah. That was a problem.

CHAPTER FOURTEEN

Monday evening brought steadily dropping temperatures, and finding a Christmas tree had been a colder event than Olivia had anticipated. Luckily, her sister, Ann Marie, had agreed to tag along, and that made things go quickly. Once they'd dragged it into the house and set it in the tree stand, then argued for ten minutes over whether or not it was straight, Olivia clicked on the gas fireplace to take the chill out of her living room. Now the lights were strung, and they were left with ornaments to hang.

"I can't believe you waited so long to do this," Ann Marie, said as Olivia handed her a Diet Coke. Ann Marie popped it open and took a slug, then pulled a glittering silver ornament from the large storage box of decorations. "You're way late."

Olivia sighed as she looked for just the right spot for the clothespin reindeer she'd made in kindergarten. "I know. Things have been so busy at work, I feel like Christmas snuck up on me. It was just Thanksgiving and suddenly—*bam*—Christmas is next week."

Ann Marie nodded, and they worked silently for a bit, the gentle sounds of instrumental carols coming from the small Bluetooth speaker on Olivia's mantel. Stockings embroidered with her name as well as Walter's dangled from red hooks, and the fireplace's cheerful glow gave the room a soft, lovely ambience. "It's a good tree," she said quietly, as if she thought her voice might disturb the peace.

"It is, right?" Olivia stood back a step. Ann Marie had wanted to go with her to pick one out. They didn't chop their own, as Olivia often did, but rather chose one from the lot at a favorite farm market.

It wasn't terribly tall—maybe five and a half feet—but it was full and lush, and Olivia's living room smelled like the outdoors.

"Mom says Hayley's coming for Christmas?" Ann Marie didn't look at her when she said it. Just kept hanging ornaments and attempting, and failing, to be nonchalant about it.

"How long have you been waiting to bring that up?" Olivia asked, with a shake of her head.

Ann Marie glanced at her nonexistent watch and said, "About an hour."

Olivia laughed.

"Mom's pretty smooth."

"God, right? I didn't even see it coming until it had happened."

Her sister let a beat go by before saying, "I like her."

"Who? Mom? I should hope so."

"Ha ha. No, Hayley. I like her."

"You hardly know her." Olivia wasn't quite sure why this conversation—this subject—made her shift uncomfortably, but it did.

"No, but I know you."

"What does that mean?" Olivia kept hanging ornaments.

"It means that you like her, too."

A scoff escaped Olivia's lips before she could catch it. "Oh, really? You had one dinner with her and me at the same table, and you were on your phone most of the time. Plus, Mom said I was rude. Please tell me how you've come to the conclusion that I like her."

Ann Marie went on as if she hadn't heard, picking an ornament from the box, hanging it on a branch, repeating. "I know what Mom said, but you work in the hospitality industry, and you have since you were a kid. You know how to be smiling and kind even when you can't stand somebody. So, the fact that you were kind of openly rude to Hayley speaks volumes." At Olivia's puzzled expression, Ann Marie rolled her eyes. "Please. If Hayley'd had a ponytail, you'd have been tugging it."

Olivia opened her mouth to defend herself. Closed it. Opened again and took a breath this time. Then closed it. Finally, she said the only thing she could think of that fit. "Shut up."

Ann Marie's laugh burst out of her like gunfire.

Later, after the tree was finished and Ann Marie had gone home next door, Olivia followed her yearly tradition. She turned off all the lights in the house except those on the Christmas tree, poured herself a small amount of warm brandy, and spent the evening with Walter looking at the tree. Christmas music still played and the snow had gone from blowing wildly to gently falling flakes. The way Olivia's tree was framed by the front window of the house, it looked like a beautiful holiday calendar shot.

Walter hopped up on the couch next to her and laid his head in her lap.

"It's a good tree, huh, Walnut?" she asked, remembering Ann Marie's words.

Olivia felt oddly unsettled. She loved Christmastime. She loved everything about it, the buildup, all the traditions, the anticipation. But she hadn't been lying to Ann Marie when she talked about it sneaking up on her this year, and now she felt a little bit like she'd missed much of it. Christmas was Sunday. Less than a week away. And she was not ready.

It wasn't like she didn't have her shopping done. She did. It wasn't that kind of not ready. It was more...an unbalancing. She sipped her brandy. Yeah, that was the right word. She felt unbalanced.

Oh, she could sit there, sip her brandy, and claim to not know why. But that would be a lie. She knew exactly why.

Hayley had unbalanced her somehow, tipped her world on its axis a little bit, and Olivia was having a hard time figuring out how to keep from sliding. She sipped again and sank down farther into the couch cushions as she watched the snow fall and thought about the changes in her life over the past month.

She shouldn't like Hayley at all. She really shouldn't, there was no question. The woman had come out of left field and taken the job that should've been Olivia's, thanks to the bigwigs at Corporate, and Olivia couldn't understand it. Mostly because, while Hayley wasn't completely unfamiliar with the business, it somehow seemed like she had never managed a Motel 6, let alone an upscale resort like the Evergreen, and the fact that Olivia could run circles around her in Hayley's own job was beyond insulting.

The physical attraction was a given. There was no way Olivia could argue. From the moment Hayley had turned to her that morning in the snow, from the very beginning of that one walk in the woods, the attraction was clear and intense. Olivia could deal with that. Being attracted to somebody didn't have to mean anything more than that, and Olivia had been perfectly okay with stuffing that down and doing her best to ignore it.

But Hayley could also be charming. And kind. And sweet. Seeing her helping Maddie Dunne navigate the art museum online had touched Olivia unexpectedly—something she still couldn't quite explain.

"Don't even get me started on the Fairy Trail," she said quietly, causing Walter to lift his head and look quizzically at her. Hayley had been beyond adorable on that trail. Her childlike, wide-eyed excitement had blended with the artistic adult in her, and the mix was something Olivia had had a hard time resisting. No, an impossible time resisting, since she actually hadn't resisted at all.

And then came the part she'd been stuck on. The part that had been playing over and over in her head on a loop for the past three days.

That kiss.

That goddamn, wonderful, ill-advised, amazing, misstep of a kiss that Olivia couldn't get past.

Before she could dwell on it more, her phone pinged with a text from Tessa.

In your driveway. You home?

Instead of typing a response, she got up and opened the front door. Sure enough, Tessa's car was sitting there, and she turned it off and headed in.

"Your lights were off," she said as she stomped the snow off her boots and then toed them off. "I wasn't sure if you were here."

"Me and Sir Walter are just enjoying some brandy and the tree. Care to join us?"

"That sounds amazing." Tessa finished peeling off all her outerwear, then blew out a breath from the effort. "It's a good thing I love winter, because all this extra clothing is a pain in the ass."

A few minutes later, the two were seated on the couch, brandy snifters in hand, Christmas tree lights on, fire casting a warm glow over the room.

Tessa was one of those friends Olivia could sit in silence with. They didn't need to talk. They were never uncomfortable if they were just quiet. It was one of the things that told Olivia how amazingly compatible they were. Silence between them never needed to be filled.

Apparently, Tessa did not feel the same way tonight.

"Talk to me," she said simply. She didn't look at Olivia, just sipped her brandy and waited, obviously sure Olivia would respond. Which she did.

"About what?"

This time, Tessa did look, all arched eyebrow and I-don't-have-time-for-your-bullshit face. When Olivia didn't answer right away, she asked, "What is going on with you?"

Olivia hadn't told Tessa about the kiss on the Fairy Trail, but she needed to. She braced herself because not only was Tessa going to flip out over the kiss itself, but she was going to be angry Olivia had waited so long to tell her.

"Okay, now you're worrying me." Tessa sat up when Olivia had evidently waited too long to answer. "Are you okay?"

Olivia inhaled deeply, held it for a count of five, then let it out before launching into the story of Friday. She told Tessa everything, from Hayley's dejected demeanor in her office, to how happy she was on the trail, how she took a million photos and how she and Olivia had talked openly about so much. Then she told her about the kiss. Every detail. She ended with the invitation from her mother for Hayley to join them for Christmas.

Tessa had stayed quiet throughout the entire telling. The only sign that it affected her in any way was the empty brandy glass in her hand. Olivia looked pointedly at it and raised her eyebrows.

"Hey, you are not allowed to judge me for downing all my alcohol while I'm judging you for not telling me any of this sooner. What the hell?" While Tessa did her best to hide the tint of hurt in her voice, Olivia heard it and felt bad, just as predicted.

"I'm sorry," she said, and meant it. "I just needed some time to sit with it. I hadn't even meant to tell my mother, but"—Olivia rolled her eyes—"you've met her."

Tessa snorted. "That woman could get an FBI agent to spill all the government secrets just by giving him a look." She handed her empty glass to Olivia. "I'm going to need more for this." When Olivia returned with the bottle of brandy and refilled both their glasses, Tessa asked, "So…how do you feel about all of this?"

Olivia gave herself time to honestly contemplate the question, to be completely open with herself. She sat back against the soft cushions of her couch. Walter decided that was an invitation and jumped up to lie down next to her. She dug her fingers into his fur and found peace in his presence, which she always did. "I don't know," she finally said. "So many things."

"Like?"

"God, I don't know. Confusion? Attraction? Potential? Fear? Resistance? Desire?"

"Okay, yeah, that's a lot." Tessa's light chuckle took away any sting. "How do you feel about Christmas?"

Olivia shrugged. "I agree with my mom. Nobody should be alone on Christmas. And I feel terrible that Hayley's family doesn't do the holiday together."

"Some families just don't. My college roommate takes a cruise every Christmas. Alone."

"That makes me sad."

"No reason to be. She's not. Maybe Hayley isn't either. Maybe she's used to this."

Olivia had to concede. "Could be."

"But she's coming, yes?"

"She said yes to my mom, so…"

"Yeah, you don't back out on Angela Santini. It's just mean." Their light laughter died down, and again, they sat quietly for a moment. When Tessa spoke again, her voice matched the relaxed atmosphere. "You okay?"

"You know what it is?" The reality didn't hit Olivia then. Rather, it seemed to float up and settle gently on her shoulders. "I don't know what to do." A lump unexpectedly lodged in her throat and she did her best to swallow it back down.

Tessa nodded, her expression knowing, as if she'd just been waiting for her friend to give the correct answer. "You hate that. It's very unlike you."

"Exactly." More silence. Then, "What do I do, Tess?"

"Well." Tessa wiggled her butt a little, snuggled more deeply into the couch, and put her feet up on the coffee table. She crossed them at the ankle, sipped her brandy, and finally looked at Olivia. "You ready for this? 'Cuz I'm about to hit you with some Granny Wanda wisdom."

"Oh, good." Olivia nodded and grinned, recalling several stories Tessa had shared about her maternal grandmother over the years. The woman had an answer for everything, and more often than not, her advice was spot-on.

"If there's one thing Granny Wanda taught me, it's the simple act of standing still."

Olivia furrowed her brow. "Explain."

"When I was about twelve or thirteen, Granny Wanda told me that in her experience, when you don't know what to do, the best course of action is to do nothing. Stand still until your answer becomes clear. And sometimes that's really, really hard to do, but every time I have, it's been the right move."

"So, you're saying I do nothing?"

Tessa tipped her head one way, then the other. "Pretty much, yeah. Have you talked to Hayley about any of it?"

Olivia flashed back to the conversation outside the fitness center, then made a sound that was half snort, half laugh. "We tried."

"What does that mean?"

"It means she brought it up and we both admitted that we like each other. We didn't get much further than that. It was kind of ridiculous, two grown women who can't manage to discuss the fact that they made out in the woods and feel strange about it."

"So, you like her." It was a statement, not a question.

Olivia nodded. Somewhat reluctantly, but nonetheless... "I don't want to."

"I get that. It could get messy."

"It's already messy."

"God, you worry too much." Tessa sat up, spread her arms out in joy. "You need to lighten up. Loosen up. Have some fun. Stop worrying about rules and appearances and just...enjoy yourself!" They looked at each other for a brief moment before Tessa brought her arms down. "Okay, some of that might have been the brandy."

Olivia laughed. She couldn't help it. "You think?"

Dialing down a notch or twelve, Tessa sighed. "Seriously, though. Just breathe. Okay? This might be awesome. It might be nothing. But there's no reason to drive yourself crazy. Just breathe."

"I'll try."

Tessa studied her face in the colored lighting for several seconds before she closed a hand over Olivia's and said, "You can just *be*, Liv. You know that, right? You don't have to *do* anything. You don't have to get all worked up. You can just *be*. That's allowed."

Those words would stay with Olivia for the rest of the night and, like the reality of the situation earlier, sit on her shoulders with considerable weight. Which was silly, because if she was supposed to lighten up and just be, what was the point of having more weight set on her?

You don't have to do anything...stand still until your answer becomes clear.

The advice made sense, but it went against everything Olivia believed in. It went against the very nature of the kind of person she was. She didn't stand still. She never had. She made decisions. She led. That's who she was. This waiting, this...indecisiveness was driving her a little crazy, and maybe Tessa was right. Maybe the indecisiveness would go away if she simply stopped trying to make a decision. She didn't have to. There was nobody waiting on one. Nothing depended on what she decided.

So she and Hayley had made out.

So they liked each other.

Nobody was holding a gun to her head and screaming at her to make a choice.

Just breathe.

❖

Renting an SUV instead of driving her cute little sporty two-door probably would've been the smarter thing to do when Hayley came to Evergreen Hills. That was the thought in her mind as she slid along the roads into town. She'd gotten her driver's license at sixteen, just like every other kid in her school, but living in Manhattan meant you didn't really need a car. She had her Beemer, of course, but she didn't use it all that often. She walked, took the subway, or used the family's car service to get where she needed to go. Driving her own car to Evergreen Hills had seemed like the independent thing to do, but now as she fishtailed around a corner, she was rethinking that choice.

Luck was with her, both on the ride and once in town, because she nabbed a parking spot only a few yards away from the front entrance to Brushstrokes.

"There she is," Ross Edwards said in happy greeting when she entered his shop. "You made it."

"I did. Barely." Hayley blew out a breath of relief as she set down her supplies and held out a hand to shake his.

"Yeah, you need four-wheel drive around here in the winter." He let go of her hand and came around the counter to help her with her stuff. "I was glad to hear from you."

She'd been painting like crazy over the past few days, but painting in her hotel suite didn't feel right somehow. Hayley couldn't put her finger on exactly why. Was it the lighting? The ambience? The mess? She wasn't tidy—she could admit that—and she felt bad for housekeeping. They'd been good about hiding their disdain at the state of her suite, but she'd caught a look or two.

The reason she'd been painting like crazy for the past few days was that she didn't know how else to channel her energy. She felt like she was all over the place, thanks to the mess her thoughts were, like a bowl of spaghetti, all tangled and twisted up with each other, and they all came back to one thing: Olivia Santini.

Ross Edwards interrupted her thoughts, thank God. "Follow me." He led her back behind the counter, through a doorway closed off with a burgundy curtain, and into a shockingly wide-open space that she hadn't expected, even though she'd known it was there. She stopped in her tracks and just took it in. Sort of a warehouse/industrial type area with a solid concrete floor and gray walls. Skylights in the ceiling told Hayley that there was likely some terrific natural light in the daytime, and she made a mental note to come here on her day off rather than in the evening after her shift, like tonight. Four people sat at easels, brushes in their hands. Workstations for six more were set up in different places along the walls.

"Wow," she said quietly. "This is amazing."

Ross stood a little taller, his pride obvious. "Right?" He carried her things to a space to the right. There was an empty easel, a small table, a few rags, a stool. "How's this?"

"It's perfect." Hayley set down the bundle of three canvases she'd been carrying and leaned them against the easel stand as Ross set her tote bag of supplies on the floor next to the stool.

"This space is yours for as long as you want it." Ross kept his voice down, seemingly to not disturb the other artists. "All I ask is that you buy your supplies here and you show up to work at least once a week."

"Seriously?" Hayley asked, completely surprised. "Can't I pay you rent or something?"

He smiled as he shook his head and waved her off with a hand. "Nope. Not how I do things here. I just want people to have a space to feel creative and do what they love to do most. It's always been a dream of mine to have a gathering place for artists like myself." He gestured to the workstation directly across from hers, which looked very lived-in with all the opened tubes of paint, palette knives, and various canvases spread around. "I'm over there. Once I close the shop at nine, that's where I'll be."

"This is amazing, Ross. I don't know how to thank you."

"Harness your creativity. That's all the thanks I need." With a nod, he left her to her art and headed back through the curtain and into the shop.

Hayley took a deep breath and inhaled the various scents of the space: paint, clay, paper, dust. She loved it instantly; it made her feel whole, like she belonged. It was the same feeling she'd had in that very first art class she'd ever taken. Junior year in high school. She'd walked into Mrs. Burton's art room and felt immediately like she was right where she was supposed to be.

She'd been chasing that feeling ever since.

The other artists in the studio glanced at her, sent smiles her way, but mainly kept to themselves. Two were painting in watercolors. One was sketching with a charcoal pencil. The fourth was sitting at a table and shaping clay with her fingers and various tools of her trade.

My people.

It took Hayley a few minutes to unpack her things and lay them out the way she wanted to. She laid out her tubes of paint, making a mental note of what colors she didn't have. She'd left a lot of her stuff back at her apartment in New York, knowing she had no plans to stay here forever, but now she was acutely aware of the things she'd left behind. She had one pallet knife with her, but not her favorite. She had a freestanding easel back in New York and loved it. When packing to come to Evergreen Hills, she'd brought a tabletop version and had been struggling a bit with it, so having a standing easel here was much better. She liked having her work up and facing her, as she preferred to paint while standing.

The one thing she needed when she was in the mood to paint, the tool she couldn't paint without, was an oversized denim shirt. It had belonged to her mother and it went everywhere with Hayley. She knew it was impossible for it to still have some of her mother's scent clinging to it, but there were days when she swore it was true, and she'd bunch up the fabric, hold it to her nose, inhale deeply, and miss her mother so badly it made her chest ache. Now she slipped her arms in and buttoned it up. The shirt was like the combined history of her and her mother's art, stained with more colors than she could count, the elbows worn thin, two buttons missing and long lost.

Her art helped her think. Hayley wasn't quite sure how that managed to work, but it did. Automatically, her focus would split evenly between whatever piece she was working on and whatever was on her mind at the time, and somehow, she'd be able to see and think clearly. More clearly than at any other time. That was the case now as she mixed three different paints with her pallet knife to get the exact shade of green she wanted for the canvas she'd been working on for two weeks now.

Sunday was Christmas, which meant Saturday night was Christmas Eve. The night she'd be having dinner with Olivia and her family. To say Hayley was nervous was an understatement. To say she was nervously *excited* was an even bigger one. Bowing out had never even been an option, and that was something Hayley found interesting. Couldn't explain it, other than to say more time around Olivia was a good thing—wasn't it? Getting to know more about her sounded perfect—should it? Spending the holiday with a family, even if it wasn't her own, sounded so much better than pretending she was fine being alone.

And how had that happened? How had Hayley been instantly, magically, totally okay accepting such an offer? It wasn't like her at all, especially given that Olivia hadn't been thrilled by the invitation. That had been so obvious to Hayley that she'd almost laughed out loud at the expression of horror that zipped across Olivia's face when her mom brought it up. But she'd covered it quickly and played the good daughter, something Hayley suspected Olivia did on a regular basis. Probably had all her life.

The complete opposite of Hayley.

The thought made her chuckle internally, even if it was a little bit sad.

Really, though, this was good. Going to the Santinis' for Christmas was good, because if Hayley wasn't alone, she'd be less likely to fall into an emotional tailspin of missing her mom like she had last year.

As she stroked her brush along the canvas, blending the green into some of the brown she'd added last week, thoughts of Olivia crowded into her mind. Because of course they did…she'd thought of little else since their make-out session in the woods last week, and—oh, my God—don't get her started on how mind-blowing that had been. What exactly was the deal with the two of them? She couldn't figure it out. Even when they'd talked about it, Hayley had left slightly confused.

There was attraction. Obviously. First and foremost. The moment Hayley had laid eyes on Olivia in the woods that very first day, she'd been taken with her beauty, with those big brown eyes and all that was held within them, with the sultry shape of her body even in the bulky winter outerwear, with the olive tone of her skin and the mystery behind her smile. It had been instant and tangible for Hayley, like never before.

She didn't really know Olivia very well. Yet. She wanted to, though. What she'd seen so far—Olivia's intelligence and wit, her kindness to others, like the woman in the fitness center, her passion for her job—she'd liked very much, and she wanted to learn more. Problem was, she wasn't sure Olivia felt the same way about her.

Hayley had the job Olivia should've gotten. That would've been obvious to her even if Olivia hadn't practically pointed it out. And while it wasn't Hayley's fault, she still felt bad, and she knew Olivia probably felt betrayed by the company she'd been loyal to for years. Hayley couldn't blame her, and she wondered if she could ever come back from that, get out from under the shadow of something Olivia most likely saw as an injustice. Hayley also had her own issues to deal with regarding Corporate—aka Dad, who she owed a phone call but was avoiding like the plague—and that was another thing that stuck with her: Olivia didn't know the truth of who she was.

"That looks great." Hayley hadn't heard Ross come up behind her, and she flinched slightly at the sound of his voice, which made him put an apologetic hand on her shoulder. "Sorry. Didn't mean to startle you."

"You'd better get used to that," the woman working with the clay said, a good-natured tone in her voice. "The guy moves like a ninja. You'll be lost in your work and then *bam*! You have a mild heart attack, because he's suddenly standing next to you."

Chuckles and nods came from the other artists.

Ross shook his head with a smile as he turned back to Hayley's canvas. "Your use of shadow among the evergreens is fantastic." His eyes moved from the photograph she'd clipped to the easel to the painting itself and back again. "Really, really nice work."

Just like that, Hayley was back in college, in the first real painting class she'd ever taken, and even though Ross was not her teacher, the approval made her stand up a little taller, assess her own work with new, more confident eyes. "Thanks," she said, feeling the blush in her cheeks. "They're much harder to capture than I was expecting."

"Nature almost always is," Ross said. "A still life is one thing. By definition, it doesn't move. But nature herself? Trees and grass and leaves and things that are almost constantly in motion? A whole different story." With that, he walked away and left her to her work.

Hayley glanced toward the sculptor, who was looking back at her with a smile and a fun glint in her eyes. With a shrug, she said, "Yeah, he does that, too. Drops little nuggets of wisdom and then walks away. He should carry around a little microphone to drop each time."

Hayley laughed, as did the others in the room, and she turned back to her piece, tilting her head to the side, narrowing her eyes, concentrating on the color, the light, the shadow, and felt utterly at peace. Which surprised her. She hadn't felt so comfortable among like-minded people since she'd entered her first ever gay bar when she was nineteen.

Yeah. She liked it here.

CHAPTER FIFTEEN

A s you well know, I've had this very same issue in the past." Mrs. Haverton was a semiregular guest at the Evergreen. Olivia was very familiar with her and also with her particular disdain for scratchy sheets.

"You're absolutely right, Mrs. Haverton. I'm very sorry about this. Why don't you head over to Split Rail and have one of those Manhattans you love so much. Tell Mike it's on the house. I'll make sure your sheets get replaced. Okay?"

There was nothing Olivia loved more about the hospitality business than taking the wind right out of somebody's sails, making it impossible for them to argue further. She smiled pleasantly at Mrs. Haverton, a seventysomething widow with more money than she knew what to do with, and waited her out. Stephanie stood next to her, also smiling.

"Fine." Mrs. Haverton looked from one of them to the other and back. Then she took her little clutch purse off the counter and clicked along the tile toward the restaurant. They watched her go.

"Who was that?" Hayley was suddenly next to her, and Olivia's entire body tingled without her permission at the proximity.

"That was Mrs. Haverton. She's a K-hack," Stephanie said, then turned to grab the phone and give housekeeping the instructions to change out the woman's sheets.

"A what?"

Olivia turned to meet Hayley's gorgeous eyes, which was ill-advised as the tingling intensified. "She's a guest we want to 'keep happy at all cost.'" Olivia kept her voice low as she made air quotes with her fingers. "K-H-A-A-C. Or K-hack."

Hayley grinned. "Ah, I get it. She's rich."

"Whatever the word is that means more money than God, that's her."

"And we want her satisfied so she'll not only keep coming here but tell all her rich friends about us."

Olivia tapped her nose. "Exactly."

There was a beat of quiet then. A moment of nothing but eye contact and closeness and Olivia felt a flutter in her stomach as her eyes dropped to Hayley's mouth, again without her permission. Her body was a damn traitor. They hadn't had any time to really talk again since that laughable conversation outside the fitness center on Monday. The week before Christmas was always a jumble of planning and preparing, and it had kept them both super busy. Olivia had fallen dead asleep the second her head had hit her pillow all week long.

"Hayley, you're here," Maddie Dunne interrupted—which was a good thing as far as Olivia was concerned—and they both turned and smiled at her, Olivia relieved to focus her gaze on something other than Hayley's full bottom lip. Stephanie moved the handset of the phone to her other ear and Maddie kissed her on the cheek, whispering, "Hi, Mom." She turned back to Hayley and held up her laptop. "I found this amazing new artist the other day."

"Yeah? Awesome. Show me." Hayley winked at Olivia, then led Maddie back into the offices. Olivia watched them go, her own smile still prominent on her face. There was something different about Hayley these past few days. Olivia couldn't put a finger on it, and maybe she didn't need to. All she knew was that Hayley had become more cheerful, a lot of fun to be around. Not that she hadn't been those things already, but they'd definitely been at a lower level. Now she just seemed...happy.

Olivia liked it. A lot.

She went back into her own office and took a seat at her desk. She could hear Hayley and Maddie talking and laughing, and something about it brought her a weird, inexplicable sense of comfort.

What the hell was happening to her?

With a literal shake of her head, she punched some keys on her computer and forced herself to focus on work. The Evergreen wasn't nearly as busy as she'd like it to be at this time of year, and while it wasn't awful, it wasn't great. They were about sixty-five percent full. Compared to eighty percent last year, it wasn't terrific news. There were so many ways they could improve the Evergreen, draw in more guests, but part of her was worried that Markham Resorts had already given up on them. The Evergreen was fairly small compared to other resorts in the area and it was out of date, as she and Hayley had discussed. And as Hayley and Alec from Marquez had discussed. But there were definitely ways to fix it, to bring the Evergreen back to the amazing jewel of the Adirondacks it had once been. It would take effort. It would take money. But it could be done. Olivia called up the new business improvement plan she'd been working on for the past couple of weeks and scrolled through it. It gave insights—in great detail—into how Markham Resorts could not only save the Evergreen but make her the most successful resort in the area. Because if Markham Resorts corporate headquarters should listen to anybody, it should be a person who knew the area, the tourist industry here, what was successful and what wasn't. It should also be a person who was passionate about this resort. A person who loved it.

That person was Olivia Santini, and she knew it.

With a nod, she hunkered down and worked some more on the proposal.

❖

It was the Friday before Christmas, and Benton Markham couldn't wait to get the hell out of Dodge. It was really the only time of year that he took a "vacation." That was how he thought of it. A "vacation," complete with air quotes. Because he'd work. He wasn't fooling anybody. He'd take his laptop and his phone and whatever else he needed to keep abreast of things, bring them onto whatever plane or cruise ship he'd be on. As long as he could get away from the city that Kerry had loved so much, especially at this time of year.

He smiled now as he sat at his enormous desk in his exorbitant office and gazed out the window at the gently falling snow. Sometimes, New York would have very little snow for Christmas, and that would bum his wife right out. She would take it as a personal affront, like

Mother Nature herself was trying to ruin the very atmosphere of Kerry's Christmas. Mostly, though, she simply loved the holiday and loved the holiday in Manhattan even more. She would drag Benton out of work and make him go with her to touristy things like Rockefeller Center or Fifth Avenue to see the decorations. She wasn't from New York, she was from Kansas, so it was like being married to a constant tourist, one who never got past the amazement of the Big Apple, eyes wide, smile radiantly permanent.

God, he missed her.

Benton swallowed hard as that familiar lump formed in his throat. Jesus Christ, was this ever going to ease up? Would he ever be able to miss his wife without wanting to throw things across the room or jump out a window? How in the world would he ever get through this? It had been almost two years. *Two years!* Yet he felt like he'd lost Kerry last week.

As almost always happened, his sorrow morphed into anger. He preferred that, if he was honest. He'd much rather be angry than a blubbering mess of emotion. Benton Markham was not an emotional guy, and he hated when he felt like one. He pressed his lips together in a thin line, flared his nostrils as he inhaled, did his best to harness that anger, to shove the sorrow aside and back into its box where he was able to keep it most of the time.

He checked his itinerary. His flight left tonight. Yes, tomorrow, on Christmas Eve, his sorry ass would be on a cruise ship, floating around the Caribbean. He'd be sipping mai-tais and getting a tan and not thinking about his dead wife or the holiday she loved so much.

Yes. This would be good.

In the meantime, he needed to give somebody a kick in the pants. Somebody who had been avoiding him for the past week. He did *not* enjoy being ignored. He picked up his cell phone and hit the right numbers. Just when he was preparing to leave a pissed-off voice mail, the call was answered.

"Hi, Dad."

"Hayley," he said, extra gruffly in order to keep the surprise out of his voice.

"How are things?"

"Things are fine. How are things there?"

"I found this very cool art studio behind that art supply store I told you about. The owner is super nice and lets me have a space there to work. And really, it's so much better than trying to paint in my suite. I can be messy and not worry about it. The lighting—"

"I meant…how are things at the Evergreen?" He'd cut her off midsentence, which was rude, he knew, but listening to her talk about her art was like listening to Kerry. Their voices were identical and Kerry had said many of the same things. The space, the light, and… he just couldn't. So he did what he did best: yanked things back into business mode.

There was a beat before Hayley answered, and he imagined she'd had to regroup slightly from his abrupt shift in subject, because why wouldn't she? There was a quiet sigh, one he almost didn't hear, and then she spoke. "It's fine. We're not as full as we were last year, Olivia says, but we're okay."

"And why isn't it as full?"

Now she was nervous. He could tell by the slight tremor in her voice. "Um. Well, there are some outdated things. Stuff that might benefit from replacement equipment. Old items and things…stuff like that."

Benton closed his eyes and rubbed his forehead with his fingertips. "You're making very little sense, you realize that, right?" Hayley started to speak and he cut her off again. "Look. Write up a report for me. A proposal of some kind telling me what needs to be fixed and why. Include cost analysis in it."

"But, Dad, I don't—"

"I'm tired, Hayley. I'm tired of having to draw you a map every time I need you to do something…"

"Dad…"

"You're on thin ice already, young lady." His voice was sharper than he'd meant it to be, but he'd had a day.

"Oh, I'm aware. Believe me. And just so we're clear, you've *never* drawn me any maps." Her anger was very slight, an edge, like she was trying to hold it back. She'd done the same thing as a kid. "By the way, Merry Christmas."

Benton opened his mouth to reply, but the line was dead. She'd already hung up on him. And he deserved it, he had to admit. He exhaled slowly as he set the phone down.

"Why are you so hard on her?" Susan's voice was gentle, not at all accusatory, but firm. Apparently, she'd been standing in his doorway long enough to hear the conversation. Pretty much the whole company had gone home for the holiday with the exception of a few stragglers. Susan was one of them. She was always one of them. His secretary—were they called that anymore?—had been with him for more than twenty years and was unfailingly loyal. If he was in the office, she was as well.

"Why are you still here?" Benton consciously softened his demeanor and smiled at Susan.

"I asked you a question first." She stepped into the office, handed him a small stack of papers, and took a seat in the burgundy upholstered chair across from him. Then she crossed her legs, folded her hands on her lap, and waited him out.

Susan Travers knew him well. Probably better than anybody. Of all the people in his life, he spent the most time with her. Sometimes, he loved how well she knew him. Others? He hated it. He sighed before answering her question with a total cop-out. "I don't know."

"Yes, you do."

With a shake of his head, Benton turned to look out the window.

"All right. Let me help." When he looked back at Susan, she was sitting forward, her folded hands on the front of his desk now. "You miss Kerry, especially at Christmas. Hayley reminds you too much of her, and you're angry about that."

He gave her a look, knowing she was exactly right.

"Honestly, I don't understand why the two of you can't just talk to each other about it." Her voice had grown in intensity, and now she seemed to consciously lower it a bit—but not a lot, because her next words held an edge. "Don't you think she misses her mother, Ben? Do you really think it's just you?"

"Of course I don't think it's just me." He said it like that was a ridiculous notion, but he also knew there was an element of truth to Susan's words. "We've just never been the kind of father and daughter who talk about…emotional things." He waved a dismissive hand. "Kerry always took care of that stuff."

"Well, Kerry's not here, and you're all that girl has left." Benton's eyes went a bit wider at the words, but Susan pressed on. "And I know you think she's all her mother, but there's a lot of you in her." She punctuated her words by pointing a red-lacquered finger at him. "She's just as stubborn as you are, you know. And she's smart, but you don't give her a chance. You put her in impossible situations and then you're mad when she doesn't come through."

Benton opened his mouth and closed it again. Held up a finger indicating he had a point to make, then lowered it again.

"You're aware that the only experience that girl has running a resort is whatever she's garnered from growing up as your daughter. Yes?"

"Yes." He said it grudgingly. There was no other way he could have. Susan was right. He knew it. She knew it, though to her credit, she didn't look at all smug about it. Rather, she looked sympathetic, and she reached across the desk to close her hand over his.

"I know you miss Kerry. I *know* it. And so does Hayley. You have to talk to her. Okay?"

He nodded, felt that hateful lump settle itself in the middle of his throat. "I can't—" he began, then did his best to clear the lump away. "I will. I just…I need a little time. To get away. This is a really rough time of year—" His voice cracked and he looked away, embarrassed.

"I know," Susan said softly. Any other employee of Markham Resorts would be horrified to see Benton Markham choking up like a child. They'd be looking for the nearest exit. But not Susan. She simply tightened her hold on his hand and waited for him to collect himself.

There was very little activity to be heard. It was two days before Christmas, the building eerily quiet as the snow fell softly outside the window, and Benton—God help him—was thankful for Susan's presence.

They sat quietly for what felt like a long while just…being. Benton tried to occupy his mind by thinking about the deal he was working on to build a resort in Sedona, the forty-five-year-old Scotch he had waiting for him at home, the cruise he'd be taking tomorrow. He did his best to focus on those things, but he wasn't completely successful because somehow, some way, his brain always shifted to Hayley.

He wondered how his daughter was spending Christmas this year.

CHAPTER SIXTEEN

O livia was nervous.

She could admit that. It wasn't easy, but she could.

It was 5:00 on Saturday. Christmas Eve. Hayley had dismissed her, promising that she had everything under control.

"Please. Everybody's checked in. Nobody's checking out until Monday. Split Rail is all set with dinner. The front desk will be manned at all times. I got this. Go." She'd seemed a little…off today, Olivia had noticed, but she'd kept things light as she made shooing motions with her hands like she was trying to wave a fly out the door. "Go. I'll see you at six thirty."

There was a big storm headed their way and it had already begun, the edges of it drifting over Evergreen Hills, dropping big, fat snowflakes that were only going to increase in volume as the night went on. But Lenny and his guys were ready to handle snow removal. He was a good guy who never minded overtime, even on a holiday, and Olivia trusted him implicitly to take care of the driveway, parking lot, and sidewalks.

She had nothing to worry about for now. Living next door to her mother had its advantages—and was such an Italian thing to do, according to Tessa. But she didn't have to drive anywhere, she could stay as long as she wanted and wouldn't worry about the snow because she and Walter would just trudge through it to their house. Ann Marie still lived with their mother while she tried to save money and pay off the loans she'd taken out for cosmetology school. Tony had his own apartment downtown, but he and Priya would probably sleep at their mom's tonight.

And then there was Hayley.

Hayley would be spending Christmas Eve with her and her family tonight. And she was invited to join them tomorrow as well, that was a given. Olivia had such mixed emotions around the whole thing that she wasn't sure what to do with herself. On the one hand, she bristled at the idea of Hayley being in her safe space, around her family, taking part in their traditions. On the other, the thought of Hayley spending Christmas alone was more heartbreaking than Olivia cared to admit. She might have balked, but the truth was, she was glad her mother had invited Hayley. Maybe she could get more out of her than Olivia had been able to in the past month and a half.

Doing her best to push all of that aside for now, Olivia got dressed. While she knew Ann Marie would most likely be the picture of comfort in leggings and an oversized sweatshirt, Olivia tended to dress up a bit for holidays. It felt like she should. It felt...respectful somehow, both to her mother and to the holiday itself. While she hadn't been to church in a very long time, she often felt a pull to go on Christmas.

Her sweater dress was black, long-sleeved with a mock turtleneck. It was warm but elegant, and she added some silver bracelets and big hoop earrings. Her mother had had the day off and had been to the house already, gathering the extra things she'd stored in Olivia's refrigerator. Olivia had taken the gifts she was giving over to her mother's earlier in the week and Walter was already there as well, probably being spoiled rotten with bits of meatballs and bites of pasta. She only had to grab one gift, then she donned her boots, coat, hat, and gloves and trudged along the path Tony had snow-blown between the houses. The wind was kicking up a bit and the path had slight drifts in it here and there.

Walking into her mother's house always enveloped her in warmth and comfort, but on Christmas? That feeling was multiplied a hundredfold. The tree was big and lush where it stood in the front window, multicolored lights twinkling happily, lighting up the dozens of homemade ornaments Olivia and her siblings had created as children. The fireplace glowed with warmth and the smells coming from the kitchen—a little savory from the meatballs, the sauce, a little sweet from the cookies and pies. There was no place in the world she'd rather be in that moment, and she felt any and all tension in her body just seep out of her and onto the floor.

"Hey, there she is." Tony greeted her from the living room couch where he sat with a beer in one hand, his arm around Priya. He got up and crossed the room to greet his sister with a hug and kiss on the cheek. Priya followed.

"I *love* this dress," she commented, rubbing the sleeve in her fingers. "It's simple but gorgeous. You look amazing."

Olivia felt herself blush and she thanked Priya, then hung up her coat and took off her boots.

"Mama?" she called as she headed toward the kitchen and the delicious smells. When she entered the room, the sight made her snort-laugh. Her mother stood near the counter where at least fifteen meatballs were sizzling in her electric frying pan. She wore an apron that had belonged to Olivia's great-grandmother and held a pair of tongs. At her feet sat Walter, looking up at her with such hope and adoration that Olivia simply shook her head and grinned. "I see now why you couldn't be bothered to come see who was at the door," she said to her dog, squatting down to pet and kiss him. He gave her a quick lick, but then moved his head any time Olivia blocked his view of the *meatballs*. "Traitor," she muttered with affection, and kissed his head before standing back up. She kissed her mom on the cheek and asked, "Need help?"

"Yes, you can open the wine. I was waiting for you before I started."

"I can do that." Olivia snagged one of the finished meatballs off the pile on a nearby plate.

"I smacked your brother for that. I'll smack you, too."

"No, you won't. I'm your favorite."

"I heard that!" Tony's voice cane from the living room.

"Not news, little brother." Olivia laughed as she pulled the cork from a bottle of Merlot and poured two glasses. "Priya? Wine?"

"Yes, please," was the response.

Tony entered the kitchen to drop off his empty beer bottle and pick up his girlfriend's wine. He wandered toward the plate of meatballs when his mother's voice stopped him in his tracks.

"I swear to God, Anthony Michael, you will lose a hand."

His eyes went wide as he met Olivia's gaze, and just like that, despite their stifled grins, they were twelve and six again.

"I'm just kidding, sweetie," their mother said, a gleam in her eye. "Why am I making them if I'm not going to let you eat them?"

"That was my question, but you Mom Voiced me, so I wasn't about to ask."

It was something Olivia loved about her family. It might seem old-fashioned to some, but there was a level of respect between the children and their mother. They never mouthed off. They always listened to her, even if they didn't agree with her advice. Angela Santini had worked hard, sacrificed so much, to raise her kids on her own, and they knew it.

"What time did you tell Hayley?" Angela asked.

Tony stopped in his tracks on his way out of the kitchen, meatball halfway to his mouth. "Hayley's coming?"

"She was going to be alone for the holiday," Angela said by way of explanation.

"Oh. Well. Can't have that." He said it seriously and gave a shrug, but waggled his thick eyebrows at Olivia before exiting the kitchen. Olivia shook her head at him before turning back to her mom.

"Any time now. I told her six thirty."

"Perfect. Oh, damn it." Her mother used the tongs to take a meatball that had split into two pieces out of the pan and placed it on a paper towel with other pieces to cool off.

"Is that the Walter pile?"

"Sure is." Angela looked down at the dog, who hadn't moved an inch since Olivia arrived. "Right, my sweet boy?"

Walter's tail wagged and he looked at Olivia's mom with such love, she couldn't hold in her laughter. "Grandma spoils you."

"That's what grandmas do," Angela said, breaking off a piece of meatball and blowing on it until it was no longer hot. She held it out to Walter, who very gently took it from her.

"So spoiled." Olivia shook her head, but with affection, and held up her wineglass. "Cheer me."

Angela picked hers up from the counter and touched it to Olivia's.

"Merry Christmas, Mama."

They each sipped, tandem Mmms emanating from their throats as they savored the smooth red.

The doorbell rang, interrupting their wine tasting and causing Walter to tremble in his spot, obviously torn between running to the door and the possibility of more meatballs. Olivia met her mother's gaze and there was something there, something in that one moment, that told Olivia her mother understood every single conflicting emotion she was having over Hayley. That her mother *got it*, and a weird sense of what could only be described as relief settled over her.

Olivia swallowed hard.

Her mother gave her a very slight nod.

She went to get the door.

❖

Were her knees knocking together?

Hayley was pretty sure they were, like a nervous teenage boy picking up his first date. At least she wasn't sweating—the drop in temperature had taken care of that.

She stood on the front stoop of Angela Santini's adorable little house, wine and gifts in hand, and—despite being a little jittery—felt oddly like she was exactly where she was supposed to be in that moment. Which was a nice feeling, because her world had felt slightly off-kilter ever since talking with her father yesterday. He had always been able to have that effect and he usually used it to his advantage. This time felt different, though.

Before she could dwell on it more—please, it was all she'd done for the past thirty six hours—the door was pulled open and Tony Santini stood there with a big smile on his handsome face.

"Hayley. Good to see you again. Merry Christmas." He pulled her into a hug before she even realized he was about to, and she gave an awkward chuckle. "Come in," he said, once he'd let her go.

She stepped through the front door and caught her breath. She'd walked into exactly what a perfect Christmas should look like.

The first thing she noticed was the warmth, both literal and figurative. It was literally warm because a fire burned in the fireplace, but it was also figuratively warm; all the dark wood and Christmas decorations joined with the delicious smell of food to create an atmosphere that Hayley hadn't felt since her mother died. Not at Christmas. Not at any time during the year. It wrapped around her like a soft blanket, made her feel welcome.

"Here, let me take those." Tony's girlfriend—Priya?—took the wine and the gifts from Hayley's hands while Tony helped her out of her coat.

"Thank you," she said to both of them, then followed Tony when he gestured for her to come on into the house. Just when she felt like she'd found her footing and the nerves had stopped vibrating in her spine, her entire world screeched to a halt.

Olivia stood in the doorway.

For the first time in her life, Hayley totally understood the phrase "time stood still," because that's exactly what happened. Time stopped, and the rest of the room and the people in it faded out of existence. There was only her and the gorgeous woman standing before her. She wore a black dress made of lightweight sweater material, and it clung to every single curve Olivia had like it was showing them off. Like the dress was talking to Hayley, saying things like, "See these hips? How they're rounded in exactly the right way? And what about these breasts? Aren't they the most perfect breasts you've ever seen?" Hayley would've liked the dress to shut up because she was staring and she knew she was staring and she couldn't seem to stop staring.

Thank God for Walter, who came skidding in happily from behind Olivia and immediately put his front paws up on Hayley in greeting. That snapped her out of the trance she'd been stuck in, and she looked down at his furry face, his happy expression, and dug her fingers into his fur. "Hi, buddy," she said softly. "Thanks for that."

"Hey," Olivia said, and when Hayley looked up, she was grinning tenderly at her.

"Merry Christmas," Hayley said, and they stood there for a moment before Angela came into the room, walked straight across to Hayley, and wrapped her in a huge hug. Over her shoulder, Hayley looked at Olivia. "Your family are huggers."

Olivia's smiled widened. "Oh, yes."

"I'm sorry, sweetie." Angela pulled away to look Hayley in the face. "I never think. I just hug."

Hayley instantly wanted to reassure her. "No, no. Please. It's wonderful. Just not something I'm used to."

"Your dad isn't a hugger, huh?"

Hayley snorted. "God, no."

"Was your mom?" Angela's dark eyes—so much like Olivia's—held her gaze. How did she do that? How did she get information out of people so easily? Because Hayley was absolutely going to answer.

"She was. She was very affectionate."

Angela hooked her arm around Hayley's and led her all the way into the living room to an overstuffed chair. "Well, we are so glad you're here. Have a seat and make yourself at home. Wine?" Priya handed her the bottle Hayley had brought. "We have a Merlot opened or I can open this one…"

"The open one is fine." Hayley cleared her throat. "Thank you so much for having me. This is great already."

Olivia appeared with a glass of wine she handed to Hayley.

"Wow. Fast service."

"I aim to please." Was that a mischievous twinkle in Olivia's eye? They touched their glasses together and sipped.

The front door blew open, startling everybody in the room.

"I'm home! Christmas can start now!" Ann Marie kicked the door shut behind her. She wore a thick winter coat and a gray knit hat, and was covered with snow that she shook off. "And just in time. It's getting nasty out there." She dropped a pile of bags on the foyer floor and, as Olivia took a step in her direction, held up a halting hand. "Nope. Nope. Stay over there. I don't want you seeing what I bought."

"Were you Christmas shopping?" Hayley asked, amused.

"I was."

"On Christmas Eve?"

"Best time to shop." Ann Marie shucked her coat and tossed her gloves and hat into the coat closet Hayley hadn't even seen when she'd arrived. "I found that out by accident." At Hayley's furrowed brow, she went on. "I was coming home from school. It was a weird year date-wise, and I ended up coming home for Christmas much later than usual. I'd been so busy that I hadn't done any shopping and my only option was to go on Christmas Eve." She snorted a laugh. "It was me and a bunch of men in the mall that evening. But they had the best deals! Like Black Friday without the insanity of the crowds."

"So, she decided to shop on Christmas Eve every year." Angela shook her head, but her expression was soft as she sipped her wine. She gestured to the bags with her chin. "If you're going to wrap those, go do it. We're going to eat soon."

Ann Marie swooped up all her bags and disappeared up the stairs.

"She's going to wrap all of those now?" Priya asked from her seat on the couch next to Tony.

"Yup," he said. "And then she'll bring them down and we'll unwrap them."

"Seems like a waste of paper." Priya shrugged, seemingly resigned to not understanding at all and being totally okay with it.

Hayley watched the whole exchange with a grin on her face and warmth in her heart. She'd had wonderful Christmases before her mother had passed, but not like this. Her brothers were quite a bit older, so they didn't have the same kind of relationship that Olivia had with her siblings.

As if reading her mind, Olivia sat on the arm of the chair, so close Hayley could feel her body heat, smell her perfume, and asked, "You have brothers, right?"

"Half brothers," Hayley said, with a nod. "Two."

"You don't spend Christmas with them? You're not close?"

Hayley took a sip of her wine. "It's not that we're not close, but there's a big age difference. They were grown and moved out by the time I was five, so we didn't really have…" She waved her hand to encompass the room. "This. Plus, they had their own mom to visit on holidays. And once they were married, in-laws. So we didn't really have a lot of Christmases together like this. It's nice to watch, though. I'm envious."

The evening went on just like that: warm, inviting, delicious. Just like the lunch of pasta Angela had shared with Hayley not so long ago, her baked ziti was amazing and her meatballs were better than any Hayley had ever had. In her life. She was pretty sure she'd died and gone to heaven every time she put a bite of one into her mouth.

None of the Santinis would let Hayley help clean up the dining room or do the dishes. Instead, her wine was refilled and she was ushered back into the living room where, rather than sit in the overstuffed chair again, she took a seat on the hearth next to it so she could soak up the fire's warmth and ambience. Walter lay down at her feet and let out a big doggy sigh, as if he'd worked *incredibly* hard today.

"Did you have as many meatballs as I did?" she asked him.

He raised his head, his brown eyes soft, and seemed to understand exactly what she'd said.

She nodded. "Yeah, I get it. I should've stopped three balls ago, but I just couldn't."

He laid his head back down on his front paws, and Hayley petted him as her gaze moved to the Christmas tree. More specifically, the ornaments. There were so many. The majority of them looked homemade, like children's crafts. She reached out to a ceramic...was it holly leaves and berries? She wasn't sure, as it was a lump of green with some red on it. She unhooked it from the branch and turned it over in her hand.

Olivia, 1993

Hayley rolled her lips in and bit down on them, suddenly filled with joy at the small ornament in her hands. Olivia had made it when she was seven years old, and something about the thought of elementary school Olivia, tongue sticking out in concentration as she painted, made Hayley go all mushy inside.

This is bad.

The thought ran through her head then, followed immediately by another one.

Isn't it?

Because...was it? This attraction she was finally accepting? Was it a bad thing? Hayley wasn't really a cautious person. She was a go-for-it type. A seize-the-day kind of girl. She didn't like to look way out into the future just so she could worry about possible—but not necessarily probable—outcomes.

"Need more wine?" Olivia's voice interrupted her thoughts, and when she looked up, Olivia was smiling down at her. Her cheeks were slightly flushed, probably from the warmth and the wine, and she looked more relaxed than Hayley had ever seen her.

"No, I'm good. Thanks." She held up the ornament and raised her eyebrows in question.

Olivia laughed and took a seat in the overstuffed chair as the others filed into the room. She reached for the ornament, her fingertips warm as she brushed Hayley's. "Oh, I was only seven when I made this," she said as she flipped it over and read the date.

"Which one?" Ann Marie asked. Olivia held it up for her to see. "Where's my macaroni Santa?"

Olivia found it, and soon, the three siblings were picking various ornaments off the tree and telling the stories of how they came to be. Hayley loved every second of it, especially the way Olivia's brown eyes glittered in the soft lighting, the way her expression was gentle. She took another ornament off and handed it to Hayley. "Mama got me this one last year."

It was a plastic molded girl in red footie pajamas, wearing a red stocking hat and holding a sign that said, "Oldest. Mom's Favorite." Hayley's laugh burst out of her as Tony and Ann Marie held up the same ornaments, only Ann Marie's said, "Middle Child. Mom's Favorite." And Tony's, which was a boy, read, "Youngest. Mom's Favorite."

Angela sat on the couch, wineglass in hand, and a smile on her face that radiated a beautiful combination of love and pride. "Presents?" she asked, and suddenly, her kids were just that again: kids. They scrambled around on the floor, reaching for gifts wrapped in silver and gold and red and green, handed them to each other, and the tearing of paper began.

Hayley was perfectly content to watch this lovely family, sitting on the hearth, Walter at her feet, feeling more comfortable and welcome than she could remember feeling, and it was a little bittersweet.

Angela spoiled her children as much as a woman who headed up a middle-class, one-income house could. Clothes and socks and a cookbook for Ann Marie— "What are you trying to say, Mama?"— heavy duty gloves for Tony, and a Crock-Pot for Olivia.

"You use the slow cooker often?" Hayley asked.

"I make a killer beef stew. Mine bit the dust last month and I was *specifically told*"—she said the last two words loudly as she glanced at her mother—"I was not to buy a new one. So, I have been stew-less for nearly five weeks."

"A tragedy," Hayley said with a grin.

"You have no idea."

The conversation was a steady buzz as the Santinis chatted amongst themselves.

Hayley leaned sideways, reached under the tree, and pulled out the gift she'd brought. When she sat back up, Olivia had a square box in her hand and was looking at her. Their gazes held for a moment before they both laughed.

"This is for you," Olivia said softly.

"And this is for you," Hayley countered, handing her the large rectangular package.

"You didn't have to get me anything," Olivia said, as she held the gift on her knees.

"And you didn't have to get me anything." Hayley grinned at her from the hearth.

"Okay, okay, nobody had to get anybody anything. We get it."

Ann Marie stood with her hands on her hips. "Maybe just open them? The suspense is killing me."

"You first," Olivia said with a jerk of her chin.

Hayley nodded and carefully unwrapped the box, which was simple, plain, and white. It was a little bit unnerving, having an entire family she really didn't know terribly well watch her unwrap a gift, but she kept her focus on the task, sliding her finger under the tape to unseal the lid, then pulling it open to reveal white tissue paper. Gently, she reached into the box and pulled the bundle out, then peeled away the tissue. And stared, wide-eyed.

In her hand was a miniature replica of a fairy house. Specifically, the one at the bridge. It came complete with a purple door, a post to represent the bridge behind it, and a little sign that warned "Beware of Trolls."

Hayley brought her fingers to her lips as she lifted the tiny house higher so she could get a better look. "Oh, my God. Olivia. This is beautiful." When she finally looked up and met those brown eyes, Olivia was smiling tenderly down at her.

"You like it?"

"Are you kidding? I love it. It will always remind me of our walk." Hayley turned the little house in her hands, admiring all the tiny detail, the little touches like the weathering of the wood and the round eyes painted on one of the windows, as if a fairy was watching from inside. "It's so intricate."

"There's a local artist who creates all of them. Replicas of all the fairy houses. I went back to the gift shop after our walk hoping they had the troll one, because that seemed to be your favorite."

"It absolutely was."

"You should've seen her," Olivia said to the room. "She got right down on her stomach in the snow to get the right photograph."

"This is beautiful, Olivia," Hayley repeated. "Thank you."

"You're welcome."

Hayley wasn't sure, but it seemed like Olivia's cheeks got a little redder. Was she blushing? Not wanting to dwell on that, she pointed. "Your turn."

With a nod, Olivia unwrapped her gift.

Hayley's heart began to pound with nerves. What if she hated it? She bit her bottom lip, chewed on it.

"Oh," Olivia breathed. And she did breathe it. It was more a sound than a word, stretched out over several seconds. "Hayley…" And right there, in front of everybody including Hayley, Olivia's eyes filled with tears. "This…this is…"

"Are the rest of us allowed to see?" Angela said, her voice light.

Olivia cleared her throat, then turned the canvas around so it faced the room. Hayley watched as mouths dropped open and more long *oohs* filled the air.

"Was this from our first walk? The first day I met you?"

"It is." Hayley hadn't even remembered taking the picture that day in the woods, snapping a shot of Olivia on her knees in the snow, holding Walter's face in her mittened hands as he looked lovingly into her eyes. He was such a great color combination, his black and white fur popping against the snow, that she'd wanted to paint him immediately. And she'd started to. But a couple days later when she'd gone through some more shots, this one had taken her breath away. She'd managed to capture that adoration on canvas, she was pretty sure, focusing on the eyes, both of Walter's and one of Olivia's, as that had been the angle from which the photo was taken, slightly behind Olivia and to her left. The combination of the various shades of the evergreens and the sparkling white of the new fallen snow had made for a gorgeously rich background, if Hayley said so herself. The focus, of course, was on woman and dog, and this painting was one Hayley was beyond proud of.

"Bring it over here," Angela said, waving Olivia toward her.

Olivia took the three steps to her mother and handed her the painting. Then, without missing a beat, she turned around, marched to Hayley, bent down, and wrapped her arms around her in a warm, tight hug. "Thank you so much," she whispered in Hayley's ear.

The world fell away.

Okay, maybe it didn't fall away, but it went all blurry and soft until nothing was in focus except for the two of them and the feel of Olivia's body in Hayley's arms. The heat of her skin under Hayley's hands. The way her hair smelled like coconuts, Hayley's nose buried in it. The intimate tickle of her breath so sensually close to the sensitive skin of Hayley's ear.

She almost didn't let Olivia stand back up. She sincerely thought about just holding tight, not releasing her grip, keeping her close forever. Olivia must've felt it because when she finally did stand up straight, the expression on her face, in her eyes when she looked down at Hayley was nothing short of fucking sexy.

Hayley swallowed hard as every nerve in her body sizzled.

What more could this Christmas bring?

CHAPTER SEVENTEEN

The evening had grown happily, contentedly quiet. Christmas music played softly from the Bluetooth speaker on the mantel. Board games had been played, too many cookies had been eaten, lots of wine had been drunk. Walter was crashed out on his side on the hearth rug in front of the fire, Hayley sitting next to him, rhythmically rubbing her hand down his side. Tony dozed on the couch, Priya reading a book as she leaned on him. Ann Marie was texting a friend on her phone. Angela had gone into the kitchen for something. Olivia stood at the front window, mug of coffee in hand, watching the snow fall and feeling incredibly blessed to be exactly where she was on exactly this night with exactly these people.

"You should stay."

She said it softly, and before she could second-guess herself, before she could chicken out, before she lost what little nerve she'd been able to grasp and pull in close to her chest. Close to her heart, which was beating extra fast. She wondered if anybody else heard it.

"What do you mean?" Hayley asked, coming to stand next to her at the window. "Oooohhh," she said as she looked out and saw that the snow had continued to fall the entire time she'd been there, blanketing the driveway and covering the cars parked in it with a good foot or more of snow.

It's now or never.

The words were loud in Olivia's head, too loud, and she spat out what she wanted to say, again before she lost her nerve. "You can stay next door." She turned and caught Hayley's eye, let herself take a moment to drown in the green. "With me."

There. It was out.

It was out and she couldn't take it back. So, of course, *now* the nerves kicked in, as did the assault of logic from her brain, which had been silent and unhelpful just three seconds ago. It shrieked at her. Things like *What the hell are you thinking?* And *This will do nothing but make your jobs worse.* And *What if she says no? How presumptuous are you?* She brought a hand to her forehead and rubbed it hard with her fingertips as she squeezed her eyes shut.

"Okay."

That got her attention. Olivia's eyes popped open. She turned her head, and it suddenly seemed like Hayley was standing much closer than she had been, though she hadn't moved. But her eyes...*her eyes.* They said everything right then. "Yeah?" Olivia asked.

"Yeah."

"Okay."

Angela sidled up to them and broke the moment as she looked out the window. "Wow. I was thinking of going to Midnight Mass, but looks like that's not happening."

"No, Mama, stay here. The plows are going to be slow tonight since it's Christmas Eve, and it doesn't look like they've made a pass yet. Stay here. God won't mind." Olivia smiled and put her arm around her mother's shoulders, suddenly feeling lighter, more assured than she had in a long time.

Which was weird, right?

Because she should be freaking out right now. Hayley was going to spend the night with her. At her house. She should totally be freaking the hell out.

But she wasn't. Not even close.

Instead, she was calm. Steady.

"It feels later than it is," her mother said quietly, her head on Olivia's shoulder.

"You must be exhausted." She kissed the top of her mother's head, then took a sip of her coffee. "We're ready to get going anyway."

"We?" Angela said, raising her head and her eyebrows.

"Yeah." Olivia cleared her throat. "Hayley's going to stay with me and Walter."

"Oh, good. Yeah, you don't want to be driving in this, sweetie." Angela reached around behind Olivia and squeezed Hayley's arm.

Olivia could read her like a book, though, and knew that while she was doing her best to remain calm, cool, and collected, inside she was doing a little dance of joy at the thought of her and Hayley. Her mother had always been very supportive of Olivia's love life—probably too supportive. She looked up at Olivia with barely contained glee and grinned.

Olivia rolled her eyes and stifled a chuckle, then turned toward the fireplace. "Whaddaya say, Sir Walter? Ready to go?"

The dog opened his eyes and looked at her but didn't move.

"Really, Mom?" Tony said in the goofy voice he used when he was doing Walter. "Do you not see this warm fire? Do you not know how many meatballs Grandma gives me? Do you not understand that it's much more fun here than at your house?"

"Aww, that's just mean," Olivia said, but laughed anyway because it was also true. She let go of her mom and went over to pet her dog, coax him up off the floor and to his feet.

"Thank you so much for having me, Angela," Hayley said as Angela pulled her into a hug. "This was amazing. I'm so full, I don't think I can eat again for a week."

"Well, you'd better run around or something, because you're coming back tomorrow and there will be more food." Angela laid a hand against Hayley's cheek.

"*More* food?" Hayley's eyes went wide with disbelief, and everyone in the room laughed.

"Non-Italians," Ann Marie said with a mock scoff and a shake of her head.

Olivia and Hayley got their stuff together, deciding to leave their gifts there under the tree until tomorrow.

"This seems silly," Olivia said as they donned boots, coats, hats, gloves. "We're only walking next door."

"Excuse me, but did you see the twenty-seven feet of snow out there?" Wide-eyed Hayley was so cute, Olivia could only grin at her.

"I noticed it."

Tony and Priya were staying at Angela's and Ann Marie still lived there, so Olivia and Hayley were the only two leaving. Tony stood. "Do you want me to shovel you a path?" he asked.

Olivia leaned forward and kissed his cheek. "We'll be fine. But thank you for offering."

Ten more minutes and they had said their good-byes and were outside, Walter running through the snow with joy like he'd never seen it before. It was up to his shoulders and he had to work hard, but he bounded through with a level of happiness that only dogs showed.

"God, it's so pretty." Hayley's voice was quiet as she stopped trudging and just stood. "Listen."

Olivia followed suit, stopped moving and stood still.

It was almost surreal. It wasn't exactly silent, but it was close. "I swear I can hear the snowflakes fall," Hayley said, in a whisper. "Can you?" She turned to look at Olivia, and her eyes were bright, delighted, her smile wide as if she'd made some amazing discovery. "Listen," she said again.

So Olivia did. She stood still, even held her breath, and Hayley was right. It was almost as if she could hear each snowflake land on the ground with a soft poof. She nodded slowly, turned to catch Hayley's gaze, and almost gasped at the sizzling shot of arousal that flashed through her body.

Yeah, she knew exactly where this was going.

She'd known since the moment the words "you should stay" had left her mouth. Judging by the expression of sheer sensuality on Hayley's face, she knew it, too.

"Come on," she said quietly, not wanting to disturb the delicate atmosphere they'd somehow created.

They trudged the remaining short distance to Olivia's back door and she let them into the mudroom, a small but useful place where she could wipe down Walter's feet if they were muddy, take off her snowy boots and outerwear, and not drag it all through her house. They did that in silence, Hayley mimicking Olivia as far as where to hang her coat, where to stow her boots. When they had both tippy-toed in their socks around puddles made by melted snow, Olivia held an arm out to let Hayley enter her home.

"Welcome to my humble abode. Again."

"This is adorable, Olivia. I didn't get a chance to tell you last time." Hayley's tone seemed genuine, and Olivia felt herself well up with pride a little bit.

"Thanks. It's small, but it's mine."

"Not at all. It's the perfect size." She stepped into the kitchen, walked across the gray ceramic tile Olivia had installed herself, and ran her hand over the granite counter top. The cupboards were white with silver handles, the sink stainless steel. "I love this kitchen." Hayley turned to meet Olivia's eyes. "Do you cook? I mean, besides a killer Crock-Pot beef stew?"

Lifting one shoulder, Olivia replied honestly. "I try. I want to. I don't have a ton of time, but every so often, I'll make homemade soup or roast a chicken."

Hayley squinted at her. "I can't decide if having a mom who can cook like yours is helpful, in that she'd teach you everything she knows, or useless, because you'd never be as good as she is."

A chuckle escaped Olivia as she crossed the room to open the cabinet above the stainless steel fridge. "Right? I'm pretty sure it's a scientific fact that food loses a little bit with each generation." She found a bottle of Frangelico and took it down, held it up so Hayley could see it, a question in her eyes.

Hayley nodded, then said, "What do you mean?"

After retrieving two brandy snifters from another cupboard, Olivia turned on the hot water tap and let it run. "I mean my grandmother's meatballs were amazing. The absolute best. And my mother's are really, really good, but they're not my grandma's. And mine are actually quite awesome…" The water was steaming, and she filled both glasses as Hayley finished her sentence.

"But they're not your mom's."

"Exactly." Olivia let the water set for a few seconds, dumped it out, poured the Frangelico into each one, then handed Hayley hers. "A little trick Mike the bartender taught me: Warming up the glass brings out the hazelnut flavor of the liquor." She touched her glass to Hayley's and they sipped.

"Mmm, that's delicious."

"I used to try to actually warm up the glasses themselves. Like, in the microwave. But they'd get too hot and make it hard to put your lips on the glass to sip."

"Well, we don't want anything happening to those lips," Hayley said. When her eyes met Olivia's, she didn't even look embarrassed or ashamed for using such a cheesy line, and something in Olivia admired that.

"Come with me. Mike also says Frangelico should be sipped by the fire."

In the living room, Olivia found the remote for both the Christmas tree and her fireplace and clicked them on as Walter went to his own dog bed in the corner, turned in three circles, and settled down with a very tired sigh.

"Does everybody in Evergreen Hills have a fireplace?" Hayley asked as the two of them sat on an area rug strewn with various pillows of different sizes and colors. "Oh, my God, this is amazing." She'd apparently arranged some pillows just right and now lounged back, her feet toward the hearth, her upper body propped up so she could sip.

"Nice, huh? This is where I love to sit and read in the winter." Olivia created a similar nest out of the remaining pillows and they lay side by side, watching the gas-fueled flames flicker, soaking up the warmth, and enjoying one another's company, the silence not at all uncomfortable.

"I had an amazing time tonight, Olivia." Hayley's voice was barely above a whisper. "Thank you so much. I know you were hesitant about having me in your space with your family, but thank you."

Honestly, Olivia was kind of shocked at how quickly she'd decided that having Hayley in her space was not only okay, but something she actually wanted. Desired. Badly. What was happening to her? She didn't know, and she wasn't sure she wanted to know, because this felt too good. Too right. Olivia was not an impulsive person. At all. She liked to take her time with decisions. Investigate all angles. List out all pros and cons before choosing a course of action. But all of that went right out the frosted window when she turned and met Hayley's eyes, their color surprisingly bright in the dim lighting. Olivia didn't stop, didn't think, didn't weigh options or analyze outcomes. She simply acted, leaning toward Hayley until their lips touched.

It was true they'd only kissed—well, made out—twice, but Olivia felt like she knew those lips, knew that mouth like the back of her hand, like she'd been kissing Hayley for years and years. The kiss began gently, tentatively, testing waters and moods, gauging response and permission. But when Hayley turned away to set her glass far out of reach, Olivia knew she had all the permission she needed, and she did the same with her own glass.

Tentative followed *analysis* right out that frosted window as Hayley turned to kiss her again, and then all bets were off as she rolled them so Olivia was on her back with Hayley above her. They kissed for long moments. Hours. Days, maybe. Olivia wasn't sure. All she knew was that she'd never been kissed the way Hayley kissed her, with such opposing qualities that shouldn't work together, but did. Taking but giving. Gently but firmly. Aggressive but submissive. None of it should have been possible, yet it all was, and Olivia wrapped her arms around Hayley, dug her fingers into Hayley's hair, and held on to her small frame as their legs entwined and their bodies pressed together.

Had anything felt this right?

In her entire life? Anything at all?

Coherent thought became sparse, because all Olivia wanted to do was give back as good as she was getting. She slipped her hand under the back of Hayley's shirt, and when her hand met Hayley's bare, heated skin, they both sucked in a breath. It seemed to spur Hayley on because she moved her knee so it was between Olivia's, then stopped and looked down at their bodies.

Olivia still wore her dress. Hayley looked at it, then looked up at Olivia and into her eyes as she slid her hand down Olivia's body. Over her hip, down her outer thigh until her fingers reached the hem of the dress. Her eyes never leaving Olivia's, she slowly pulled the dress up, and Olivia lifted her hips to help. Hayley stopped with the dress just high enough that it bared Olivia's black underwear—and more importantly, gave Olivia free rein to open her legs. Which she did.

Hayley smiled and settled her knee between them. Then she pressed it upward, gently, and Olivia gasped…a sound Hayley caught with her own mouth, and then they were kissing again.

If anybody had asked Olivia to recall a time in her life when she'd completely let go, ended her grip on control, on logic, on what made sense, and simply gone with the flow, she'd have drawn a blank. The truth was, she'd never done that. She didn't feel safe when she didn't have control. She didn't like somebody else deciding which way her day, her week, her life went. She was the one who would dictate that, thank you. No, Olivia Santini did not let go, had never let go, not once in her entire life.

Until now.

She stifled her inner voice, the one that worried about *everything*. She stifled any concerns she had about where this thing with Hayley was going, should go, could go, if anywhere. She stopped thinking ahead to what would happen after. Tomorrow. No, she let it all go and simply...*felt*.

And it was magnificent.

Olivia had been with other women. Of course she had. She was no prude. She'd even had a relationship. But being with those others? None of them felt like this. Hayley felt...right. Hayley's mouth, kissing her with such expertise that part of Olivia marveled at the fact that she'd never been this turned on in her entire life and Hayley had barely touched her.

And then that thought was gone as Hayley's fingers brushed over Olivia's breast, pushing a small whimper from her own lips.

Hayley tugged at the fabric of the dress and whispered, "Do you think we could take this off?"

All Olivia could do was nod.

She sat up. Hayley, on her knees, already had the hem in her hands, and she pulled the dress up and over Olivia's head in one smooth move, tossed it up onto the couch. Then she turned back to Olivia and simply stared, lips slightly parted, eyes hooded, dark.

Olivia swore she could feel Hayley's eyes on her just as if they were fingertips, softly brushing over different parts of her body, her bare skin, causing goose bumps to erupt along her arms, but not because she was cold.

"My God," Hayley breathed out. "You are the most beautiful woman I have ever seen." And she meant it. Olivia could tell. There was nothing sarcastic or even a little patronizing in the statement. There was nothing but awe, and in that moment, Olivia had never felt so attractive, so sexy, or so wanted. Ever.

And she wanted Hayley. Good God, did she want Hayley.

Suddenly, her inner control freak was back, but not in the way it usually was. Not in a way that halted all action while it weighed pros and cons. Not in a way that made her sit and analyze the situation for an hour. No, this time, Olivia's inner control freak simply did what it was supposed to: It took control. And apparently surprised them both, as in the next thirty seconds, Hayley's red sweater and black pants had joined Olivia's dress on the couch, and the two of them stared at each other. Breath ragged, both in their underwear. Their eye contact was intense. Olivia had noticed over the past few weeks that eye contact wasn't one of Hayley's stronger qualities, but right then? On the floor in front of the fire half-naked? Hayley held her gaze, didn't falter, didn't look away, barely blinked. And when she whispered, so softly Olivia almost didn't hear it, "I want you so badly," that was it.

Olivia fell back against the pillows in a blur of arousal and Hayley was on her again, kissing her hard, tongues battling, hands traveling over skin and inconvenient fabric that eventually disappeared, though she wasn't sure when or how. And when Hayley closed her mouth over Olivia's bared nipple, the cry pulled from her was a sound Olivia had never heard herself make before. Every nerve in her body tingled and she was so wet, she absently wondered if she was ruining the rug.

That thought was instantly chased away when Hayley's fingers found their way between Olivia's legs and toward that wetness, the heat that she'd created. Olivia's hips began rocking on their own, as if they had no faith in Olivia and wanted to help Hayley find the right spot.

But Hayley teased her.

She used a fingertip to trace a path all around Olivia's center, circling but never touching that perfect spot. Olivia's hips moved a little faster, but Hayley had taken all the control back. Olivia was completely at her mercy and she knew it. And it wasn't frustrating. Well, okay, that was a lie. It was a little frustrating. But it was also delicious and exhilarating and so fucking sexy. Olivia opened her eyes to find Hayley watching her face, a mischievous smile on her own as she trailed her finger around and around and around.

Olivia swallowed hard, her breaths coming in ragged gasps as she looked at Hayley.

"Tell me what you want," Hayley commanded softly, fingertip still moving maddeningly close to where Olivia needed it—but not close enough. She groaned and Hayley smiled tenderly. "Tell me."

Olivia wasn't a beggar. She didn't plead. She had strength. Pride. Nobody told her what to do… "Touch me. God, please, Hayley. Touch me."

And Hayley did.

When her finger slipped into the wetness, directly over her swollen, sensitive flesh, it only took two strokes before Olivia tipped over the edge and into oblivion. Her eyes squeezed shut as her hips lifted off the rug. She crumpled a pillow in one fist, the fingers of her other hand digging into Hayley's back as a low, guttural moan emanated from her throat in a long, gravelly note of mind-shattering pleasure.

Olivia seriously wondered if she'd blacked out for a few seconds because she felt like she was waking up from unconsciousness as her body came down, settled back to the pillows, her muscles beginning to relax.

"Oh, my God." She said it quietly. She said it over and over again, apparently the only three words of the English language she could remember. "Oh, my God."

She was spent. Complete and utter jelly. Her entire body felt like it had somehow lost all bones and she was just a quivering pile. When Olivia finally pried her eyes open, Hayley was right there, propped on an elbow, tracing her fingers over Olivia's bare stomach, and smiling with such... Olivia swallowed hard, not quite ready to go there yet.

"Well," Hayley said, her voice soft, her eyes filled with tenderness. "*That* was something to behold."

Olivia blushed. She could feel it, the heat the crawled up her neck and warmed her cheeks. She covered her eyes.

"No," Hayley said and gently moved Olivia's hand away. "Don't do that. Don't be embarrassed. You have nothing to be embarrassed about. That was the most gorgeous thing I've ever seen." Her smile was so sincere that it brought tears to Olivia's eyes.

"That was..." Olivia shook her head slowly, words eluding her. "I don't even know."

"I will take 'I don't even know' any day of the week." Hayley's face was glowing. Olivia couldn't read everything in that expression, but it was definitely all good. All very, very good.

They lay there for a long time, looking at each other. Again, Olivia was amazed by their eye contact, how intense and...raw it was. Hayley's fingers still traveled Olivia's body and it felt so glorious, the gentle tickle that crossed her stomach, went up her side, over her shoulder, down her arm and back. They stayed that way for a long moment... until Hayley's fingers took a detour across one of Olivia's nipples and her breath caught in her throat.

"Oh, no," she said, even as she felt her arousal uncurl deep in her body, preparing for another round. "I believe it's *my* turn to drive *you* a little crazy." With that, she pushed herself up and over so this time, Olivia was the one on top. Hayley's eyes had gone from bright and tender back to hooded and dark. "We are so far from finished," Olivia whispered just before crushing her mouth to Hayley's.

CHAPTER EIGHTEEN

The sun wasn't up yet, but the sky had gone from dark to a slight pinkening, the promise that daylight was on its way. Hayley could only see a tiny bit through the living room window from where she lay, still on the floor, cushioned by pillows, a fluffy and super-cuddly fleece blanket, and Olivia.

Hayley didn't move. Instead, she took this time awake to catalog everything she could feel, as Olivia's deep and even breaths indicated she was still asleep, lying on her back beneath Hayley, her bare skin so warm and soft. Hayley was on her side, her head cradled on Olivia's shoulder, Olivia's arm wrapped around her almost protectively. Hayley's leg was thrown over Olivia's, her knee tucked snugly between Olivia's legs, their bare feet touching. Hayley's arm was bent, on Olivia's midsection, but her hand up near her shoulder, fingers entwined in some of Olivia's dark, tousled hair.

I never want to move from this spot.

Hayley smiled as the thought crawled slowly through her head. She was used to things zipping, moving quickly, but right now, everything was at half speed, easy and relaxed, and Hayley loved it. Last night had been...

God. Last night.

Hayley inhaled quietly, filled her lungs up as full as she could, then let the air back out very slowly, just letting herself revel in this feeling. In the slight chappedness of her lips. In the tender ache in her thighs. In the pleasant soreness between them. The idea of moving upstairs to the bedroom hadn't even crossed their minds. No, they were too focused on what they were doing, in how amazingly well they fit together, and in how they played each other's bodies like musical instruments, strumming and plucking and stroking until one of them sang and then it was the other's turn.

She'd lost track of how many orgasms they'd had. Three each? Four? They'd only collapsed in utter exhaustion an hour or two ago, and Hayley knew the second Olivia opened her eyes, she might very well pounce on her. Because these memories from last night, these moments she was reliving in her head, were turning her on all over again. The gentle and insistent throbbing between her legs was a pretty good indicator.

Hayley had never had sex under a Christmas tree before, but she would highly recommend it. Even now, as dawn was close to breaking, the multicolored lights bathed the room in a fuzzy, welcoming glow that spoke of love and happiness. The fire still burned in the gas fireplace, though they'd turned it down a bit, given the sweat they'd worked up— and Hayley's brain tossed her *that* image: Olivia's naked and glistening body above her, those dark eyes looking down at her as her fingers toyed with Hayley's nipple until she gasped.

So, yeah. *That* would be in her head forever.

A muffled snorfling sound caught her attention, and in the next moment, Walter was standing over them, his tailless rear end wagging, knocking into the bottom branches of the tree as he looked from Hayley to Olivia and back again. As if they had some kind of telepathy, the dog and his person, Olivia opened her eyes after only a couple of seconds and Hayley waited as she took a quick moment to assess her situation.

"Hi," Olivia finally said, turning to look at Hayley with those dark, dark eyes. The arm around Hayley tightened, pulling her closer as Olivia pressed a kiss to Hayley's forehead.

"Hey," Hayley said back, one corner of her mouth pulling up. "Merry Christmas."

"Merry Christmas." Their gazes held for a beat before Olivia said, "I have to put this boy out and feed him breakfast."

"Okay."

"But don't go anywhere." And the twinkle in her eye had Hayley's body already thrumming with want.

"I'll be right here." She heard Olivia let Walter out, then scoot upstairs. Hayley's eyes moved along the living room ceiling as she heard Olivia's travels. In a couple minutes, she was back down. Hayley yelped as a pile of fabric landed on her face.

A long-sleeved T-shirt so worn and soft it was almost threadbare. Hayley could barely make out "Evergreen Hills High," the print was so faded. She put it on, inhaling the scent of laundry detergent.

Pushing any overthinking aside—or at least trying to—Hayley propped up a couple of pillows, tucked the blankets around her bare legs, and listened to what morning sounded like in Olivia's house. The back door opening and closing, Walter's tippy-tapping nails clicking across the floor, a scoop of dog food being dropped into a bowl, gentle murmurs from Olivia to Walter. Other sounds occurred as well, and before long, the wonderful aroma of freshly brewed coffee filled the air. And while Hayley didn't exactly consider herself a romantic, she found herself wondering what it might be like to wake up like this every day, to hear these sounds and smell these smells.

And see this sight, she thought as Olivia returned in black leggings, and a Life Is Good T-shirt, and carrying two cups of coffee. She'd pulled her hair up into a messy pile on top of her head and looked nothing short of breathtaking. Adorably tousled. Sensual in an "I had a lot of sex last night and my cheeks are probably still flushed" kind of way. And they were.

"You look beautiful," Hayley said, before she could stop herself.

Olivia's olive skin flushed even more. "Well, I'm glad you think so because I avoided any and all mirrors while upstairs." She handed Hayley a Santa Claus mug and sat down next to her, her own snowman mug clutched in both hands. She draped one leg over Hayley's, like it was the most natural thing in the world to do. The sound of Walter crunching his breakfast was oddly comforting as they sat in companionable silence and sipped their coffee.

"I love Christmas morning," Olivia said after a moment.

"Yeah? How come?"

Olivia inhaled slowly and let it out as Hayley watched her face, watched her think about her answer. "Because it's so...perfect. It's interesting to me how one particular day can actually feel different from others. It's warmer." She tapped a finger against her chest where her heart was. "I mean here, not out there." She jerked her chin toward the window. "It's warmer in that we're all a little nicer to each other. I love knowing the day that's coming, spending it with my family. Eating and drinking and talking and just being together. I think a lot of people might find that boring. Or even frightening—I know not everybody gets along with their family. But I'm very lucky, and I think on Christmas morning, I'm more aware of it than on other days." With a glance at Hayley, she scrunched up her nose and asked, "Does that make sense?"

Hayley nodded. It really did. "I felt like that when my mom was alive," she said quietly. "She loved Christmas so much." The last thing Hayley wanted was to bring the whole mood down by being too melancholy, so she focused on the best parts of Christmas with her mother. "She would drag my father all over Manhattan to look at the decorations. And he would bitch and complain that it was all touristy stuff, but I think he secretly loved it because he would go. Every single time." She smiled at the memory, sipped her coffee. Then her smile turned to laughter as another memory hit. "And we'd make these god-awful cookies!"

"What?" Olivia laughed with her.

"Oh, God, yes. My mom wanted so badly to bake Christmas cookies with me, and she so was *not* a baker. But every year, she'd try a new recipe, and every year, they came out terrible. Maybe if we'd stuck to the same one, we'd have been able to get them right eventually. But as I got older, it became another holiday tradition, and I actually looked forward to it. Which cookie can we completely ruin this year?"

They were both laughing now, and suddenly, Hayley felt so grateful. She turned to Olivia and just looked at her, watching as Olivia's laughter quieted, then stopped.

"What?" she asked softly.

"Thank you."

"For?"

"Everything. The time with your family. The massive amounts of food. Insisting I stay here instead of going back to my place alone."

"What about having amazing sex with you?" Olivia arched one eyebrow, and Hayley laughed. "Don't I get thanked for that?"

"Oh, that, too. That, the most." Her laughter faded and she looked into Olivia's dark eyes, eyes that had once seemed so closed but now were completely open, almost vulnerable. "Thank you for helping me love Christmas again."

"You're welcome." Olivia's voice was barely above a whisper as she leaned toward Hayley and kissed her softly. She pulled back and looked into Hayley's eyes for a beat—there was so much there, so many things, but Hayley didn't get a chance to absorb any of it before Olivia kissed her again.

Coffee cups were set aside.

Clothes were again discarded.

They were late getting next door.

Very late.

❖

"I insist." Hayley's tone was extra firm even to her. She impressed herself.

"Hayley." Olivia arched that eyebrow again, and Hayley made a mental note that she needed to be careful of that thing. It was a deadly weapon that she suspected would get Olivia pretty much anything she wanted from her.

But not today.

"No." Hayley held up a hand as she stepped into her boots. "I have to go back there anyway, so it's silly for you to come in. You stay here and enjoy the rest of the evening with your family. I will take care of things at the Evergreen. Okay?" Her voice had softened by the end of her reasoning, but she was pretty sure she'd made her point.

"Okay," Olivia said on a sigh. "But I don't like it."

"You don't have to." Hayley winked at her. She hugged Angela. Then she hugged Ann Marie and Tony and even Priya, the feeling that she'd known the Santinis for much longer than a few weeks settling into her heart and soul. She thanked them all profusely as Angela loaded up her arms with containers of leftovers.

"Come see us again soon," Angela said, then took Hayley's face in both her hands and kissed her cheek.

Hayley felt tears spring into her eyes and quickly looked down to blink them away.

"I'll walk you out," Olivia said as she stepped into her brother's boots and grabbed her coat out of the closet.

The day had been nothing short of gorgeous. The snow had stopped and the sun had shone, giving the world a sparkle that seemed appropriate for the day. The plows had made their runs through the town, cleaning up all the neighborhood streets. Tony and Priya had taken it upon themselves to snow-blow the driveway and shovel the walk while Ann Marie had brushed off all the cars. All Hayley had to do was get in and drive away.

Which she didn't want to do, much to her own surprise.

She opened her car door, got in, and keyed the engine. Then she sat there, one leg out with a foot on the driveway, and looked up at Olivia. "So."

"So." Olivia smiled hesitantly down at her, but then darted her eyes away.

"Thank you. Again."

Bringing her gaze back to Hayley's, Olivia's smile seemed to grow. Solidify. "You're welcome. Again."

"I'll see you tomorrow?"

"You will."

"I'll text you tonight."

Olivia nodded. Then, as if doing so before she could change her mind, she leaned into the car and gave Hayley a quick kiss on the lips, then stood back up. At Hayley's raised eyebrows, she explained, "My family is probably standing in the window watching us."

Hayley let her gaze travel in that direction. "Ah. Yup. All four of them, like a little audience."

Olivia closed her eyes and shook her head, and the color that tinted her cheeks was beautiful.

"You're very sexy when you blush."

"Stop it," Olivia whispered, but when she opened her eyes, she smiled at Hayley, her expression soft. She took a step back. "Okay. Go. Drive carefully. I'll talk to you later."

"Deal." Hayley made herself pull her door shut. Olivia stayed in the driveway, arms crossed over her chest against the cold, and watched her, until she drove away, then she lifted one hand in a wave. Hayley drove for a minute or two before the weight of the past twenty-four hours finally sat on her. "Holy shit," she said, to the emptiness of her car.

But then she smiled. She couldn't help it. And she kept smiling all the way back to the Evergreen. Maybe she was going to smile like this forever.

She was okay with that.

The atmosphere inside the Evergreen was jubilant. Festive. There wasn't a huge number of staff working, but there were some, as guests still needed to be taken care of. Not to mention, Tessa had an amazing Christmas dinner spread that Hayley was sure was currently knocking the socks off every guest with a seat in Split Rail.

She took the back halls to the elevators and zipped up to her room first, as putting on clean clothes that weren't sweats that belonged to Olivia was necessary. Once in her room, she tucked her leftovers into her minifridge, unboxed her miniature fairy house and set it lovingly on her dresser, changed quickly into something not too worklike but still presentable, donned her manager name tag, and headed down to see how things were going. On the elevator ride down, her phone vibrated in her back pocket and she realized she'd silenced it yesterday and had left it that way. She pulled it out and took a look at the newest text. Olivia.

Come back. I miss you already.

Hayley felt herself flush with heat as she remembered their night. And their morning. She swallowed hard and texted back. *I miss you too.* And damn if that wasn't the absolute truth.

It was pretty much the first time she'd even looked at her phone since arriving at the Santinis' yesterday, and now she saw she had several unanswered texts along with a couple of calls. There was a text from Serena, asking if she was in town—meaning Manhattan. Another from her brother Max, wishing her a Merry Christmas. She sent him a quick one back. A voice mail from her brother Jason—Hayley gave him extra points for taking the time to actually dial his phone and speak. A voice mail *and* a text from Guinevere.

"Oh, joy," Hayley muttered as she scrolled to find the voice mail. From Guin. Who never, ever left voice mail messages because she thought they were "too primitive. What is this, 1994?" Hayley hit Play and put the phone to her ear.

"Merry Christmas, you gorgeous thing. I hear you're up north. Are you celebrating all alone up there in the mountains of East Jesus? Listen, honey, I know we've had our issues, but the truth is…" Here, Guinevere paused, seemed to hesitate, and then her voice softened. "I miss you. I miss us, and I think you probably know that maybe you were hasty in suggesting we take some time apart."

Hayley shook her head. This was such typical Guinevere Aston. If there was one thing she'd excelled at during their short time of dating, it was telling Hayley what she thought and how she felt, as if Hayley was confused and needed clarification on her own brain.

"Anyway," the voice mail went on. "Come home for New Year's Eve. I'll take you out and then we'll head to the Ritz where Carlo's throwing his usual amazing bash. I already told him we were coming, so…wouldn't want to disappoint him and his crew, right, sweetie? Call me." Then there was the smacking sound of an air kiss and the message ended.

Five different responses flew through Hayley's head—none of them pleasant—so she simply pocketed the phone and decided she'd make some rounds, then spend an hour or two in her office on email and such. Christmas dinner with the Santinis had happened at noon, so it was still only early evening, and when Hayley peeked into Split Rail, she was happy to see it was almost full. Their rooms might not have all been booked, but they'd obviously gotten some outside guests for Christmas dinner.

She wandered around, went back upstairs to check on the rooftop bar, which had a handful of guests and a stunning view now that the snow had cleared out and all the lights outside were visible. She checked in with the cheerful bartender on duty and thought how nice it was that even the staff who had to work today were happy and smiling.

Jacob, the dorky young guy Hayley remembered, was working the front desk, and as Hayley approached, she noticed that he seemed to have gained a little confidence. Or maybe it was holiday spirit. Either way, she liked his presentation, the way he stood tall instead of hunching. The way he looked the guest he spoke to in the eye instead of letting his gaze dart around with uncertainty.

"Hey, Jake," she said, clapping him on the shoulder and nodding at the guest as she passed by them.

"Merry Christmas, Hayley," he said, then went back to what he was doing.

Hayley slowed her pace as she entered Olivia's office. It was weird how she felt different now, how she noticed things. She could smell Olivia in here. Even though she'd left yesterday and hadn't been back, her scent lingered. Cinnamon. Musk. It immediately made Hayley's throat go dry and sent a pulse to beat low in her body. She could envision Olivia sitting in her chair, squinting at her computer monitor, and suddenly, Hayley missed her like crazy. Instead of continuing on into her own office, she took a seat at Olivia's desk. Sat back in the chair, rubbed her palms over the smooth desktop. A foam stress ball in the shape of a tiny beach ball sat on the desk, and Hayley picked it up, squeezing it a few times as she sat there and looked at Olivia's workspace, feeling a new connection to her after their night together.

There was a photo on the corner of the desk of the Santini family, young versions of Olivia and her siblings along with two adults. Taken before her father died, obviously. Hayley reached for it, jostling the computer's mouse as she did so, which woke up Olivia's computer. Hayley brought the photo frame closer and studied the family, smiling as she scanned over Olivia's not quite teenage face. All her current features were there, especially her big, dark eyes, which she'd obviously had to grow into. Hayley smiled as she ran her fingertips over the glass, then glanced up at the computer screen as she set the frame back in its place.

On the screen was a document, a list of paragraphs and numbers and totals. Hayley looked closer and read for a moment or two before realizing what it was. Olivia had typed up a plan. A viable plan complete with costs, returns on investment, and total increased profit for the next five years at the Evergreen. And while Hayley was not at all well versed in this type of thing, it seemed to make sense. She did a little searching through Olivia's computer files and discovered this was her seventh version, each one written six months or more apart. Had she sent them? If no, why not? If yes, were they getting into the right hands?

Benton Markham's voice boomed through Hayley's memory right then.

Write up a report for me. A proposal of some kind telling me what needs to be fixed and why. Include cost analysis in it.

She had protested—or tried to—because she had no idea how to come up with a cost analysis. And now here one was, right in front of her, all worked out right down to the last penny. Then she heard him again.

You're on thin ice already, young lady.

Her stomach churned a bit, as it always did when her father sounded like that with her: annoyed, impatient, and her favorite—disappointed.

Before she could think about it, she emailed the document to herself from Olivia's computer.

CHAPTER NINETEEN

The week between Christmas and New Year's Eve was always a bit chaotic at the Evergreen. Many of the guests who'd stayed over Christmas tended to stay through New Year's Day. There were also many guests who came just for the night, to celebrate New Year's Eve at Split Rail or on the rooftop bar, dance into the night, and crash safely in a hotel room rather than trying to drive home. In fact, New Year's Eve was one of the Evergreen's busiest nights of the year, so a lot of planning and prep work went into it.

Due to all that work, Olivia hadn't had a ton of time to spend with Hayley. Sometimes, she felt like that was a good thing because they'd really kind of jumped into things on Christmas Eve—not that she regretted it for one second, because she *so did not*—and maybe slowing down was a smart move. Other times, she'd see Hayley from a distance, talking or laughing or something and she'd get a flash of Hayley beneath her, breathing ragged, blanket balled in her fist, Olivia's name on a whisper over and over again...

"Hey." Hayley's voice interrupted Olivia's very naughty thoughts as she peeked her head out of her office. "Are you free for lunch?"

Olivia cleared her throat, hoped her face wasn't as red as it felt. A hope that was useless, judging by the amusement of Hayley's expression. "Um. Lunch. Let me see." She grabbed her phone, scrolled to her calendar, not because she didn't know if she had an appointment but because she'd suddenly lost track of what day it was. Okay. Friday. Got it. "Yes. I have about forty-five minutes until I have to meet with Tessa about the New Year's Eve schedule for tomorrow night."

"Forty-five minutes, huh?" Hayley gave one nod and stepped out of her office fully. "That should work." She gestured to Olivia to follow her out of the offices and past the front desk, where Stephanie was checking somebody in. The lobby was bustling with skiers just getting ready to head to the slopes. "Come with me. I have something to show you."

"Where are we going?" Olivia asked as she stepped onto the elevator with Hayley and five guests.

"My room," Hayley said, not looking at her.

Every drop of moisture in Olivia's body went south and she swallowed hard, instantly turned on and amazed by the fact.

Four minutes later, they were in Hayley's suite, kissing like two schoolkids trying not to get caught. The instant the door had closed behind them, Hayley had been on Olivia, beating her to the punch by a mere second or two. Olivia pushed Hayley's blazer off her shoulders and left it on the floor near the small kitchen as they stumbled together, never breaking the kiss, across the living room and into the master bedroom. They fell onto the bed, and soon, shoes thumped to the floor, clothes flew, and a struggle for power ensued.

Olivia won, smiling down from above Hayley as she slid her fingers inside and Hayley cried out. "I'm taller and stronger," she whispered in victory, her lips nearly touching Hayley's as she began to move her hand. "I win."

The pace of Hayley's breathing picked up, her hips beginning to move with Olivia's rhythm. "Or maybe I'm the one who wins," she said through clenched teeth as her orgasm then ripped through her body, her fingers digging into Olivia's hair as she pulled her down on top of her.

"My God, that was fast," Olivia commented, and she could admit to feeling rather pleased with herself. "I'm surprised."

"I've wanted you for four days," Hayley said, smiling, eyes closed. "I'm not."

And before Olivia could utter another word, Hayley flipped their positions, pushed Olivia's bare legs apart, and ran the wet, hot flat of her tongue over Olivia's center, from bottom to top. Once. Slowly.

"Oh, my God," were the only three words Olivia could come up with, so she said them over and over until Hayley picked up her pace and Olivia arched off the bed like the string on a bow. She blindly grabbed for a pillow and held it over her face as more sound than she'd ever made in bed in her life exited her lungs with startling force.

There wasn't much time left for cuddling, but they managed to work some in. Olivia pulled Hayley onto her shoulder, held her tight, and marveled at how perfectly their bodies fit together, as if they were made specifically to lie in this position.

"I would love nothing more than to stay right here all day," Olivia said, then sighed. "Unfortunately, I have to be downstairs in…" She turned her head to glance at the clock, and her eyes flew open wide. "Shit. Ten minutes."

Hayley lifted her arm and leg and rolled to her side, effectively unlocking Olivia from the bed. Then she propped herself up on one elbow and watched as Olivia scurried around the suite, grabbing all her articles of clothing, dressing as she went.

"Have you seen my underwear?" she asked. When she looked up at Hayley, the white lacy bikinis were dangling from one finger. Olivia grinned as she snatched them back. "Thank you, baby." She gave Hayley what was meant to be a quick kiss on the lips, but Hayley hooked a hand around the back of Olivia's neck and held her long enough to make it much more. "God," she said, out of breath—again— as she freed herself, took a step back and stood up straight. She stepped into her panties, then her pants. Once she was fully dressed, she allowed herself a moment to just…stare. Because Hayley, lounged on the bed like that, on her side, hand propping up her head, completely naked? The sexiest thing Olivia had ever seen. Like, ever.

She waved a finger in the general direction of Hayley's form. "That, by the way? An excellent look for you."

"Yeah? Why, thank you. You should come over here and take a closer look."

"Ha! I've met you, and I am fully aware of what would happen if I came one inch closer." She loved the expression on Hayley's face in that moment. Sated, sexy, happy. Olivia's entire body relaxed a bit. "You look gorgeous," she said softly.

Hayley's cheeks reddened and she looked down, almost shyly. "Thank you."

"I've gotta run. See you downstairs?"

Hayley nodded, and with a quick wave—because Olivia wasn't

kidding about what would happen if she'd stepped within grasping reach of Hayley's naked body—she left the suite.

Luck was with her, as the elevator was empty when she stepped in, and she looked at herself in the mirrored wall, wondering if somebody could tell what she'd just done simply by looking at her. The face that stared back at her was… Olivia felt the grin spread across her face even as she watched it appear on her reflection. Her face was happy. That was the best way to describe it. Her lips were a little swollen; she'd grab some lip gloss on the way to the restaurant. Her hair was tousled, and she finger-combed it as the car stopped on the third floor and picked up a middle-aged couple. Her cheeks were flushed, but it could easily be that she'd been…working vigorously. Yes, that was it. She turned and smiled at the couple.

"Are you enjoying your stay?" she asked, gave them her best open assistant manager expression, and tried to ignore the gentle throbbing that still pulsed between her legs.

❖

The kitchen at Split Rail often reminded Olivia of a beehive. Worker bees buzzed all around, chopping, sautéing, preparing, while the queen bee (Tessa, of course) directed their actions, pointing here, ordering there. Olivia knew the best thing for her to do was stay off to the side until she was noticed. Otherwise, she'd get stung.

She'd stopped by her office quickly on the way, avoiding what she was sure was a knowing look from Stephanie—though how could it be?—to stroke on some lip gloss and grab her tablet. Now, she stood in the corner and waited for Tessa to finish whatever she was showing her sous chef and notice her. Which she did.

A few moments later, they were headed to an empty conference room just a couple doors down the hall. They sat down, Tessa squinted at Olivia, then pointed. "You got laid," she said, so matter-of-factly Olivia sat blinking at her for a full ten seconds.

"What?" It was the only thing she could think of to say, and she infused it with as much indignation as she could.

Tessa laughed right in her face. "Seriously? You think I don't know you by now? Your hair is flat in the back, your eyeliner is smudged…"

"Maybe I put a hat on and...had to go outside in the cold, which could smear my makeup."

"Your shirt's on inside out."

Olivia gasped and looked down. "Shit." With a groan, she got up, closed and locked the door, and righted her shirt.

"I don't have a ton of time." Tessa jerked her chin toward Olivia's chair. "Sit. Spill."

And Olivia did. She told Tessa every little tiny detail from the moment Hayley had arrived at her mother's house right up until how Olivia had been flat on her back in Hayley's bed less than half an hour ago. Everything. All of it.

Tessa sat quietly, did a lot of blinking, but let Olivia talk until she was finished. After a moment, she said, "Wow." Then more blinking. Then "Wow" again. Then she nodded. "Okay. Well, there you go. Your course of action became clear." Then she let go of a soft laugh.

Olivia stayed quiet.

"Oh," Tessa said, more serious. "Oh, okay. You don't just like this girl, you *like* her."

The lump that lodged in Olivia's throat was unexpected, and she tried—unsuccessfully—to swallow it away. The look she tossed at Tessa was a large portion pathetic and she knew it and she hated it. She was not pathetic. That was not one of her go-to emotions. But this? The whole Hayley thing? She was at a loss.

"Talk to me," Tessa said, and purposefully pushed Olivia's tablet aside.

With a shake of her head, Olivia did. "I just don't even know. There's so much around this that...God, so complicated."

"Like?"

"Our jobs, for one?" Olivia didn't actually add a *duh*, but it was there.

"Mm-hmm. What else?"

"Well." Olivia stared at her as she thought. Looked down at the table. Over toward the door. Back to the table. Up to Tessa's amused expression, eyebrow arched.

"Exactly. Honey, you need to chill the hell out. I am serious as a heart attack right now." She stared at Olivia until she was apparently satisfied that she'd been heard.

"Okay." Olivia breathed in, breathed out, nodded. "Okay."

"Listen to me." Tessa folded her hands on the table in front of her. "I know you're Miss Control Freak." When Olivia opened her mouth to protest, Tessa held up a hand, palm out. "Don't even try to argue with me on that because we both know it's true." She waited while Olivia closed her mouth again. "Mm-hmm. As I was saying, let me put it simply. You, my dear, are a control freak, and this whole thing? This is completely out of your control."

Olivia waited for more. When it didn't come, she raised her eyebrows expectantly. "That's it?"

"That's it. You can't control the heart. People have been trying to do that since the damn dawn of time. Nobody has managed to."

"You can't control the heart? *That's* the advice you have for me?"

"No, my advice is to take a deep breath and stop worrying so much. If you like this girl and think you want more, then talk to her about it. Does she like you?"

The smile came all on its own. "Yeah. She does."

"Then it sounds like you have a date for New Year's Eve...which we need to talk about right now if you expect your guests to have anything to eat."

"Okay, okay." Olivia slid her tablet back in front of her. She didn't feel a ton better. She was still anxious. Confused. Wary. So wary. Hayley had breezed in out of nowhere, taken Olivia's job, fudged much of her responsibilities, and as much as Olivia had fought the attraction, Hayley had won her over. At least her body...

Oh, who was she kidding. Hayley had won over much of the rest of her as well. Quickly. So quickly, Olivia felt completely off-balance and once again thought it felt like the world had tilted just enough to make her slide a little bit to one side or a little bit to the other with each step she took, making it impossible for her to move forward in a straight line. It was driving her slightly mad.

She and Tessa finished things up, and Tessa hugged her tightly before she all but bolted back to her kitchen. Olivia didn't really have time to sit and ponder, and for that, she was grateful. She needed to stay busy, and there was certainly a lot to do.

Two parts of her battled between avoiding Hayley at all costs and actively seeking her out.

She settled for shooting her what she hoped was a smoldering look as she passed by the front desk where Hayley was helping Stephanie with incoming guests.

Judging by the way Hayley's cheeks colored, Olivia called it a win.

❖

Why couldn't every place he went be seventy-five degrees and sunny? It wasn't the first time Benton had pondered the silly question. And he knew the solution: He had enough money that he *could* move to someplace that was seventy-five degrees and sunny on a regular basis. He and Kerry had talked about retiring someplace nice. Someplace like Key West, where he was right now.

It was the last stop on his cruise, and he loved the artsy little island off the coast of Florida. He cruised a lot, and there were definitely stops where he didn't get off the ship to explore. He preferred to stay on board, work, have a cocktail, whatever. He wasn't interested in shopping. He wasn't a sightseeing kind of guy. But Key West was different. Key West was an attitude. A mood. He always got off the ship here and he always wandered the streets, stopping into various bars and restaurants, starting up conversations with the locals.

Kerry had loved it here. No, they'd never come over Christmas—there was no way she wanted to be away from her beloved Manhattan at this time of year—but they'd come to Key West on several occasions, and she'd fallen in love with its color, culture, atmosphere just as he had.

He sat at a bar in a small place completely open to the beach and savored the East Coast IPA, a beer the bartender had recommended. What was it about the ocean that he loved so much? Benton knew it wasn't uncommon for a person to feel peace and relaxation while on the beach listening to the waves. But it was uncommon for him to feel peace and relaxation anywhere. They weren't go-to feelings for him and never had been. But when he was near the ocean, when he could see the waves roll in and hear them crash against the shore, it was as if all his troubles and worries faded into the background and only the most important things became clear.

Key West was a sort of artist colony, and there were many galleries along the streets and pieces of art in various yards. Benton took another slug of his beer and noticed a man down the beach a bit. He had an easel set up in the sand and he sat facing the water, brush in hand, tipping himself to one side so he could see around his canvas, then sitting back up straight and stroking the brush across his work. Benton couldn't see the man's painting, but part of him wished he could.

A flash of movement caught his eye and he looked to the left and up. Another easel sat on a balcony of the building next to the bar. A woman wearing a flowing white shirt of some sort was also painting, facing the same direction as the man on the beach, doing the same look around her canvas, then painting.

It was the sun over the water, of course. The blazing yellow-orange ball hovering in the sky, causing the water to twinkle and glitter as if iridescent. In another hour or two, the beach would be crowded with people, as everybody in Key West cheered and drank to the sunset. For now, these two artists had some time.

Benton's mind went to his daughter. Honestly, she hadn't been off his mind all week. Not since the email she'd sent and the things she'd said in it. He'd been rolling that around in his head pretty much nonstop. But now, he was thinking about how Hayley was so much like Kerry. So much and in so many ways. Art and paintings always did this to him, sent him off on this particular tangent. Hayley was good. He knew that. He didn't tell her often—okay, he'd hardly ever told her—but she was. She had talent. It amazed him at times how his genes had ended up in such a creative soul as Hayley's. Benton could barely color in a coloring book.

The bartender got him a second beer but put this one in a plastic cup so Benton could go out onto the beach, and he wandered toward the water. His skin had bronzed nicely over the past week, and it occurred to him as he looked down at his own legs how much healthier he looked with a bit of a tan. Working in an office twelve to fifteen hours a day did nothing for his complexion except make sure he looked pasty.

When he was close enough that the ocean waves rolled over his bare feet, Benton simply stood and watched. Breathed. Remembered...

It was years ago. Him, Kerry, and Hayley. On a different beach, but still here in Key West. Miraculously, there had been few people that day, and the space felt like theirs and theirs alone. Hayley couldn't have been more than six, playing with her plastic toys in the sand, creating a pretty elaborate sandcastle for a kid whose age was still in the single digits. He sat in a lounge chair, head back, eyes closed, soaking in the warmth of the sun. Kerry was in the chair next to him, her hand in his across the space between them.

"Hey, Benny?" Kerry's voice was quiet, as if she didn't want to disturb the peace in the air.

"Hmm?" He'd opened his eyes and turned to her, his beautiful wife, as she took her sunglasses off. Her skin had tanned to a deep bronze, and her emerald one-piece bathing suit only accentuated the green of her eyes.

"This is the happiest I have ever been in my life." Her voice was still quiet, but it overflowed with emotion. "This moment. Right here."

As if on cue, Hayley looked up from her construction, a big smile on her face, and waved at them. "Hi, Mommy! Hi, Daddy!"

They waved back to their daughter in unison. "Hi, baby," Kerry called to her. When she turned back to Benton, her eyes shimmered with unshed tears. "One day, when I'm on my deathbed and looking back on my life, *this* is the moment I'll remember. *This* is the memory I'll take with me. You. Me. Her. Our family. It's the most important thing, Benny. *She* is the most important thing."

He'd listened to her. With a stroke of his thumb, he'd wiped away the one tear that had escaped down her cheek. He'd loved her so much right then. He'd loved her always, of course, but that moment was…intense. He hadn't thought about it in a long time, but there was something about this place, this time of year without her that turned him melancholy and cerebral.

She is the most important thing.

And it hit him.

He didn't know what exactly *it* was, but it hit him. Hard. Square in the chest like he'd caught a punch from a boxer. Made him step back to maintain his balance. He blinked as he looked out over the water. Blinked some more as he marveled over the fact that everything was suddenly so much clearer, and he had no idea why.

He did know, however, exactly what he needed to do.

He pulled out his cell and dialed, waited.

"You're on a ship, you're not supposed to be calling me." Susan's voice held the hint of a scolding, but she mostly sounded happy to hear from him. "Everything okay?"

"Everything is fine," Benton said, then amended his words. "No. Not fine. Great. Everything is great. Better than it's been in a long time."

"Wow. Well, that's definitely good to hear."

Benton poked the sand with his toe. "I need you to change my flight."

"Okay. To what?"

"To tomorrow. Out of Key West."

There was a moment of silence on Susan's end. Benton could almost hear the gears in her brain whirring. "You're sure everything's okay?"

"I promise. I'm heading back to the ship right now to collect my things. Get me a flight from here to whatever airport in New York gets me closest to Evergreen Hills."

"You got it." This time, he could hear the smile in Susan's voice, the unspoken joy and approval. "I'll let you know when everything is set."

"Thank you, Susan. For everything."

Benton slid his phone back into the pocket of his shorts and finished the last of his beer. He stood a few moments longer, looking at the ocean, listening to the waves. The beach was starting to fill up in anticipation of the sunset, the buzz of conversation around him increasing in volume, but he didn't care. He was content. Certain. About life, about his heart. He hadn't felt this calm and sure around anything but work since before Kerry was diagnosed, and he'd forgotten how good it felt. Also, strangely, he felt *her.* A definition escaped him—Her presence? Her essence? Her spirit? He normally didn't believe in such mumbo jumbo, but there wasn't a doubt in his mind. He felt Kerry, right there with him. So, there was that.

He allowed himself another minute or two to bask in the beauty of nature. Then he turned and headed back into the bar where he paid his tab. His walk back to the ship was brisk with excitement.

He had so much ground to make up.

CHAPTER TWENTY

This was Olivia's eighth New Year's Eve celebration at the Evergreen, and just like every year before, she was a mixture of excited, nervous, anxious, and joyful. There was so much to do. So much that needed to be monitored, directed, and managed that she barely had time to breathe, let alone eat. By late afternoon on Saturday, her stomach felt gurgly and she knew she needed to find some food to tide her over until the festivities began.

She wasn't the only one brimming with anticipation. She could feel it throughout the resort as she made her rounds. The spas were full and there were a couple of guests relaxing in the pool. The rooftop bar, where folks would watch the ball drop and count down to midnight, was well stocked and clean, the tabletops shining, the daylight beginning to wane outside. There were two bartenders on, Mike and a young guy named Ari. A third would arrive at six, which was a good thing, as there were already a dozen patrons seated in various spots. Also behind the bar was Hayley, tablet in hand, pointing at different bottles and chatting with Mike, their backs to her. Not wanting to interrupt, Olivia allowed herself ten seconds to enjoy the view, the way Hayley's black pants hugged her ass, how the matching blazer tapered in at the waist so nicely, how Hayley's hair was a waterfall of browns and golds cascading past her shoulder blades. A surge of arousal hit her, settling low in her body and causing a gentle throbbing there.

So. Yeah.

God.

With a hard swallow and a quick shake of her head, Olivia headed back downstairs before she was seen, and detoured, taking the back hall to Split Rail. Only a few tables had occupants, but that would change soon. Tessa was serving New Year's Eve dinner at eight, and a quick glance at the reservations told Olivia they were packed full. Thank God. They may not be booked, but people from Evergreen Hills had come through once again with their outside reservations for dinner. She gave the hostess a nod, then headed toward the kitchen, knowing it wasn't so much a beehive tonight as it was backstage at a huge production, and she needed to stay the hell out of everybody's way.

She found her usual corner and felt a small smile spread onto her face. Olivia loved watching the kitchen staff work like this, when there was a big meal or event about to happen. They were the epitome of a well-oiled machine. Somebody dropped a stainless steel bowl, which hit the floor with a clang, and then the entire staff shouted, "Oh-pa!" and went on with their work.

At the end of the steel prep table, Tessa glanced over and saw her. She held up a finger—the universal sign for "Hang on a second"—and disappeared into the walk-in refrigerator. She came out with a plate covered in plastic wrap and handed it to Olivia. A quick peek told her it was a turkey sandwich and a small bowl of Tessa's homemade cranberries. Olivia's mouth watered and she looked up at her friend in surprise.

"I've met you," Tessa said quickly. "I know you're running around like a crazy person and have probably had nothing but coffee." She made a shooing motion with her hand. "Go. Eat it. I'll see you later tonight."

"You're the best!" Olivia called out as Tessa was absorbed back into the fray.

Her walk back to the office was peppered with greetings to guests and short conversations with others, and what would normally take three minutes took closer to twenty. Olivia never avoided guests. She always stopped and made the time to listen to them, whether they had a complaint or just wanted to say hello. It was important to her to be approachable.

The shuttle bringing people back from Clearpeak Mountain had just emptied out, and the lobby was filled with people in various colors of coats and hats milling around. Some carried skis, some carried snowboards or snowshoes. Everybody seemed extra energetic, as often was the case when New Year's Eve approached. Finally getting past the crowd and shooting Stephanie one of their shorthand, "Do you need help?" looks—Stephanie gave a subtle shake of her head—she made it back to her office.

Dropping into her chair felt like all weight came off her shoulders in that moment, and Olivia just sat. Took a deep breath in and let it out slowly. Then she uncovered the plate and took a huge bite of the sandwich...which pulled moans of ecstasy from her as she chewed. How was it that Tessa could make something as simple as a turkey sandwich taste like heaven on a plate? Opening her desk drawer, she took out a spoon and dug into the cranberries.

More moaning.

Stephanie popped her head through the open doorway. "Everything okay in here?" she asked, eyebrows raised in expectation.

Olivia laughed and held up the sandwich.

"One of Tessa's?"

Olivia took another bite. Nodded.

"I figured." Stephanie turned to go, then came back. "Hey, can you forward me that email you sent last week on vacation schedules? I think I accidentally deleted it." She clenched her teeth and made an *oops* face.

"On it." A scoop of cranberries later, Olivia sat up straight and woke up her computer. A burst of laughter came from the front desk. She recognized Stephanie's but not the two others and figured they must be guests. She smiled at the sound, loving when her staff was enjoying themselves, especially on a day that could be so stressful.

Three clicks and she was looking at her Sent folder, scanning for the email she'd sent to Stephanie, when something else caught her eye. It was an email she'd sent to Hayley, and it had an attachment.

Except she couldn't remember sending Hayley anything lately that had an attachment. She went to the email itself, which had no subject line and no body, just her own standard signature that went at the bottom of all emails she sent: name, title, resort name, address, phone number, and email.

She clicked to open the attachment.

It blossomed onto her screen, and her brow furrowed. First, there was confusion as she looked at her own proposal for ways to improve things at the Evergreen. Her breakdown of each department. Her suggested ways to modernize. Her comparisons to other resorts of similar size. Her cost analysis. She'd spent months and months writing it up. Countless hours, both here and at home, on her own time.

It was obvious Hayley had emailed it to herself—who else would?—and Olivia remembered leaving it open earlier in the week when she'd been reviewing it and had been called away from her desk unexpectedly. What in the world would Hayley need it for? And why wouldn't she just ask Olivia for it?

She sat there, staring, for several moments, brow furrowed, head jumbled. And then her brain went to bad places. She couldn't stop it; it was like it had, ironically, a mind of its own. She started to think about Hayley's inexperience. Her incompetence with regard to how a resort was run. Her deer-in-the-headlights look at staff meetings. The complete blank she'd drawn when it came to the budget. What if she was worried about her job already? It was true she'd gotten better as weeks had gone by, but...what if she was getting pressure from Corporate and Olivia didn't know? What would Hayley do in that case? Would she go so far as to steal—

"Hey." As if Olivia had conjured her up, Hayley walked into the office wearing a big smile and looking—*God help me*—stupidly sexy. Her green eyes sparkled with obvious excitement. "The rooftop bar is good to go. It's going to be so cool up there tonight." She crossed through and toward her own office, still talking. "I need to make a couple of calls and then maybe we can talk about what we want to do tonight." She tossed a wink over her shoulder and disappeared into her office.

Olivia sat motionless, blinking at the empty doorway to Hayley's office. Her brain, which had been so quick to throw her every worst-case scenario possible, was now quiet. That was almost worse, as long moments went by and Olivia made no moves at all. Ten minutes. Fifteen. Twenty. She could hear Hayley chatting away with somebody on her phone, laughing that laugh that Olivia loved so much.

Okay. Stop it. Just ask her. What's the matter with you? Just. Ask. Her.

Yes. That was the right course of action. With a slight nod of determination, Olivia pushed her chair back from her desk, but was stopped short by a raised voice coming from the front desk.

"Markham. M-A-R-K-H-A-M." It was a woman's voice, and she

was obviously irritated and rapidly approaching annoyed. Olivia stood up and went out to see if Stephanie needed help.

The lobby was still bustling. The hum of conversation mixed with the sound of suitcases being wheeled along the granite floor to create a steady buzz. Three people stood in line behind the older gentleman Jacob was taking care of and the angry blonde across the desk from Stephanie. The woman was pretty, albeit heavily made up, her long, dark lashes far too lush to be real, accentuating bright blue eyes that might have been pretty if they weren't flashing with anger in the moment.

"Hi there," Olivia said, as she stepped next to Stephanie. "I'm Olivia Santini, the assistant manager here. Is there a problem?"

The woman sighed. "Apparently, yes. I'm trying to locate a guest of yours. Ms. Markham—"

"I told her we don't have anyone by that name checked in," Stephanie said, her own irritation clear to Olivia. Stephanie was always calm, cool, and collected, so Olivia wondered how long she'd been dealing with this woman before voices were raised.

"And I told *her* to look again. Because of course she's checked in. Her family owns the damn place. Markham Resorts?"

Stephanie looked to Olivia, who stared back at her.

The woman gestured to Stephanie's keyboard with her manicured hand, red nails flashing in the holiday lighting. "Look again. Hayley Markham. M-A-R-K—"

Olivia felt her eyebrows raise up toward her hairline as she did her best to understand, to compute what she was hearing. *Hayley* Markham? Well, that would be a weird coincidence...

"Oh, you know what?" the woman said, stopping Stephanie mid-type. "Sometimes she uses her mother's name if she's trying to fly under the radar. Try Boyd. Hayley Boyd." Then, suddenly, "*There* she is. Good God, babe, where have you been?"

Stephanie's fingers froze and she turned her head slowly toward Olivia, who turned to look toward the offices.

Hayley stood in the doorway, eyes wider than seemed possible, face blooming with bright red splotches, lips parted in a small "O."

Time stopped then.

Just stopped. Olivia felt like everybody had frozen around her and she was the only one able to move…except she couldn't. She could do nothing but stare into those green eyes she'd grown to look forward to seeing. To trust. To—yes. To love. And all Hayley did was stare back, looking just as confused and shell-shocked as Olivia felt. There was a beat, two, as their gazes held, and then it was as if somebody had hit the play button again and movement resumed.

"Where have you been?" the woman said to Hayley, coming around to the side of the desk where the doorway was and stepping through it without permission, without even asking for it.

"Why are you here?" Hayley asked, but her voice was so quiet, Olivia read it on her lips instead.

"I've been texting and calling. Did you lose your phone again?"

But Hayley wasn't looking at the woman any longer. She was looking at Olivia again. Olivia, whose feet were still, apparently, rooted to the floor. Hayley opened her mouth, then closed it again. She tilted her head to one side. It wasn't until she took a step toward her that a word finally escaped Olivia's mouth. Just one word. A question.

"Markham?" She said it quietly, but clearly.

Hayley pressed her lips together, rolled them in and bit down. She looked at the floor.

"I told you," the woman said. "Her family owns this place." There was a hint of pride in her voice as she smiled the kind of smile reserved for wealthy soap opera characters when they speak to a member of the hired help. A smile that was polite but didn't reach her eyes. A smile that said she was making an extra effort to speak to somebody beneath her, and that should be appreciated. Apparently done giving her attention to the staff, the woman turned back to Hayley, reached out her hand and wiggled her fingers, then took a step closer to Hayley and grabbed her hand. "Babe. Seriously, come here and kiss me. I haven't seen you in weeks."

Olivia's stomach churned sourly and there was a split second where she thought she might throw up right there on the floor of the lobby for all to see. She swallowed down the bile that had risen in her throat and just looked at Hayley. For her part, Hayley looked stunned, at a loss for words, and downright miserable.

She should.

Olivia had to get out of there or she was going to lose it in some way. Her heart was hammering in her chest and she felt like she couldn't get a full breath. How could this be happening? How had she not only not seen this coming, but never even suspected Hayley might not be telling the truth? Not only was she not who she said she was—*my God, she's part of the Markham family?*—but *she had a girlfriend.* Maybe they were married. How the hell would Olivia know? Hayley obviously hadn't told her the truth from day one.

"Excuse me," Olivia said quietly as she pushed past the woman, sidling by in an attempt not to touch her.

"Olivia, wait." It was Hayley, but Olivia couldn't bear to look.

Once she was through the door, it was all she could do not to run, not to sprint as far and as fast as she could away from that desk. Away from the expressions of surprise. Away from the glimpses of a possible future she'd stupidly allowed herself to see.

Away from Hayley.

She speed-walked, keeping her head down, until she got to the only place she knew that she wouldn't be seen or walked in on or heard. A small supply closet in the back of the building on the way to the maintenance area. She opened the door with her master key card, went inside, and shut it behind her. She left the light off. The smells of cleaning solutions assaulted her—bleach, lemon-scented furniture polish, hand soap. But Olivia didn't care. The only thing she was aware of was the rising tide of grief that wouldn't be held back any longer and she finally let it out, opening her mouth wide in a silent scream of pain as the tears came and her knees buckled and she sat on the floor.

And she cried.

CHAPTER TWENTY-ONE

"What the hell are you doing here?"
Hayley said it quietly but fiercely, through clenched teeth and with clenched fists. She couldn't get the image of Olivia's face out of her head, her disbelief, the look of betrayal, the way her sparkling eyes dimmed. All of that happened while she looked right at Hayley. The realization of what she'd done had hit Hayley hard, went right down to the pit of her stomach and sat there like a rock. If the walls of the office had started to literally crumble around her in that moment, Hayley wouldn't have been even a little bit surprised. Her entire world was imploding and there wasn't a damn thing she could do about it, because she'd caused it all.

Guinevere stood there looking a multitude of things. Stunned. Hurt. Insulted. Wide-eyed. All of that shifted a bit until anger was added to the mix. "Do *not* talk to me like that," she said, a low almost growl. They were both aware that Stephanie, Jake, and the others in line might not have been looking at them, but ears were open and working, and Hayley did *not* need everybody in the lobby witnessing her emotion. At least, not any more of it.

Her hand on Guin's elbow, she tugged her—not gently—through the front desk area, through Olivia's office, and into hers where she shut the door. Then she whirled on her.

"What the *fuck*, Guin?" At Guinevere's widened eyes and slight lean back as if avoiding a blow, Hayley went on. "What are you doing?"

At one time, Hayley had found Guinevere Aston very attractive. Her blond hair was pin straight, bluntly cut in a bob that angled up from her jawline. Her eyes were large, brilliant blue and wide-set. Her nose was perfect, thanks to a nose job five years ago. She wasn't tall but had a very nice figure from years of yoga and Pilates. An admirable fashion sense was icing on the physical appearance cake. Guin definitely turned heads when she walked into a room, and she had turned Hayley's once, long ago. But not anymore.

"I have been texting you." Guin's voice held an edge of indignation. "I have called. I have been worried sick."

Hayley sighed. "You haven't been worried sick. Serena told you I was fine."

Guinevere wasn't able to catch the quick flash of surprise that zipped across her face. "I see."

"What, you thought my best friend wasn't going to tell me you were hounding her about me?" Hayley sighed, understanding that it might have become unbearable for Serena. "Did she tell you I was here?"

Guinevere at least had the decency to look slightly embarrassed. "I may have overheard her talking to somebody, and I put two and two together." Then she straightened and waved a dismissive hand. "But that's not the point here. The point is you've practically ghosted me. Why?" It was as if her face couldn't decide between a hurt expression or an angry one, so it tried to do both, and the result seemed a bit unnerving. "I thought we had something."

It became clear to Hayley right then, in that very moment. Finally. It was possible Guinevere would never understand, wasn't it? That she would just...never get it. That something in her brain wouldn't allow her to actually hear the words being said. Was that a possibility? Could Hayley do or say anything at all to make herself clear?

All Hayley wanted to do was go find Olivia. Explain. Beg. Plead. God, she'd get down on her knees if she had to. But she was not going to leave things like this, with Olivia thinking she was a lying, deceptive imposter.

Even though that's exactly what I am.

The sudden feeling of utter hopelessness and defeat drained her energy so quickly, she had an instant of wondering if she'd died. Had a stroke or an aneurysm or simply ceased to exist. Hayley dropped into her chair, and the breath left her lungs as if she'd had it knocked out of her.

"Honey? You okay?" Guinevere squatted next to the chair, laying the back of her hand across Hayley's forehead as if she was a child with a fever. Hayley pushed the hand away.

"You have to stop calling me honey," she said quietly, doing her best to keep any irritation or edge out of her voice. She was frustrated and angry at Guin, yes, but she wasn't an asshole. "I'm not your honey or your babe or your sweetheart. We do *not* have something. You are *not* my girlfriend. We dated a few times. We made out once. That's all." She forced herself to look into Guin's eyes, even as they filled with tears. It was the least she could do. "I'm sorry."

"But there was that time..." Guin stood up and kept talking, walked around the office picking things up and setting them back down.

Hayley let her voice fade until it was nothing more than background noise. She had to let Guinevere work through it; she owed her that much for not being clear enough from the start. She should've listened to Serena months ago. A glance at her watch told her it was nearing six. There was so much to check on for tonight, and she knew she couldn't sit here listening to Guin forever. She needed to give her a time limit.

God, she needed to talk to Olivia.

❖

Olivia had no idea how long she sat in the dark supply closet, but she'd finally stopped crying. Man, she had started to worry that maybe she wouldn't. That maybe she'd just cry forever and never be able to stop.

But she had.

Her eyes were scratchy and her nose was running and she was certain her face was a big, splotchy mess, but at some point, she had to go back out front and do her job, and she'd have to face Hayley sooner or later.

Goddamn it, she knew she shouldn't have gotten involved. She knew it! Everything in her had warned her not to get caught up. Not to be sucked in by Hayley's charm, by Hayley's beauty, or by her own loneliness. How could she have been so stupid? Olivia considered herself a strong woman, but this? This was a lot. This was too much.

Hayley was a *Markham*? God, she'd never in a million years seen that coming. And why wouldn't Hayley have told her? Why was that a secret? Was Markham Resorts running a test of some sort like that show...what was it? *Undercover Boss*? Was that it? But a test for what? And had Olivia failed?

God, of course she'd failed. She'd slept with her boss. Duh.

Olivia used a nearby metal shelf to haul herself to her feet. There was so much running through her head right now. Through her heart. Confusion, mostly. Confusion and hurt because she didn't understand what had happened. She didn't understand any of it. At all. And she wanted to. She desperately needed to. But it was almost six, and things were happening in the Evergreen and she was in charge. Well. Sort of in charge. She was in charge behind Hayley *Markham*, who... Olivia stopped. Felt her brow furrow. Did Hayley actually *not* know how to run a resort, or was that just an act? Another lie to add to the pile?

My God, what a mess.

She snatched a tissue out of the box she'd opened and used it to blot her face, blow her nose. She couldn't remember a time in her life when her brain had ever felt so crammed full of disconcerting information, and she felt like it was literally about to leak out of her ears.

Her phone buzzed. Stephanie.

Where are you?

Olivia sighed. She took a moment to get her bearings before typing a response. *Near maintenance. Needed a minute.*

"Okay, Liv," she whispered to herself as she blew her nose one more time. "Pull it together. There's work to be done. You've gotta shelve all this crap for a later time. Just...pull it together." Inhaling slowly through her nose, she filled up her lungs and held it for a beat. She slowly blew it out through her mouth, reached for the doorknob, and let herself out of the supply closet and into the hallway...

...where she nearly ran right into Stephanie.

"There you are," Stephanie said, not missing a beat and making no indication that she thought it was strange to find her boss exiting a closet. "Are you okay?"

Not wanting to get into it, Olivia tipped her head from one side to the other and shrugged. "I'm fine for now."

"Well, good." Stephanie took her elbow and steered her back toward the front of the building. "Because there's a man from Markham Corporate here."

With a slight roll of her eyes that happened before she could catch it, Olivia said, "Why not just send him to Hayley?"

"He's specifically asking for you."

"He is?" That was a surprise. Olivia was pretty sure people at Corporate barely knew her name, let alone would come here to speak to her in particular. Olivia wasn't a nervous person—she was pretty calm and cool in stressful situations—but the nerves kicked in right then. She swallowed down the lump of anxiety that had formed, chewed on the inside of her cheek. What could this man want? Corporate rarely visited. The manager went to meetings twice a year with the higher-ups, but that had never been Olivia. Roger had always gone. When he'd come back, he'd have new policies or budget revisions to share with her. But she couldn't remember the last time somebody from Corporate actually showed up in Evergreen Hills.

Was he here to fire her?

It didn't make a lot of sense. Wouldn't they just have Hayley do it? She was Olivia's superior, after all. Unless… Olivia closed her eyes and swallowed hard. Unless they knew that she and Hayley had a sexual relationship, and that led them to believe that Hayley wasn't in any position to let her go. Maybe they were both going to get fired!

Her brain was running away with her. Olivia knew that, but she couldn't seem to stop it. The worst-case scenarios in her head, impossibly, just kept getting worse.

They walked quickly, Olivia and Stephanie, their shoes clicking along the floor, Olivia doing her best to smile at guests as they passed. She had a job to do, despite the turmoil her head and heart were now in, and goddamn it, she would do it. Right up until the bitter end.

They rounded the corner and Stephanie picked up her pace, scooting back behind the front desk to help Jake. Luckily, aside from the older couple he was waiting on, there was nobody in line. The atmosphere was still festive throughout the lobby, the holiday lights twinkling—both inside and outside—now that it was dark. Guests all decked out in their party clothes flowed from the elevators past the front desk and around toward Split Rail, where Mike was running a big happy hour with tons of drink specials before dinner.

Olivia looked at Stephanie, who gestured with her chin toward a gentleman in a suit who stood, one hand in his trouser pocket, the other holding a black leather briefcase. He stood gazing out the lobby window. From the back, he had thick salt-and-pepper hair and broad shoulders.

Straightening her frame so she stood as tall as possible, she took a deep, fortifying breath and approached him.

"Excuse me?"

He turned to look at her, his light brown eyes soft. He smiled at her, vaguely familiar somehow.

"I was told you were asking for me. I'm Olivia Santini, assistant manager." She held out her hand and he grasped hers. As he shook it, he said the last words in the world she expected to hear.

"It's so nice to finally meet you, Ms. Santini. I'm Benton Markham."

She blinked at him, speechless. This wasn't just "a guy from Corporate." This wasn't even "*a* bigwig from Corporate." Benton Markham was *the* bigwig at Corporate. Founder. President and CEO. He'd built Markham Resorts from the ground up and into a Fortune 500 company. The man was a business legend.

And now he was standing in front of her, smiling and shaking her hand, and she couldn't seem to make a single word come out of her mouth for a good ten seconds. Finally—*finally*—she found her voice. "It's an honor to meet you, sir, and welcome to the Evergreen." Suddenly, everything in the world about the Evergreen ran through her head. Were the floors clean enough? How about the windows? Were the valets wearing their entire uniforms, including the hats they all hated? Had Jake been polite and helpful to the guest while Markham was within earshot? Somehow, she managed to yank herself back to the moment at hand. "What can I help you with, sir?"

Markham looked around. "Is there someplace we can talk? A conference room or…?" He left the sentence for her to finish.

Olivia's first thought was her office, but it was small and possibly messy, and a conference room was a much better idea. She hesitated for a second before asking, "Should I get our manager to accompany us?"

He shook his head. "No, no need. Just you."

"Okay. Follow me." She led Markham back toward the front desk where she introduced Stephanie, who somehow managed to keep her face carefully blank, though Olivia could see the wideness of her eyes. "We'll be in the conference room around the corner."

"You're not fully booked," Markham said, as he walked next to

Olivia, and she felt her heart drop. "But it seems you've got a really nice crowd." The way to the conference room took them past Split Rail, so he could see all the patrons in the restaurant and at the bar.

Relieved, she nodded. "We have a really good reputation with the local residents and we get a lot of them in for dinners and holiday events. Our rooftop bar is also pretty full. People will be up there at midnight to watch the fireworks display."

"You'll have to show me after we sit down."

Okay, that seemed at least a little bit positive, right? He wouldn't fire her and then expect her to show him around more. Would he?

Olivia used her master key card and let them into the small conference room and closed the door behind them. They each took a seat. Markham set his briefcase on the table and loud snaps cut through the air as he opened the fasteners. From inside, he pulled out a folder, and from that folder, a small stack of papers.

Wordlessly, he slid the papers toward Olivia and pulled out a second small stack—which she assumed was a duplicate—for himself.

When she looked down at the top sheet, her blood ran cold. It was a printout of an email. The recipient was Benton Markham. The sender was Hayley Boyd. The body of the email consisted of one sentence.

Here's the report we discussed.
—H

And below that was Olivia's entire proposal for changes to the Evergreen, complete with cost analysis and budgeting suggestions. Hayley had done exactly what Olivia had thought: She'd taken Olivia's work and sent it in to Corporate on her own.

Benton Markham folded his hands on top of his papers and looked at Olivia, his eye contact intense. "I'd like to talk about this."

CHAPTER TWENTY-TWO

"Guin. Listen." Hayley stood up, crossed the office to where Guinevere now stood, and reached out and touched her upper arm. She looked a little bit lost, a little bit confused, and a little bit sad. Briefly, Hayley wondered if she would've preferred Guin to be angry because then maybe she herself would've felt better. Less guilty. Less awful. Guinevere faced her, forced a watery smile, her blue eyes much dimmer than they'd been earlier.

"It's okay," she said quietly. She nodded once, and it was obvious it took effort on her part to keep the smile in place. "I jumped in with both feet. Way too fast." She lifted one shoulder in a half shrug and let go of a bitter chuckle. "It's kind of what I do."

A million things zipped through Hayley's mind in that moment, a million responses, a million things to say to make Guin feel better. But she stopped herself, because she knew that anything remotely positive or anything that attempted to contradict what Guin had observed about herself would open the door just enough for her to kick her way in. That was the last thing Hayley wanted. So she said the only thing she could think of. "I'm sorry."

Guinevere tipped her head to the side and again tried to smile. "I know."

They stood quietly, eye to eye, for what seemed like a long time. Finally, Guinevere took a deep breath and seemed to visibly shake off her sadness. She glanced at the expensive watch on her slim wrist.

"Well, if I leave now, I can probably get to Carlo's party in time for midnight." Hayley had no doubt Guinevere would easily find somebody to kiss when the ball dropped. She wouldn't be alone for long. She never was.

"The roads should be pretty clear, yeah?" *When all else fails, talk about the weather or the driving conditions.* Hayley internally rolled her eyes at herself.

"They should, yes." They stood for another moment, then Guinevere stepped forward and wrapped Hayley in a hug. The familiar floral scent of her designer perfume filled Hayley's nostrils as she hugged her back. Not too tightly, but not too loosely. "You take care of yourself, Hayley," Guin said softly, her lips close to Hayley's ear. When they parted, she held on to Hayley's shoulders. "And fix whatever mess you made with that girl."

Hayley felt her eyebrows raise up toward her hairline.

Guin gave a snort. "Please. I saw how you looked at her." Picking up her coat from the chair where she'd draped it, she slid an arm into a sleeve. "You should go find her. It's New Year's Eve." With that, she gave another tentative smile and took her leave.

Hayley followed her out of the office, staying a few steps behind, and Guinevere never looked back as she made her way across the lobby, through the small groupings of guests. Some were moving, some were standing in little cliques and talking, but the feeling in the air was palpable. Excitement. Anticipation. Joy.

She had to find Olivia.

Stephanie was poking at keys on her keyboard as she checked in a guest, her back to Hayley. Stepping up behind her, Hayley asked quietly enough so only Stephanie could hear her, "Do you know where Olivia is?"

Stephanie turned to look at her and held her gaze. Hayley swallowed hard beneath it, as this was so very obviously what she would call a mama-bear stare.

"I know," Hayley said. "I know. I really need to talk to her."

Stephanie stared for another beat or two before giving in, obviously not happy to. "A guy from Corporate showed up to talk to her." She turned back to her keyboard and poked more keys.

Hayley's brow furrowed. "From Corporate? Why didn't you tell me?"

The poking stopped. The stare returned. "Because he didn't ask for you. He asked for Olivia."

Hayley blinked at her, having no idea what to make of this information, wondering why her father—or somebody—hadn't given her a heads-up. "And?" she asked Stephanie. "Where are they?"

"Conference room." Stephanie turned back to the guest and spoke to him with cheerful apology.

Conference room. Hayley bolted out from behind the front desk and hurried across the lobby, dodging and weaving, smiling at guests but doing her best to move quickly enough that she wouldn't be expected to stop and chat. People were coming in through the glass double doors of the front entrance. Some milled around, some joined what seemed like a flowing river of bodies heading for Split Rail. Any other time, Hayley might have stopped and marveled at how busy they were. But right now, all she wanted was to see Olivia, to look in her eyes, to explain.

God, what if she can't forgive me?

Hayley didn't want to think about that, but she knew it was a possibility. She'd lied. A lot. Right to Olivia's face. On more than one occasion. Yes, she had good reason, but still. A lie was a lie. Lies broke trust, and Olivia had trusted her. How was she going to come back from that?

The simmering anger she felt toward her father when all of this began seemed to heat up until it was closer to a boil. As she reached the conference room door, she thought about how she was going to have some choice words for him the next time she saw him. That was for sure. She took a deep breath, rapped on the door with her knuckles, then turned the knob and entered the room—and stopped dead in her tracks.

Blinked.

Stared.

Blinked some more.

"Hello, Hayley," he said, from where he sat at the table across from Olivia.

Hayley swallowed hard, found her voice. "Hi, Dad."

Olivia's dark eyes went so wide it was almost comical. "Dad?" she asked, in glaringly obvious disbelief. She pointed across the table at Benton Markham. "This is your *father*?"

And right then, Hayley realized that was yet one more lie added to the giant pile in the middle of the room.

"Jesus, Dad, you didn't tell her?"

Something weird happened then, something Hayley had never seen in her entire life. Her father, Benton Markham, self-made millionaire and head of one of the biggest resort empires in the country, looked chagrined. And ashamed. And sorry.

Before Hayley could get her bearings, before she could wrap her brain around that weird turn of events, it got weirder. He stood up, took the four steps to reach her, and wrapped her in a tight hug without saying a word.

She almost struggled. She almost tried to wiggle out of his grasp. It had been so long since she'd felt her father's arms around her, holding her, protecting her, that it seemed foreign. Wrong somehow. But seconds went by and he held on. Then more seconds. And Hayley felt herself slowly relax. The familiar spicy scent of his aftershave—the same one he'd worn ever since Hayley could remember—enveloped them, spoke to her of love and safety like it had when she was little.

What is happening?

Then she felt him press a kiss to the top of her head, stroke her hair with his big hand, and she was mortified to feel tears spring into her eyes. She swallowed hard, got herself just about under control, and then he yanked the emotional rug right out from underneath her.

"I'm sorry, Hayley," he said. His lips moved against her hair, and his voice was so quiet and gentle, Hayley wondered if Olivia could hear him at all or if she was still simply sitting there in confused anger. "I'm so sorry for everything. I've been so hard on you—some of it deserved, mind you," and he chuckled at that, "but mostly not. I just…" He stopped talking and Hayley could hear him swallow.

She pulled back to look up into his eyes and was shocked to see unshed tears shimmering there. "Dad…"

He didn't let go of her, but shifted his gaze toward the ceiling in what seemed to be an attempt to collect himself. "I miss your mother so much," he said as he returned his gaze to her, and Hayley felt her own tears well up, her own lump lodge itself in her throat. "And you are *so much* like her. You look like her. God, you *sound* like her. You're stubborn like her." They both grinned at that. "I know I haven't handled that well. I couldn't. It was just…it was too hard. But…" He hesitated and Hayley waited patiently, somehow understanding how difficult saying these words to her was for him. "I forgot that you lost her, too. You know? I was so caught up in my own grief, so flattened by it, that I couldn't seem to remind myself that I had you. That you'd lost your mom and could really use your dad around to help with that." He looked down at his shoes then, shaking his head slowly.

Hayley blinked several times, her own tears spilling over and down her cheeks as she stood there, trying to reconcile how she'd never, ever in her life seen her father look the way he did in that moment: ashamed.

"Do you remember our trips to Key West when you were little?" Hayley nodded, not trusting her voice.

"I was there yesterday. I was standing on the beach, looking out at the water, and I could see you playing in the sand. In your little frilly pink bathing suit with your plastic toys, working so hard on your sandcastle, your little tongue poking out while you concentrated. And as I stood there, lost in my own memories, I heard your mother's voice." He looked at Hayley, his dark eyes wide with surprise. "Like she was standing right next to me, I *heard* her, and she reminded me of what's important in life."

Hayley couldn't speak. Couldn't find words. Couldn't find her voice.

"I came here today for two reasons. The biggest one was to ask your forgiveness. For not being there for you since she passed. For making things harder on you. For not listening to you. I love you so much, Hayley. I need you to know that." He cleared his throat, and his voice went very, very quiet. "Can you ever forgive me?"

They were words Hayley hadn't even realized she'd been waiting for, waiting to hear. "Of *course* I can." She stepped back into his arms, wrapped her own around him. "I love you. You're my *dad*. Of *course* I can."

Hayley wasn't sure how long they stayed like that, father and daughter in a warm, loving embrace. She'd have happily stayed that way for hours, making up for lost time. Finally, she loosened her grip on him, extricated herself, and took a step back so she could look up into his eyes. He smiled down on her with more love than she'd felt from him in much too long.

Something occurred to her then. "What was the second reason?"

His thick, dark brows knit together above his nose. "Pardon?"

"You said you came here for two reasons. What was the second one?"

"Oh!" His eyes went wide and his face lit up as he turned back to the table and began shuffling through papers.

Hayley felt something akin to a jolt of surprise as she remembered that Olivia was still sitting there. She was chewing on her bottom lip and looked slightly uncomfortable. Because why wouldn't she? She met Hayley's eyes and Hayley gave her a small smile. She did not return it.

"The second reason," her father said, as he sat back down, "was to meet this woman whose praises you sang so loudly."

That got Olivia's attention. Her dark brows lifted and she sat up a little straighter in her chair as she cleared her throat. "I'm sorry?"

Benton tapped a finger on the packet of papers he'd given to Olivia where it still sat on the table in front of her. "Yes, absolutely. Hayley emailed this to me earlier in the week. She told me how hard you'd worked on it, how much the Evergreen means to you. She said you're the one who should have the manager job." He glanced down at his own copy, flipping through a couple of pages. "She's not wrong. This is excellent work."

Olivia made no comment, just sat there looking dumbstruck. Blinking. Hayley had to admit that she liked seeing Olivia surprised in a good way.

Hayley's father folded his hands and placed them on the table, a move she knew meant *serious talk* was coming.

"I'm going to be completely up front with you, Ms. Santini. I haven't had a lot of faith in this resort. It's been the last one on my mind for a long time, and I've been entertaining the idea of either shutting it down or selling it off or both for more than a year now."

If that surprised Olivia, she hid it well. Hayley stood off to the side watching her face. Her expression stayed neutral. Her body language didn't change. She gave one nod.

"But reading your proposal, your suggested updates, your ways to improve profit ratios as well as the cost analysis you included…" Benton smiled, and Hayley recognized it as genuine, not one of his sharklike smiles he reserved for the moment he was about to eat somebody alive. "I've changed my mind."

Olivia blinked and her brows raised again, this time clearly broadcasting her surprise, and rather than keeping her focus on Benton, she turned a shocked look toward Hayley—who felt the same way and took a step back to regain her equilibrium, as she felt suddenly off-balance.

"What?" Hayley asked.

Her father nodded and seemed absurdly pleased with himself and the reactions of the two women in the room. He held up the report. "I wasn't kidding when I said this was excellent work. You were right to send it directly to me. I have no idea how it kept getting lost among my staff. You can bet I'm going to do a little investigating around that."

He looked from Hayley to Olivia and back, his smile still wide and still firmly in place. Then he put both palms on the table and pushed himself to his feet. "Listen, it's New Year's Eve and I know you two, as managers, have a lot to take care of. I'm going to get out of your hair, but I've decided to stay until Monday morning. I know tomorrow is a holiday, but I'd like to sit down with you and go over your new position, if you don't mind."

He was talking to Olivia, and for only the second time since Hayley had entered the room, she spoke. "I was planning on working tomorrow anyway, so I'm happy to meet with you."

"Perfect. I'll text you in the morning. Meantime..." He snapped his briefcase shut. "I'm going to go check out Split Rail. The reviews on Yelp are stellar."

"I recommend the filet," Olivia said as she stood up and held her hand out to Benton. "Sir, I just want to say thank you so much. I'm still in a state of shock here, but I'll be in better shape when we meet tomorrow. I promise."

Hayley watched her father shake Olivia's hand, and it was weird how perfect everything suddenly felt. Well. Almost everything.

"I'll see you later?" he asked, as he sidled past Hayley and put his hand on the doorknob. She nodded and then he was gone and she was alone in the room with Olivia.

CHAPTER TWENTY-THREE

So," Hayley said and made a face that came off as half smile, half grimace.

"So," Olivia said, not sure where to even begin. Her head ached, it was so full of shock, questions, confusion, delight, disbelief.

They stood.

They stared.

"You're a Markham." Olivia said it quietly, barely above a whisper. At Hayley's nod, she added, "Not just a Markham, you're the daughter of *the* Markham."

"Yes."

More silence.

"You could have told me," Olivia finally said, voicing the largest issue for her in five simple words.

"I know." Hayley looked down at her shoes.

"You *should* have told me." A much more accurate statement.

"I know," Hayley said again.

"And your girlfriend?" Olivia tried not to sneer the last word. She wasn't entirely successful.

"She's not my girlfriend. And she's gone now."

"Mm-hmm." More silence. More standing and staring. Olivia swallowed the lump that had suddenly appeared in her throat. "You should have told me," she repeated. She really was at a loss for any words beyond those. Her stomach felt sour, and she could feel a headache starting in the base of her skull.

"I know." Hayley nodded. "You're right. I should have. There were reasons, though."

"Oh, really? Reasons for hiding your true identity? Are you a superhero?"

"No." Hayley's scoff wasn't sarcastic, it seemed more self-deprecating. "My father wanted me to show him that I could be responsible, that I deserved to be a part of the family business *without* getting special treatment because of my name. He put a freeze on my spending."

Olivia felt the surprise roll through her but wasn't sure she bought the story. "Wow. What did you do to warrant that?"

Hayley sighed and Olivia's phone vibrated. "It's a long story and I will gladly tell you, but we've got to handle things around here first. It's a busy night."

She was right, Olivia knew that, but a big part of her didn't want to stop the conversation here. Now. She had so many unanswered questions. So many things she needed to say. A new job to prepare for. Her phone buzzed again and she glanced at it. An issue in housekeeping, apparently.

"What's going on?" Hayley asked, indicating the phone.

"Housekeeping is shorthanded."

"I'll take care of it."

"Really?"

Hayley nodded. "Yeah, I got it. Go over to Split Rail. I know you said your mom's coming for dinner. Go mingle. I'll take care of housekeeping and whatever else there is." She stopped talking, swallowed hard, wet her lips—which Olivia watched.

Olivia was furious with her, but that insane attraction she had didn't seem to be affected at all, and that ticked her off. She had to tear her gaze away. "Okay." She made a move for the door but was stopped by Hayley's hand on her arm.

"Wait." Hayley didn't speak until Olivia looked her in the eye. "Would you meet me at the rooftop bar later? Please?"

Those green eyes were pleading with her, the expression on her face one of regret and apology and sadness and worry. Olivia wanted to say no, wanted to tell Hayley what she could do with all her lies and deception.

But she couldn't.

Goddamn it, she just couldn't.

"Fine," she said, on an exhale. And then, she had to get out of there. Away from Hayley so she could catch her breath and regroup. She didn't look back as her heels clicked down the hall toward the buzzing of commotion and festive conversation and the whole time she walked, only one question rang through her brain.

What the hell had just happened?

❖

Split Rail was bustling. Not completely packed, but very close to it. Only a few tables were unoccupied. The bar was taken up and people were standing behind those sitting on the barstools. It was loud but not unbearably so, and the heavenly aromas wafting up from plates and from the kitchen made Olivia's mouth water, despite the fact that she was sure her roiling stomach wouldn't allow her to eat.

She put on her happy manager face, aware that her name tag was visible, and smiled at guests as she passed. She stopped to chat with regulars she knew as well as locals who'd come in for dinner. It turned out to be a good way of taking her mind off the current turmoil in her brain and in her heart.

Olivia finished checking in with the Barnards—a couple she knew because Mrs. Barnard had been her English teacher in high school—making sure their dinner was to their liking (it was). Then she craned her neck to see if she could find her mother. It was almost seven, and she'd told Olivia she'd be there by six thirty. Olivia pushed herself to her tiptoes to see over a group of friends standing near the bar, and finally she saw her mother at the corner of the bar, talking animatedly to somebody. Her smile was big. Radiant. It made Olivia smile to see it, and she sidled past customers as she made her way to her mother... and then stopped.

"There you are," Angela said, reaching out a hand to Olivia. She had half a martini in front of her and her cheeks were flushed, leading Olivia to believe it probably wasn't her first one.

Olivia took Angela's hand and reluctantly let herself be pulled toward her mother.

"This is my oldest daughter," Angela said, to the man in the expensive suit she'd been chatting with. The man who had apparently been making her smile so big.

"Olivia is your daughter?" Benton Markham said, his eyes

widening for a split second, then settling to a twinkle. He chuckled, and his grin looked so much like Hayley's right then, Olivia caught her breath. "We met not an hour ago."

"You did?" Olivia's mom looked puzzled as her eyes went from Olivia to Benton and back.

"We did. Mama, this is Benton Markham. The CEO of Markham Resorts." She cleared her throat. "And, also, Hayley's father."

"Hayley's father—what?" She was clearly confused, but Olivia didn't have it in her to explain. Everything was so raw, and there was a moment—a horrifying moment—when Olivia thought she might start crying right there in front of them.

"Yeah, it's a long story." She squeezed her mother's shoulder. "Listen, I need to take care of some stuff. New Year's Eve is so busy. But I'll see you on the roof later?" Her mother nodded as Olivia bent to kiss her cheek. Then she escaped. She had no choice; she had to get away and think. Absorb. Deal.

She wished badly to be able to sit down with Tessa and spill the whole story, but she knew the kitchen was a bustling madhouse of activity tonight and there was no way she could expect Tessa to stop what she was doing and help manage her emotional tornado.

Mike was behind the bar, martini shaker in hand, pretending he didn't see the admiring glances of some of the women, which made Olivia smile. Mike caught her eye as he strained the drink into a glass, added a garnish, and handed it over. Without a word, he pulled out a shot glass, filled it with the mango habanero whiskey he knew Olivia loved, and slid it her way. At her raised eyebrows, he simply said, "You look like you could use this." Then he was off to take another order.

He wasn't wrong.

Olivia picked up the glass and downed the shot, savoring the sweet taste of the mango, waiting for the kick from the habanero on the back end. She set the shot glass back on the bar and left Split Rail, feeling the slight burn from the whiskey on her tongue, the alcohol settling into her blood and calming her as she walked back to her office.

She prayed Hayley wasn't there, because she didn't know where else to go. She needed to be available to do her job but couldn't imagine putting on a happy face with Hayley right now. She needed a little time to sit and sift through her head. She crossed the lobby, feeling Stephanie's concerned eyes on her as she came behind the front desk. A squeeze of reassurance to Stephanie's shoulder, and she went back into her office. Her prayer was answered, as she was alone, and she dropped into her chair as if she hadn't sat in days.

There was so much to contemplate, so much to roll around in her head that she didn't even know where to begin. It was mind-blowing, really.

Hayley had lied to her. About her identity. About why she was there. About who she really was.

Did she lie about her feelings for Olivia as well?

That was the big question. Was it all a lie? Was Olivia some pawn in Hayley's daddy issues? Was she something Hayley had used to blow off steam? Was everything an act? Could she have been pretending the whole time?

As Olivia's eyes welled up, her gaze landed on the painting Hayley had given her for Christmas. *God, was that only a week ago?* She allowed herself to focus on it, to study it. The colors and the detail and *the love*. That was the thing that stood out. Olivia's love for Walter was so apparent. Could Hayley have painted that if she didn't actually feel something for her? Was it possible to fake emotion that was so obvious in a piece of art?

The questions plagued Olivia. She knew she needed to focus on something else. She'd thought taking some time alone to absorb it all would be helpful, but it was making things worse.

Her phone buzzed and she snatched it out of her blazer pocket. Lenny needed her in maintenance.

"Thank freaking God," she mumbled, as she jumped up from her chair and beelined out of the office. She hoped Lenny's problem was a big one, then made a face at herself for that.

But seriously. Anything to take her mind off Hayley.

It was New Year's Eve. In a few hours, the slate was wiped clean and everybody had a chance to start fresh.

Somehow, that didn't make her feel any better.

CHAPTER TWENTY-FOUR

It was nearly eleven thirty.

Any problems that had arisen and needed Olivia's attention had been dealt with. Everything else could wait until tomorrow. She was officially calling herself off the clock, even though she never really considered herself that, especially if she was still on the premises. She'd left her blazer with her name tag on it draped over the back of her chair in her office and headed up to the rooftop bar in black slacks and a white button-down top. She'd rolled up her sleeves and ordered herself an extra-dirty martini with three gorgonzola-stuffed olives as soon as she walked in.

The place looked beautiful. Twinkling lights, soft holiday music, tons of windows with the outdoor Christmas lights visible from any spot in the room. Fresh pine garland with tiny lights was draped lushly everywhere—on the windowsills, along the front of the bar, lining the lit shelves behind it—and the big, full tree in the corner still looked like it had just been chopped down that morning. The whole place smelled of pine and cinnamon, and the festive atmosphere let Olivia relax. At least a little bit.

"I was wondering when you'd get here." Olivia's mom suddenly appeared at her elbow holding a glass of white wine. She put an arm around Olivia's waist and gave her a gentle squeeze.

"Now." Olivia sipped her drink, which was deliciously strong and burned its way down her throat.

Angela looked at the drink and raised an eyebrow. "A martini, huh? That can't be good."

Olivia's eyes tracked the room, watched the different groupings of people. "What do you mean?"

"I mean I have only ever seen you order a martini when something is bothering you. I asked you about it once and you said, and I quote, 'Numbs my soul, Mama. Sometimes, I need that.'"

Olivia couldn't help but smile at the vocal impression her mother did of her, furrowing her brow and lowering her voice. "Yeah. Well."

When Olivia glanced at her, Angela was holding up a finger toward somebody at the bar, signaling, "I'll be there in a minute."

Following her mother's gaze, Olivia saw Benton Markham ordering drinks, and she let her shoulders sink a bit. "You guys an item now?" she asked, hoping it came off as playful and not sarcastic. Judging by the stern look Angela gave her, she failed.

"You watch your tone with me, young lady."

Olivia sighed. "You're right. I'm sorry."

"If you must know, he's a nice man and I am enjoying his company. I'm allowed to do that."

"You are. Absolutely." She'd struck a nerve in her mother, and the guilt washed in like water flooding her system.

Angela gave it a beat, then nodded once and said, "So. Why does your soul need numbing?" When Olivia didn't answer, she ventured a guess. "Is it Hayley?"

Olivia turned to look at her and, not for the first time, was shocked by how much knowledge her mother's dark eyes held. It always amazed her, and when she was a small child, she was sure her mother knew everything there was to know about everything in the world. Olivia had never been able to lie to her mom, not when Angela was looking directly at her like that.

She nodded, tried to keep her eyes from welling up by blinking a lot.

"Can I tell you some things that I know?"

More nodding.

"I've been chatting with Benton for the better part of four hours now. He had no idea you and his daughter were a thing, and I didn't tell him. At first."

"Mama."

Angela held up a hand. "Wait. Let me finish." She threw another glance Benton's way. "The man has needed to unload for a while now,

I think. I know much more about him than most people." Olivia wasn't really surprised by this, as her mother was somebody people felt safe opening up to.

"Do you need rescuing?"

"Oh, no. He's actually quite charming. In fact, I'm very much enjoying my time with him."

Olivia took a big sip of her drink and didn't comment.

"He and Hayley have been through a lot the past couple of years." Olivia knew this, obviously, but let her mother keep talking.

"He said he put her in an impossible situation here."

That got Olivia's attention. She took another sip and this time, made eye contact with her mother as she spoke.

"He said she's never run a resort, that she grew up in them as a kid but was never really interested in joining the business. That he threw her into the deep end here and expected her to swim, and he should've known better, that she's got an artist's heart. That's when I told him about having her over for Christmas, about that gorgeous painting of you and Wally, how she made you light up in a way I haven't seen in a long time."

That damn lump was in her throat again, and she had to swallow several times to get any relief from it. "She lied to me, Mama. A big lie."

"I know." Her mother nodded, sipped her wine. "But she was forced into it. Ben admitted that as well. Keeping her identity a secret was his rule."

So, Hayley hadn't lied about that. "Did he say why he made such a rule? I mean, I know he didn't want her getting special treatment because of her name, but why?"

"Apparently, she'd been very irresponsible with her money since her mother passed. Rang up a lot of what Ben considered unnecessary expenses. Nightclubs. Restaurants. Impromptu weekends away."

"Did it not occur to him that maybe she was blowing off steam because her mom died?" Olivia's sudden defense of Hayley surprised her. And didn't. "They were really close, from what she's told me."

"I said the same thing to him, though a little gentler than you." Angela grinned to take away any sting. "He said he realizes that now, but at the time, all he had was anger. And I pointed out that—"

"He was still grieving for his wife and maybe taking it out on his daughter."

Her mother gave Olivia the same smile she'd used when she was a kid, the one that said she'd gotten the answer right. "He feels terrible and says he has a lot of ground to make up with Hayley."

"Well, it's good that he realizes it."

"He was also very impressed with you."

One corner of Olivia's mouth turned down and she gave a half shrug, coupled with a subtle scoff.

"No, really. He said the way Hayley talked about you in her emails? He knew there was something more. He said he hasn't heard her sound so passionate about anyone or anything since she began painting." Angela paused to let Olivia absorb that before she added, "I think he'd be very pleased with your pairing."

With a sigh, Olivia slowly shook her head. "I don't know, Mama."

"I'm sorry, and please correct me if I'm wrong, but…didn't she just get you the job you thought should've been yours to begin with? And, at the expense of her own?"

Olivia had actually put that on a shelf for a bit, and the reminder jarred her slightly. Hayley had done that. She'd told her father that Olivia should be managing.

"Have you talked to her about all of this?"

"Not really."

Looking past Olivia, Angela gestured with her chin. "Well, it's almost midnight, and your chance just walked in."

Olivia spun around to see Hayley at the doorway, scanning the crowd with those eyes, her expression…nervous? Olivia wasn't sure, but she did know one thing: Every cell in her body seemed to relax at the sight of her. How could that be? After everything they'd gone through today, all the revelations and the lies, how was it possible? How could laying eyes on Hayley from across a crowded room just feel…*right*?

Hayley's gaze landed on her, and the smile that followed—one filled with relief and joy and so much more—told Olivia that Hayley most likely felt the same way.

So, there's that.

As Hayley gave a small wave and walked toward her, Olivia realized her mother had left. She craned her neck to find both Angela and Benton looking in her direction, and she couldn't help but shake her head with a grin at how obvious they were.

"Hi."

Hayley was tired. Olivia could tell by how drawn her beautiful face was.

"Hey."

"Got a minute?"

Olivia glanced at her watch, gave Hayley a half grin. "Got about eleven." It was almost midnight.

Hayley gave one nod, then led Olivia to a corner of the room where they were out of the crowd. "I thought maybe we could hear each other better over here."

It was a good call; the walls that made the corner seemed to block some of the sound around them, and Olivia bent her head a bit so she could hear Hayley's voice.

"I want to apologize again. For keeping the truth from you. Yes, I had my reasons, and I didn't do it to hurt you—God, never in a million years would I want to do that. But it was still wrong, and I still should've told you."

Olivia nodded slowly as Hayley spoke, listening to every word, to the sincerity in her tone. Olivia didn't think for one second that Hayley was doing damage control. The open, uncertain look on her face made that clear.

"And the only reason I took the report was because I knew if I got it into my father's hands, it would be seen instead of being kicked around the corporate offices endlessly. But—"

"You couldn't tell me he was your father."

"Right."

"I mean, you *could* have…" Olivia let the sentence hang. Hayley looked miserable as she agreed, and Olivia bumped her with a shoulder, wanted to alleviate that. "It's okay. I forgive you."

"Yeah?" The way Hayley's face lit up was almost comical, and Olivia's own smile grew.

"Yeah. Just…don't lie to me again, okay?"

"I won't. I swear."

"We have a lot to talk about, you know." It was Olivia's way of saying that this wasn't exactly over—they needed to talk about the girlfriend that wasn't, according to Hayley—but she was okay tabling some things for now. The truth was, she was simply happy to be standing next to Hayley as midnight approached.

"Absolutely. Whenever you want. I look forward to it."

Olivia focused on Hayley's face, on how her green eyes sparkled under the twinkling Christmas lights, as the crowd began to count down the last ten seconds of the year. Neither woman spoke. They simply held one another's gaze, and for Olivia, it was intense and charged and perfect. And when the crowd screamed out "Happy New Year!" in unison, Olivia did the only thing she wanted to do.

She bent her head down slightly and captured Hayley's lips with hers.

It was the most perfect of kisses. Olivia had always read about such a thing, about how pure a kiss would be when you were with the right person, but she'd never experienced such a thing, never given it much credence. It seemed like the stuff of fairy tales and romance novels. But this? Right here? Kissing Hayley at midnight, tucked away in the corner of a very crowded room, with the promise of something hanging in the air around them?

It was perfect.

She pulled away slightly but held eye contact with Hayley, who smiled like she was the happiest woman on the planet. "Happy New Year, Hayley."

"Happy New Year to you. I'm looking forward to..." Hayley paused as if she had so many things to say. But she seemed to think better of it, and her smile grew even wider. "I'm just looking forward."

They'd been through so much in such a short time, but there was definitely something between them. There was no denying it. Hell, Olivia didn't want to deny it. Instead, she wanted to explore it, to follow it along and see where it led. And she wanted to do that with Hayley's hand in hers.

The realization startled her, but also made her smile.

"I'm looking forward, too," she said, then kissed Hayley again. And it was the truth.

EPILOGUE

That looks amazing," Ross said, his voice very quiet. He'd learned, over the course of the past few months, not to sneak up behind Hayley and startle her, or she was likely to turn around and poke him with her wet paintbrush. Which she had done four or five times before he laughingly changed his behavior. "You've come such a long way with your use of shadow and depth of field."

The compliment filled Hayley with pride, not for the first time. Ross's approval was something she'd grown to crave, and now, as she sat on her stool, tilted her head, and really looked at her work, she realized he was right.

The canvas depicted a shot of the woods, the exact same shot she'd painted in winter, but this time, it was spring. More color, no snow, the yellow heads of wild daffodils poking up through the soil, tiny green buds on the trees. She planned to paint the same shot in the summer and again in the fall, creating a series of seasons in four paintings.

Walter lay at her feet, giving a little snuffle as he resettled himself in the dog bed Hayley had bought for him.

It was early evening, and the waning sunlight streaming through the windows of the studio was a warm, deep yellow and very focused in spots. On the wood floor stained with paint. On the old exposed brick walls. Five other artists, including Maddie Dunne, were at work. They were people Hayley had grown to know and become friends with. Maddie, she'd talked into grabbing a corner and designating some time for her art. She'd only started a couple weeks ago, since her classes ended, but she seemed ridiculously happy to just be there. Another artist walked through from the shop, smiling at them both as he passed and headed toward his assigned spot. More would soon follow, coming in after work or even after dinner.

"Listen," Ross said, still quietly, then waited until Hayley turned to him and he had her full attention. "I have the paperwork."

Hayley blinked at him, waiting for him to go on, but he didn't. "What?"

Ross gave one nod, his smile wide.

"Ross. You're sure?" she asked, the same question she'd asked him about a hundred times over the past months.

"I'm positive. This is the right move. I feel really good about it."

"You're absolutely, one hundred percent, without a shade of doubt sure?" Hayley felt her heart begin to hammer in her chest, and her palms became clammy.

"I am absolutely, one hundred percent, without a shade of doubt sure."

Hayley wasn't a girl who squealed in delight, but she did just that as she set down her brush, stood, and threw her arms around Ross, who laughed heartily as he caught her in a hug.

They had the attention of the room, and Hayley looked at Ross to see what his plan was. This was his deal, she knew, and she didn't want to overstep. She waited as he cleared his throat.

"I have some news," he said, and the six artists with their gazes trained on him, various creative supplies in their hands, waited for him to speak. He gestured at the small whiteboard on the wall that read, in red marker, "57 days left." "You're all aware that my plan has been to close the shop over the summer. I love it here so much, but both of my kids are in Nashville, and my wife and I would like to be near them, so closing up and retiring seemed like the next step in my life."

The folks present knew this already. Ross had been clear, feeling it only fair to let them know they'd need to think about a different space to work. Gentle nods went around the room.

"But there's been a slight change of plans." At that, Hayley watched the artists perk up a bit, expressions of curiosity on their faces. Ross turned to her, held out his arm, and wrapped it around her shoulders. "Hayley's going to buy Brushstrokes and everything in it."

The curiosity changed over to surprised gasps.

"Seriously?" asked Margo as she sat at her pottery wheel, her hands brown with clay, and happy exclamations went around the studio. "That's amazing!"

Hayley nodded enthusiastically, smiling at her. "My plan is to keep things as is, but maybe modernize a bit." She bumped Ross with a hip, acknowledging their many discussions about how dated the shop was.

They went over a few details and answered questions, three more artists coming in to work and were filled in, and the overall atmosphere was one of joy, happiness, and relief. Hayley felt all of those things and more. She cleaned her brushes and packed up her things, wanting badly to share the news with one particular person first. She left with a copy of the papers, Ross promising his lawyer would send hers everything she needed, and they'd set a date for solidifying things.

Once in her car and driving, Hayley let out a whoop of pure happiness. It was happening. It was happening. The path for a future she'd never even considered was now laid out in front of her.

All she had to do was follow it.

❖

"You've got to be freaking kidding me," Olivia muttered under her breath as the contractor walked away from her after telling her he'd need another week to complete the job. The job he was supposed to have finished two weeks ago. Olivia realized this was a typical issue when it came to dealing with construction, but it definitely took the very precise planner in her and tossed her into chaos. Which she did not handle well.

She blew out a breath that made her lips flap, then turned away from the spa wing to head back to her office. A glance at her watch told her it was after six and she should go home, having come in twelve long hours ago. She was exhausted from not getting enough sleep because her brain wouldn't shut off at night. Her feet were killing her—maybe cute shoes with heels were *not* worth this kind of pain. She hadn't eaten since wolfing down a granola bar that morning, but she'd had way too much coffee.

With a nod to Jacob, who was manning the front desk tonight, she headed toward her office. The door was closed, but she didn't think about it as being odd, mostly because her brain was fried from the day.

She'd had terrific ideas for updating and expanding the Evergreen, and Benton Markham had let her run with them. Only she'd had *no earthly idea* how stressful it would all be, from making decisions about things as small as fixtures to trying to wrangle contractors and workers. Still, she was the manager of a fairly successful, soon-to-be *very* successful resort, which was what she'd wanted for years, and she was damn proud of that. Exhausted as she was, she was also happier than she'd ever been with her job.

The smell hit her first, but she didn't really register it until she opened her office door and saw the place setting laid out on her desk. Roast chicken, a baked potato brimming with sour cream and cheddar, a small salad, and a flute of what looked a lot like champagne all sat waiting for her. Across the office, Hayley lounged in a chair reading a book. When she looked up and smiled at her, Olivia's heart melted right there in her chest. It had been five months, and she kept waiting for the time to come when that didn't happen any longer. So far, it didn't seem like that time would ever arrive.

"Hi, gorgeous," Hayley said as she closed her book and sat up.

Olivia crossed the room and gave her a soft kiss on the mouth. "Hi yourself. What's all this?"

"Dinner. I had Tessa make you up a plate because odds are, you forgot to eat again."

"Odds are, you're right. Oh, my God, I'm gonna drool all over myself." She took a seat at her desk and dug in, making various humming noises as she ate. When she glanced up at Hayley, she noticed the ice bucket with a bottle in it and Hayley's own flute.

"I dropped Walter off at your mom's," Hayley said as she filled her glass. "She reminded me that my dad is coming this weekend and they want us to come over for dinner on Saturday."

Olivia grinned. "She must have talked him into not taking her out to someplace fancy."

"Please. One bite of her meatballs and they'll never go out for dinner again."

Olivia chewed the chicken, savored the seasonings Tessa used— some Olivia could pinpoint and others were a mystery, the way Tessa liked it—and cocked her head. "Will it ever stop being a little weird?"

"What, our parents dating? Probably not." Hayley looked at her and they both grinned because the truth was, neither of them had seen their parents this happy in years. Taking the chair in front of Olivia's desk, Hayley sat down and said, "You look tired, baby."

Olivia nodded, her mouth full of potato, and willed herself to slow down rather than shoveling food into her face like a starving person. "Exhausted," she said, hoping Hayley could make out the word around the food in her mouth.

"Well." Hayley picked up Olivia's flute and handed it to her, then hoisted her own. "I have something for us to toast, too."

"You do? Tell me." Olivia loved when Hayley looked like this: excited, a little flushed because of it, trying to keep her smile small, but wanting to let it bloom into a much bigger one. "Tell me," she ordered with a chuckle as Hayley reached into the back pocket of her jeans. She put a small batch of paper, trifolded, onto the desk.

Olivia set down her fork, picked up the papers, and unfolded them. She didn't have to read any further than the first page, which said at the top in big, bold type, "Deed of Sale."

She blinked at it, looked up at Hayley, back down at the paper and double-checked the details. She blinked some more as her very tired brain struggled to make the words come out of her mouth. She managed to make a sound of some sort as she pointed to the paper, then looked up at Hayley expectantly.

"Yes! He decided to take me up on my offer!"

In the seven months she'd known Hayley, Olivia had never seen her look quite this happy. Her eyes were bright, her smile was huge, and she seemed almost lighter somehow, like something had been pressing her down slightly and had now lifted off her. Olivia got up, went around the desk, and caught Hayley in a huge hug, felt her eyes well up.

Taking Hayley's face in both hands, she held it, looked her in the eye. "I am so proud of you, sweetheart."

Hayley had been waiting for this. Olivia knew it. Yes, they were very happy as a couple, even in these still-early stages of a relationship, but it was always clear, at least to Olivia, that something was still missing for Hayley. When they'd talked several weeks ago, she began to understand. Hayley had stepped down from managing the Evergreen, had bowed out of employment there altogether, and had taken a part-time gig at Brushstrokes. Benton hadn't been thrilled, but he'd eased up a lot on his daughter since the holidays. Olivia was also pretty sure her mother had some influence there. Above the shop was a small apartment, and Hayley rented it, wanting to stay in town with Olivia but knowing it was much too soon to be living together. And for the most part, she seemed happy.

But still, it always seemed to Olivia that Hayley was missing... something.

Now she knew what it was. A purpose.

"My God, I have so many ideas." Hayley's eyes darted around. "I want to update the shop, make it look more modern. I'm going to start contacting some new vendors, see what kinds of new gadgets we might be able to sell. Maybe run some workshops and classes. There are so many artists that come here! I want to be a staple for them. A place where they feel comfortable and understood and free to work."

Olivia watched her as Hayley paced the office, using her hands to talk, almost spilling her champagne in the process, ideas flowing out of her like water from a spigot. When she finally turned to Olivia and saw the expression on her face, she stopped.

"What?" Hayley asked, grinning like a small child on Christmas morning.

"You." Olivia shook her head in wonder. "I am so very happy for you." Hayley's face softened as Olivia held up her glass. "Come over here and let's toast so I can actually drink some of this."

Hayley crossed the room and went around the desk until she was standing only a few inches from Olivia. Speaking softly, Olivia said, "To the new owner of Brushstrokes, the woman I love."

Their glasses made a pretty tinkling sound as they touched, and both women sipped, eyes locked on each other.

"I was thinking," Olivia said, as she sat back down.

"Uh-oh," Hayley teased, her standard reply.

"Now that you'll be a respected business owner in the community, maybe...you could move out of that tiny apartment above the shop?" She posed it as a question intentionally so Hayley wouldn't feel any pressure. "I mean, I know Walter would love it. Me?" She shrugged. "I don't really care."

That got a smile as Hayley set her glass down, turned Olivia's chair, and sat in her lap. She looked into Olivia's eyes, stayed that way for a moment, and Olivia felt seen. Warm. Loved. "Are you asking me to move in with you?" Hayley asked.

"Only for about the twenty-seventh time...but yes."

Again, Hayley stared at Olivia for what felt like a long time. Olivia would never tire of looking into those beautiful green eyes, picking out each individual shade of green, noticing the small gold flecks and the dark circle around the green.

"I love you, Olivia," Hayley said softly, and Olivia would never tire of that either—hearing that most gorgeous of phrases.

"I love you, too," she whispered back. "Move in with me."

"Okay."

Olivia felt her own smile spread wide across her face. "Yeah?"

Hayley nodded, her smile just as big. "Yeah." Then she leaned in and kissed Olivia. Softly, but full of promise. Gently, but full of sweetness and love. And Olivia knew. Right then, in that moment, she understood that one innocent walk in the woods in the middle of winter had changed the course of her life. Just like that. Forever.

She would never need anything else. As long as she had Hayley, nothing else mattered. Hayley was hers.

Her heart.

Her love.

Her everything.

About the Author

Georgia Beers is the award-winning author of more than twenty lesbian romances. She resides in upstate New York, where she was born and raised. When not writing, she enjoys way too much TV, not nearly enough wine, spin classes (aka near-death experiences), and loving all over her dog (much to his dismay). She is currently hard at work on her next book. You can visit her and find out more at www.georgiabeers.com.

Books Available From Bold Strokes Books

30 Dates in 30 Days by Elle Spencer. In this sophisticated contemporary romance, Veronica Welch is a busy lawyer who tries to find love the fast way—thirty dates in thirty days. (978-1-63555-498-4)

Finding Sky by Cass Sellars. Skylar Addison's search for a career intersects with her new boss's search for butterflies, but Skylar can't forgive Jess's intrusion into her life. Romance is the last thing they expect. (978-1-63555-521-9)

Hammers, Strings, and Beautiful Things by Morgan Lee Miller. While on tour with the biggest pop star in the world, rising musician Blair Bennett falls in love for the first time while coping with loss and depression. (978-1-63555-538-7)

Heart of a Killer by Yolanda Wallace. Contract killer Santana Masters's only interest is her next assignment—until a chance meeting with a beautiful stranger tempts her to change her ways. (978-1-63555-547-9)

Leading the Witness by Carsen Taite. When defense attorney Catherine Landauer reluctantly becomes the key witness in prosecutor Starr Rio's latest criminal trial, their hearts, careers, and lives may be at risk. (978-1-63555-512-7)

No Experience Required by Kimberly Cooper Griffin. Izzy Treadway has resigned herself to a life without romance because of her bipolar illness but wonders what she's gotten herself into when she agrees to write a book about love. (978-1-63555-561-5)

One Walk in Winter by Georgia Beers. Olivia Santini and Hayley Boyd Markham might be rivals at work, but they discover that lonely hearts often find company in the most unexpected of places. (978-1-63555-541-7)

The Inn at Netherfield Green by Aurora Rey. Advertising executive Lauren Montgomery and gin distiller Camden Crawley don't agree on anything except saving the Rose & Crown, the old English pub that's brought them together. (978-1-63555-445-8)

Top of Her Game by M. Ullrich. When it comes to life on the field and matters of the heart, losing isn't an option for pro athletes Kenzie Shaw and Sutton Flores. (978-1-63555-500-4)

Vanished by Eden Darry. First came the storm, and then the blinding white light that made everyone in town disappear. Another storm is coming, and Ellery and Loveday must find the chosen one or they won't survive. (978-1-63555-437-3)

All She Wants by Larkin Rose. Marci Jones and Tessa Dalton get more than they bargained for when their plans for a one-night stand turn into an opportunity for love. (978-1-63555-476-2)

Beautiful Accidents by Erin Zak. Stevie Adams doesn't believe in fate, not after losing her parents in a car crash. But she's about to discover that sometimes the best things in life happen purely by accident. (978-1-63555-497-7)

Before Now by Joy Argento. The instant Delaney Peyton and Jade Taylor meet, they sense a connection neither can explain. Can they overcome a betrayal that spans the centuries to reignite a love that can't be broken? (978-1-63555-525-7)

Breathe by Cari Hunter. Paramedic Jemima Pardon's chronic bad luck seems to be improving when she meets police officer Rosie Jones. But they face a battle to survive before they can find love. (978-1-63555-523-3)

Double-Crossed by Ali Vali. Hired thief and killer Reed Gable finds something in her scope that will change her life forever when she gets a contract to end casino accountant Brinley Myers's life. (978-1-63555-302-4)

False Horizons by CJ Birch. Jordan and Ash struggle with different views on the alien agenda and must find their way back to each other before they're swallowed up by a centuries-old war. Third in the New Horizons series. (978-1-63555-519-6)

Legacy by Charlotte Greene. In this paranormal mystery, five women hike to a remote cabin deep inside a national park—and unsettling events suggest that they should have stayed home. (978-1-63555-490-8)